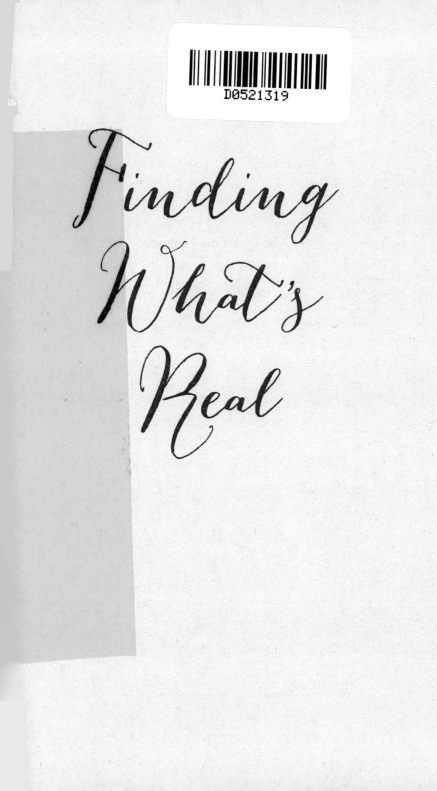

Finding What's Real

Also by Emma Harrison

Escaping Perfect

Finding What's Real

EMMA HARRISON

SIMON PULSE

NEW YORK   LONDON   TORONTO   SYDNEY   NEW DELHI

SIMON PULSE

An imprint of Simon & Schuster Children's Publishing Division
1230 Avenue of the Americas, New York, New York 10020
First Simon Pulse paperback edition March 2018
Text copyright © 2017 by Simon & Schuster, Inc.
Cover photo-illustration copyright © 2017 by PixelWorks Studios
Also available in a Simon Pulse hardcover edition.
All rights reserved, including the right of reproduction in whole or in part in any form.
SIMON PULSE and colophon are registered trademarks of Simon & Schuster, Inc.
For information about special discounts for bulk purchases, please contact Simon & Schuster Special Sales at 1-866-506-1949 or business@simonandschuster.com.
The Simon & Schuster Speakers Bureau can bring authors to your live event. For more information or to book an event contact the Simon & Schuster Speakers Bureau at 1-866-248-3049 or visit our website at www.simonspeakers.com.
Cover designed by Karina Granda
Interior designed by Tom Daly
The text of this book was set in Adobe Garamond Pro.
Manufactured in the United States of America
2 4 6 8 10 9 7 5 3 1
Library of Congress Cataloging-in-Publication Data
Names: Harrison, Emma, author.
Title: Finding what's real / by Emma Harrison.
Other titles: Finding what is real
Description: First Simon Pulse hardcover edition. | New York : Simon Pulse, 2017. | Sequel to: Escaping perfect. | Summary: Cecelia Montgomery returns home but faces new challenges, including her mother's Presidential campaign—headquartered in Sweetbriar—and the effects of her fame on her best friend, Fiona, and boyfriend, Jasper.
Identifiers: LCCN 2016030220 | ISBN 9781481442152 (hc) | ISBN 9781481442176 (eBook)
Subjects: [1. CYAC: Runaways—Fiction. 2. Fame—Fiction. 3. Presidential candidates—Fiction. | 4. Dating (Social customs)—Fiction. | 5. Friendship—Fiction. | 6. Family problems—Fiction. | 7.Tennessee—Fiction. | 8. Social Issues / New Experience. | JUVENILE FICTION / 9. Social Issues / Friendship. | JUVENILE FICTION / Family / Parents.]
Classification: LCC PZ7.H2485 Fin 2017 | DDC [Fic]—dc23
LC record available at https://lccn.loc.gov/2016030220
ISBN 9781481442169 (pbk)

For Matt

Finding What's Real

1

"BUT YOU MUST HAVE KNOWN YOUR PARENTS WERE looking for you—that the whole nation was looking for you." Kitty Wolf's brow was appropriately concerned, her posture tipped forward in interest. The colorful overhead lights made her pore-free, latte-colored cheeks glow. "Why didn't you let them know you were all right?"

Heat seared my skin, even though I could feel the relentless whoosh coming from the air-conditioning vent behind my head. My manicured fingernails dug into the leather seat at my sides and my mother's eyes twitched. I folded my hands in my lap and plastered on a smile. Outside the plate-glass window, some mom from Ohio shouted, "Give 'em hell, Cecilia!" If only.

"I just want to say I'm very sorry for any stress I caused my parents, or anyone else for that matter," I recited. "My grandmother and I were very close and after her death . . . I made some bad choices. But I'm back now, and I'm as committed to my family as ever."

There was some truth in there somewhere, at least. Sandwiched between the publicists' lies. My mother reached over and briefly placed her cold, dry hand on top of mine, giving it a wide-fingered squeeze like one of those claw mechanisms inside an arcade machine. Comforting, it was not. Though I'm sure it looked that way to *Good Day America*'s ten million viewers.

"More than anything, we really just want to focus on getting Cecilia to her high school graduation tomorrow and start looking toward the future both for her and for this country," my mother—the great Senator Rebecca Montgomery—said. She gazed directly into the camera. "We're so grateful to the people of this great nation for supporting us through this crisis. You've really shown us the best side of America, and we hope that you'll now respect our privacy as we mourn the loss of my husband's mother and work to piece things back together."

Gag. And as if anyone in this great nation of ours had ever respected anyone's privacy.

"God bless America," my father added.

Gag. Barf. Gag.

Kitty Wolf sat back in her chair with a satisfied smile. "And on that note, we'll go to commercial." She looked into the camera and ducked her chin in the way of professional newscasters everywhere. "For *Good Day America*, I'm—"

"Wait! One more thing!"

The words came out of my mouth before I could stop them. It was like a switch in my head had flipped. And now, every single person in the studio held their breath. I saw two boom operators exchange a look like I'd just lit myself on fire in the middle of the set. But what was I supposed to do? No one had mentioned Jasper. Or Shelby. Even though news footage of the two of them being dragged out of Jasper's house in handcuffs had been playing practically on loop for the past two days.

Kitty and her producer exchanged a shrug, and then the green light on top of the camera that was aimed at me turned on.

"Jasper Case and Shelby Tanaka did not kidnap me," I said, looking Kitty steadily in the eye. Or as steadily as possible when the rest of my body was shaking. "They're just friends I made in Sweetbriar. Every allegation leveled against them is false, and they should be released immediately."

Kitty's smile was stiff. I'd leaned forward, so I couldn't see my mother's face in real life, but I could sort of make it out on one of the monitors. She looked about ten years older than she had two seconds ago. Wrinkles. Lines. Ire.

"All right then," Kitty said brightly. "Rebecca, David, Cecilia, thank you so much for joining us and for sharing your story. I'm sure I speak for the entire viewing public when I say we're so glad you're safe, Cecilia, and we can't wait to see what you do next."

Was it just me, or was there a sort of evil glint in her eyes when she said that last bit?

"For *Good Day America*, I'm Kitty Wolf."

The theme music started up and Kitty launched herself

out of her chair, ripping off her microphone. "God, I need to pee."

She quickly shook my parents' hands, gushing about how nice it was to meet them, then wished me luck, kicked off her puce-colored heels, and ran as best she could in her tight-ass pencil skirt, a team of makeup artists chasing after her.

"Well. That wasn't too painful now, was it?" my father asked, straightening his suit jacket. The caked makeup on his dark skin was a shade too light, making him look like he was wearing a latex mask that was slowly peeling off.

"If lying doesn't bother you, then no." I glanced at my mother and I could tell a tirade was building. There was this very subtle shade of purple-pink creeping up her neck. It would not make it to her face. It never did. The woman had an intense amount of control in public.

"Greenroom," she said through her veneers. "Now."

I turned away from my parents just as the PA who was in charge of us appeared to usher us down the hallway. My mother walked behind me, her heels click-clacking primly, and I could practically feel the rage emanating off her. But of course she wouldn't say anything out here, where anyone could hear her. As soon as we were alone she would unleash the beast. Or alone with her assistant, Tash Miyaka, a twenty-something professional butt-kisser who wore nothing but black shift dresses and pearls and always had two phones and an iPad on her. She was waiting in the greenroom and jumped out of her chair when we arrived, sending the iPad bouncing across the carpeted floor. She scrambled on hands and knees to pick it up.

"You guys can feel free to relax in here while I check on your car," the PA said with a kind smile. Then she closed the door and was gone. I ripped off the itchy pink-and-white-plaid jacket my mother's stylist had chosen for me and threw it at the nearest garbage can, then fished in my new Louis Vuitton bag (a smaller version of my mom's, also provided by the stylist) for my phone. Until I remembered that my mother had taken my phone five seconds after we were reunited two days ago.

"What the hell was that? You just hijacked that interview!" my mother snapped. Her body trembled, but her helmet of blond hair stayed freakishly still. "We had the perfect sign-off and you had to muck it up by pushing your cause."

"My cause?" I blurted. I felt hot all over from the effort of standing up to her. It wasn't something I'd done much of in the past few years—hell, in my entire life. Honestly, since I was ten years old, I'd barely ever seen her. But things were different now. They were going to be different. After everything that happened, they had to be.

"You mean my boyfriend who you had arrested for no good reason?"

"Don't turn that around on me! You're the one who ran away, leaving me to clean up the mess. Did you really think I wasn't going to find a way to spin the story?"

"By throwing two innocent people under the bus?" I

asked. "They're in *federal prison,* Mother. And for what? For being kind to me? For being my friends? Is that such an awful offense?"

"Enough!" my father shouted. Everyone in the room flinched in surprise. "Rebecca, Cecilia is right. This charade has gone on long enough."

I beamed. My father was taking my side. He was standing up to my mom, for *me*.

"You have to get those two kids released before one of them gets the idea in their head to sue for wrongful imprisonment."

Oh. So it wasn't about me. It was simply the lawyer in him protecting the family. As always. Sometimes I wondered if my mother had pursued my father back in college simply because she knew he was going to end up in law school. Because she knew she'd have him around to fight her battles for her for the rest of her life.

My mother took in a breath and blew it out—a short blast of indignant, but acquiescent, air. "Fine. I'll make the call. But you . . . ," she said, turning on me with a finger raised. "You better start toeing the line and get on message if we're going to make this work."

"Make what work? You really think I'm sticking around for whatever torture you devise for me next?" I demanded, on a roll. "I'm eighteen, Mom. You can't make me do anything anymore."

"I made you come here, didn't I?"

I clenched my teeth and willed myself to not explode. "I

came here because it was the right thing to do. But now I'm out."

I grabbed my bag and headed for the door, never really believing she'd let me go. When her fingers closed around my arm it was all I could do not to turn around and deck her with the heavy leather purse. Honestly, I don't even know why I was taking it with me. There was nothing useful inside of it. No cash, no credit cards. Even the makeup wasn't in brands or colors I would ever buy for myself.

"Maybe we should get away for a few days. To the Cape?" my father suggested. He was sweating as he eyed the door. "Just the three of us, so we can sort this all out."

Tash, who had retrieved her iPad, froze with her fingers over the screen. She looked completely confused. Not that I could blame her. As long as I'd lived, no one had ever suggested that the three of us do anything alone together. She was probably imagining all the appearances she'd have to cancel, the meetings she'd have to push, her perfectly color-coded calendar being blown to bits.

"Now's not the time for a vacation, David." My mother dropped my arm and yanked down on her gray suit jacket. "I'm about to announce."

The room went still. Ice water trickled into my veins. "Announce what?"

My mother rolled her eyes. "This little power play of yours couldn't have come at a worse time, Cecilia," she said. "After the funeral I intended to tell you that I am going to run for president."

"What!?" I blurted.

I sat down and my butt hit the very hard arm of a black couch. Okay, I had always known this was a possibility. Of course it was. My mother was one of the most popular senators in Congress, and she was Rebecca Montgomery, for God's sake. She could sew up the women's vote, the black vote, and the I-just-want-to-vote-for-someone-famous vote without lifting a finger. But this was huge. I hadn't even heard any rumblings or rumors about it.

"When was this decided?" I asked.

"We've been in the exploratory period for over a year, but the final decision was made in February."

Oh, right. When I was locked away in the ivory tower that was the Worthington School, where no one communicated anything to me, ever, other than my schedule and their expectations of me. Which trickled down either through my bodyguard or a tutor or came via e-mail from Tash.

"You're not taking off again," my mother intoned. "Not now. I need you by my side on the campaign trail."

I laughed bitterly.

"Did you just *laugh*, young lady?" my mother demanded.

Even though my insides felt like they were being corroded by acid, I managed to rise to my full height, which, thanks to my father's genes, was a good two inches taller than my mother's, and today, thanks to the heels she'd made me wear, I was even taller.

"I am *not* going out on the campaign trail with you," I

said. "What do you want me to do? Get my picture taken playing with sick kids? Visit nursing homes or failing farms or crumbling factories?"

One glance at Tash's face and I knew I'd come seriously close to the truth. She tucked her iPad behind her and I got the distinct feeling that she'd been about to show me an itinerary that looked a lot like the plan I'd just laid out. My confidence welled.

"No. Not a chance. There's no way I'm going to go around telling everyone what a perfect family we are . . . what an incredible mother you've been," I raged.

"Cecilia! For God's sake, keep it down!" my father said through his teeth.

"Why, Dad? Why? Who the hell cares what the random person walking by thinks of us?" I shouted, my voice cracking. "Isn't it actually a positive thing for people to realize we're a real family? That nothing is as perfect as even her spin doctors can make it seem?"

"Stop it right now, Cecilia," my mother hissed. "We still have your little hick boyfriend in custody. I haven't made the call *yet*. And I heard he's supposed to open for some big act this weekend. I wonder what happens to the hot new thing on the music scene if he simply doesn't show up for an important date."

I whipped around to glare at her. "You wouldn't. You couldn't! You have no evidence against him because he did nothing wrong."

"As if that matters." My mother leaned toward me. "You

really have no idea how powerful I am, do you?"

"Leave Jasper out of this," I said, all that resolve I'd just built up beginning to crumble. "Be reasonable."

"I would *love* to be reasonable, Cecilia," my mother said. She sighed and reached for a bottle of water, which she handed to Tash. Tash opened it, poured it into a glass, added some ice, and handed it back before I could even blink. "But you took that option away from me when you stole one of my cars and fled your grandmother's funeral."

"I only did that because you wouldn't listen to me!" I shouted. "Why couldn't you have been reasonable *then*?" I shoved my hands through my short curls and barked a laugh. "Wait a minute, what am I talking about? I know why. Because you don't give a crap about me. All you care about—all you ever cared about—is yourself. I wonder what the voting public would think if I went out there and told them that."

"Stop it, Cecilia. Everything I've ever done, I've done to protect you."

"Well, it's just too bad there was no one around to protect me from *you*."

My mother's jaw dropped slightly. Suddenly, the anger was gone. The perfect mask was gone. For a second, I saw hurt in her eyes. Actual, human hurt. But then the door opened, and she plastered on her politician's smile again.

"Your car's here, Mrs. Montgomery," the PA said.

"Thank you, Melissa."

She always remembered everyone's name. It was one of

the things people loved about her. She made it so easy for the
public to adore her, and so difficult for her own daughter to
sit in the same room with her.

My mother picked up her purse while Tash scrambled to
shove her makeup kit and other paraphernalia into a small
rolling suitcase.

"We're going to the airport," my mother told me. "You
have graduation tomorrow."

As she breezed by me out the door, she tugged something
out of her pocket and handed it to me. A red, white, and blue
button that read MONTGOMERY: FOR OUR FUTURE.

It was the slogan she'd used when she'd run for senator last
term, so it didn't technically give anything away. But the logo
was brand-new. She'd probably had a million of them made
up to distribute once she made the announcement.

"Put that on and I make the call to have your boyfriend
released."

It hadn't escaped my notice that although she remembered the PA's name, she'd yet to speak Jasper's.

But then, she wasn't good enough to know Jasper.

I took the pin, shoved it through the expensive white silk
shell top I was sporting—thereby ruining it entirely—and
put on my fake smile.

"Happy?" I asked through my teeth.

My mother slung her bag over her shoulder and tossed
her head. Her hair still didn't move. Her mouth was set in a
grim line. "You have no idea."

* * *

Every senior at the Worthington School was partying. At least, that was how it sounded from inside my locked dorm room filled with freshly packed and neatly labeled cardboard boxes. The ten-by-ten room smelled stale and dry, and it had been stripped of any and all traces of me. I wondered when my mother had sent her little elves here to pack my life away. How much of my stuff had they simply tossed in the trash? Was it before they found me? After? Actually, I didn't want to know.

Somewhere down the hall, a girl screeched, and it was followed by a round of boisterous laughter. I was semi-itching to investigate, but I hardly knew these people, even after six years of attending classes with them. And besides, my new bodyguard, Alexis, was stationed right outside my door. Alexis. It had always sounded like a prissy little girl's name to me, but not anymore. The moment I'd met this six-foot-two, two-hundred-fifty-pound woman, my first thought had been, *Help me.*

But worse than the cell and the smell and the guard was the fact that my chest felt like it was being compressed under forty-two tons of bricks. It had felt that way ever since my mother and her FBI squad had swarmed Jasper's house back in Sweetbriar and dragged him and Shelby Tanaka off to be questioned. I hadn't talked to Jasper in three days. Three whole days. I didn't know where he was—not exactly—or how he was being treated, what he was thinking, what he was feeling. I didn't know if he still loved me or missed me or never wanted to see me again. I would have given anything in that moment just to talk to him—just to hear his voice, even if he *was* pissed off. But the phone he'd given me was gone, and there was no landline in the room.

There was another round of laughter and suddenly hip-hop music shook the walls around me. Apparently no one cared about the rules anymore on the night before graduation. I heard Alexis talking outside my door and wondered if she was making nice with the other bodyguards, or if she was chatting on the phone herself.

Maybe I could mug her for her phone. Yeah, right. I may have held a black belt in three martial arts, but I still had the feeling she could flatten me with one eyelash.

A very quiet ding got me sitting up in bed, my heart pounding. My laptop. Of course! What the hell was wrong with me? Maybe that was Jasper texting me right now.

With a glance at the door, I swung my legs over the side of my bed and ripped my computer off the desk. I still wasn't sure how it had gotten here—it was one of very few things from my apartment down in Sweetbriar that had magically appeared in my dorm room. I hoped my mother's minions hadn't scared the crap out of my roommate, Britta Tanaka, when they'd come for my stuff. Which didn't include any of my new clothes from Second Chances, or the violin Jasper had given me. Not surprising. It was as if the past two weeks of my life—the best two weeks of my life—had been entirely erased.

They had also been the only two weeks of my life during which I'd been my own person—made my own choices. The message my mother was sending by obliterating them from existence wasn't lost on me. She was telling me that what I wanted didn't matter. That who I really was didn't matter.

I opened the laptop, but the ding hadn't been an incoming message. It was a reminder. I was supposed to be at work at Second Chances early in the morning to clean old merchandise off the shelves. The heaviness inside my chest seemed to thicken.

Okay. Deep breath. All was not lost. That ding had at least inspired me. I didn't know why I hadn't thought of this before, but I could text Jasper through my laptop. I could even FaceTime him! Actually, I did know why it hadn't occurred to me—because I'd never done either of these things, because I'd never had real friends to communicate with. But now, I did.

I hovered the cursor over the FaceTime icon, but then froze. If I could hear Alexis talking, she would be able to hear me talking. So no. No calls. But texting? That was silent.

I muted the sound on my computer, opened up the text box, and typed in a message to Jasper, hitting the keys slowly and cringing at every quiet click.

You okay? Where are you? I'm so sorry. Please write back and just let me know you're okay.

Glancing at the closed door, I hit send. Then I held my

breath while I waited for the reply. And waited. And waited. Finally, I had to take in some air, so I did, and then bit down on my lip. I waited so long that I drew blood.

He wasn't replying. How much did he know about why he was arrested? Was he mad at me? Or still in custody? Yes, my mother had promised me they'd let him go if I wore her stupid button and fell in line, but what did a promise from dear old Mom mean? I had kept my end of the bargain, of course. I'd picked up my ceremonial commencement gown and accompanying valedictorian tassel, both of which now hung on a hanger on the outside of my closet. I'd promised not to tell anyone she was running until she made her big, official announcement (as if I had anyone to tell). If she was true to her word, Jasper should have been a free man by now. I had to hope she wasn't insane enough to have him detained in jail for a crime that hadn't been committed.

So why wasn't he replying?

Not wanting to dwell on the answer, I opened up Safari and Googled "Jasper Case." The very first hit was a newsfeed video of him and Shelby being released from a Washington, D.C., police station earlier that day. They'd brought them all the way to D.C. from Tennessee? Why? How? Had they been flown commercial with handcuffs and guards? Bile rose up in the back of my throat.

I fumbled in my bag for my headphones and plugged them in before hitting play. I couldn't tear my eyes away from

Jasper. He wore dark sunglasses and his favorite black cowboy hat, his head ducked as he hurried toward the limousine. His publicist, Evan Meyer, was at his side as he dove into the car and it sped off.

"Jasper Case, a freshly signed artist on the Blue Peak record label, was released from custody today and cleared of all charges in the kidnapping of America's Sweetheart Cecilia Montgomery," the voice-over said. "He is returning to his home in Sweetbriar, Tennessee, where a representative from Blue Peak tells us he is eager to get back to work on his debut album and put this unfortunate experience behind him."

Put this unfortunate experience behind him. Did that include me?

They didn't even mention Shelby, but I caught a glimpse of her in the background as Tammy and Britta put their arms around her and squired her off. They must hate me now. All of them. Britta, my roommate and friend. Tammy, my boss at Second Chances and one of the few adults who had ever really noticed me. I bet they were back home in Sweetbriar now, cursing my name.

But it didn't matter. What mattered was Jasper and Shelby were free. They were going to be okay. I glanced at the text message box. It was still blank except for my sent message bubble, forlornly awaiting a reply.

The video ended and a vaguely familiar news anchor guy appeared on the screen.

"In a related story, new footage of Cecilia Montgomery's time away has surfaced this evening, calling into question the official story that she went to Sweetbriar simply to visit her deceased grandmother's best friend and to mourn in peace."

Until that moment, I'd had no idea it was possible to choke on one's own saliva.

Grainy, blurry footage filled the small video box. It was me, on stage at The Mixer on my first night in Sweetbriar, playing that borrowed violin. At first the picture was so bad that there was no way anyone could have ever confirmed it was me. But then it suddenly zoomed in, blurred, and then sharpened, and there I was, clear as day. My chin, my skin, my gangly figure. Only my freshly shorn and dyed hair was hidden, underneath the very same cowboy hat I'd just seen on Jasper's head as he was released from custody.

I stared at the screen, and once the panic subsided, I realized I didn't sound half bad. Go me.

But then the footage suddenly stopped and snapshots of me and Jasper flipped onto the screen one at a time, each slightly overlapping the last. There was one of the two of us talking backstage at the theater where Jasper had played the showcase, another of us kissing in the seats at the same theater, a third of us standing outside the dressing room at Bridgestone Arena. People had clearly been trolling their cell phones all night, checking to see if they'd managed to snap pictures of the newly famous couple. I wondered how much the news channels were paying for this stuff. My pulse thrummed loudly in my ears—so bad I couldn't hear what the newscaster was saying. But still, the message was clear.

Cecilia Montgomery hadn't been in mourning. She'd been on a joyride. She'd been slutting it up with the hot new country music star. She'd made all of America worry, while she stuck her tongue down some guy's throat.

This sucked, big time. Why did anyone care? All I'd been doing was trying to live my life. Also, I really hated the person who'd first decided to put a camera inside a phone.

Suddenly, the anchor was back, staring out at me with a very practiced look of concern.

"So, you decide, America. Is Cecilia Montgomery a girl who went into seclusion after a devastating loss, or a selfish, entitled princess who took the entire country for a ride? We'll have more on this story as it develops."

I pressed my tongue against the dry roof of my mouth and closed the laptop. The worst part about it was, everything the man had said was true. I had taken the country for a ride. I had been selfish. But it wasn't like I'd intended to hurt or mislead anyone. At least not anyone outside my own family. My mother had kept me under lock and key and under the watchful eye of a bodyguard/jailer for the past eight years of my life. I'd just needed some time. Some freedom. A life. I'd seen my opportunity, and I'd seized it.

I turned out the light and lay flat on my back, but I knew there was no way I was going to be able to sleep. My mother's retribution for small infractions tended to be swift and hardly ever matched the crime. I could only imagine what her reaction to that news story might be.

2

THE SUN WAS BARELY PEEKING THROUGH THE BLINDS
on my window when the door flew open, the lights blazed on,
and no less than five people barreled into my room. The first
two were big, muscle-bound men in blue coveralls who went
right for the boxes. The second pushed a rack full of colorful
clothing in clear plastic bags ahead of her, so all I could see was
a shock of pink hair atop her head. The fourth toted a tackle
box and tugged a rolling suitcase, his biceps bulging against
the short sleeves of his light blue polo shirt. The fifth was Tash,
armed with her two cell phones and wearing a sensible, sleeveless tweed dress—black with just a touch of gray. For her, this
was really mixing things up.

"Great! Yes! Get the boxes out of here so we have some room
to work," Tash micromanaged, placing her phones next to each
other atop my desk. She pulled out her iPad and scrunched her
nose at me. "You're not up? Get up!"

I'd never heard Tash give an order before, only take them.
The shock of it made me jump to my feet, even though the

back of my skull still felt like it was full of cotton candy. Also, I was wearing my pajamas. The two-piece menswear-style set printed with rainbow hearts.

"What's going on?" I asked.

"Don't ask questions," Tash snapped. She wore a deep red lip color and had painted tiny wings at the end of her eyeliner. Her black hair was slicked back so tight it was tugging at her eyebrows. "This is Matilda. She's your new stylist."

Matilda of the pink hair also wore square glasses with plaid frames, a nose ring, and a far-more-boring-in-comparison pencil skirt with a silk shell top.

"Pleasure to meet you, Cecilia. A real pleasure," she said, pumping my arm up and down like she was trying to raise water from a well. Then she dropped my hand, pulled out a measuring tape, shoved my arms into the air, and wrapped the tape around my breasts.

"Um, boundaries?" I said.

"Sorry, hon. It's my job."

She started to mutter numbers under her breath as Tash snapped her fingers at the tall black gentleman with the tackle box.

"Oh, no, Tash my love. Let us not forget that I am here as a favor to you. You snap that cheap gel manicure of yours at me again and I'm walking right out that door."

Tash gritted her teeth. "It wasn't cheap, trust me."

"Well, then, someone's getting ripped off." He touched the tip of his finger to her nose.

One of the movers bumped Tash aside while removing one of the bigger boxes and I bit back a laugh. She breathed in deep through her nose, then turned to me.

"Cecilia, this is Max, your—"

"Hair and makeup?" I guessed, offering my hand as Matilda dropped to her knees to measure my waist.

"Transformation specialist," he amended, but smiled as he shook my hand. Firm grip, wrist tattoo of Roman numeral MMIV, definitely wearing eyeliner and possibly also mascara, though it was hard to tell. Either way, his eyelashes were enviable.

"I am going to have some fun with you," he promised, flicking his assessing gaze over my face. "Those cheekbones alone."

He hummed quietly as he tossed his rolling luggage onto my dresser, unzipping it with a flourish. The movers grabbed the last of the boxes and swept out, leaving the door wide open. Matilda began unzipping the clear plastic bags and whipping out clothes, holding them up under my chin and pursing her lips as she studied me.

"Interesting. You are definitely a winter . . ." She produced an ecru linen dress. "With just a hint of summer."

That was me. A total contradiction.

"Tash," I began, "could you please tell me—"

"Okay, so today you have breakfast with your parents at eight, then your mother is taking you into D.C. to shop at Tiffany for your graduation gift."

I blinked. "Wait, what?"

"We've got an interview with the Huffington Post at eleven, then to Georgetown for lunch with the Westinghouses." She looked up from her iPad briefly. "You remember Chet Westinghouse? He's graduating as well, but from Windsor. That should be a great photo op. Talk about cheekbones."

She glanced over her shoulder at Max, who *mmm-hmmm*ed his agreement.

"Photo op? Are you—"

"Then we're back here by three to prep for the ceremony, which is at four. You and your parents will pose for pictures with the dean and other families from your graduating class." She looked up again. "Strictly A-list, of course, but you don't need the particulars."

Roger that. Why tell me which peers I'm suddenly fake friends with? But even more disturbing was the number of times she'd mentioned "pictures" and "photo ops." I hadn't had my photo taken outside of the annual family Christmas gathering for years. My mother strictly forbid it and freaked out whenever there was a camera in my vicinity. Thanks to her, I *hated* having my picture taken. The very sight of a lens gave me PTSD.

"And then there's the after-party at the boathouse, where you'll stay for an hour and a half to make it seem genuine. You'll leave directly from there for your charter flight back to Boston. And of course, Alexis will be accompanying you every step of the way."

Alexis, who was currently standing in the open doorway in

her sensible blue suit, eyeing Max as if he was piecing together an Uzi, not clattering around with makeup brushes. Did this woman never sleep?

Tash looked up and tilted her head. "Any questions?"

"Shoe size?" Matilda asked.

"Not you," Tash snapped. "Cecilia, do you have any questions?"

"First of all, I'm a nine," I told Matilda, who actually shuddered. With height came big feet; what could I say? "And yes, I do have a question."

Behind Tash's shoulder, Max was lining up bottles and compacts and atomizers on my dresser, still humming quietly—an upbeat song, though I couldn't quite pick up the tune. He paused, popped open a small mirror, and checked his pores. I caught his eye in the reflection and he snapped the compact closed.

"Cecilia?" Tash prompted.

"Right," I said. "So for the last ten years my mother has kept me hidden away from the world like some kind of Quasimodo and now, suddenly, she's decided to let every person in America know exactly who I am?"

"No, sweetie. You're the one who decided to do that," my mother replied, striding into the room. "I'm just making the best of it."

Max flinched and knocked half his bottles to the floor with a serious crash. Alexis stuck her head back into the room.

"Everything okay, ma'am?"

"We're fine," my mom replied with a pleasant smile.

Max went about cleaning up his mess while my mom casually flicked through the clothes on the rack. Matilda backed away toward the wall, hands clasped behind her, as if afraid to startle the rare and dangerous creature who had just entered our midst. I wondered what she thought of my mother's style. Dark gray suit jacket, light pink silk sheath, shiny black heels. Impeccable. Timeless. Intimidating.

"You're the one responsible for getting your face splashed all over the papers and across every news broadcast, are you not?" my mother said, the clink of metal hangers punctuating her words. I knew from experience that it was a rhetorical question. "There's no taking it back. And now we're in the position of having to change the conversation. Photos of you at a respectable lunch with respectable people will go a long way toward doing that. Let's put you and your newfound fame to good use."

She met my eye steadily and I bit back the two-dozen retorts that pressed against my lips. Put me to good use. What an awesome way to make me feel like an inanimate pawn in some ridiculous game. We stared each other down for what felt like an eternity, but I refused to blink first. I was done being subservient. All I'd ever wanted was a normal life. A small, happy, life. And for two weeks I'd had it. I'd had everything I'd ever wanted—friends, an apartment, a job that I loved, a *guy* that I loved—and she was the one who'd obliterated it.

"Tash?" Her gaze flicked to her assistant. "Please take your team out into the hall. I'd like to speak to my daughter alone."

Tash grabbed her phones and iPad and led the retreat, followed quickly by Max, who was clearly sweating, and Matilda, who tried to make herself smaller by sliding sideways into the hall. I was grinning as the door closed behind them.

"What are you so happy about?" my mother asked.

"I won."

She narrowed her eyes, faking confusion, but she knew what I meant. The woman was a lifelong politician. Half her career was about not blinking first. She sighed and gestured at the bed.

"Cecilia, please sit."

I hesitated a second, not wanting to give back an inch, but then did as I was told anyway. I was shocked, however, when she sat next to me. On an unmade bed. Giving up the position of power. My mother always stood when others were sitting, and if she had to sit, she took the highest perch she could find—a stool instead of a chair, the arm of a couch instead of the seat—or at the very least, the head of the table.

"Cecilia, do you remember your first day of kindergarten?"

This was not what I was expecting. "A little," I said. "I remember that blue sailor dress I wore. And playing on the playground. It had this big jungle gym thing that looked like a—"

"A flower."

How the hell did she remember that?

"What I remember about your first day of kindergarten

is that your father and I were worried you wouldn't want to go," she said. "You'd been home with us and your nanny for five years. We'd never left you at a playdate or a music class or anything, really. One of us was always with you."

I swallowed hard. What was going on here? What was her angle?

She lifted her hand from the bed and it hovered over my knee. Both of us froze. Was she really going to *touch* me? But no dice. After a suspended moment, her hand found its way to her lap.

"But you didn't bat an eyelash," she said, looking me in the eye. "You didn't cry or beg to come home with us. You didn't even look back. You just ran over to that big flower and started to climb."

"Mom—"

"I'm the one who cried," she said, looking down at her hands briefly, before shooting me a tight smile. "Your father sat there with me in that parking lot for fifteen minutes while I sobbed like a baby."

The prickling in my throat made its way up to my eyes. "No way."

"It's true. Hardest day of my life. Until the day you were almost kidnapped." Her eyes shone and she cleared her throat. "The thing is, Cecilia, I wasn't raised to be a crier. I wasn't raised to have any emotions, really. In my house, with my father being who he was and all those brothers looking over me, crying was considered a weakness. We didn't talk about how we felt. The Montgomerys have always been doers, not . . . ."

"Feelers?" I suggested.

And she snorted a laugh.

"Exactly. If I kept you at arm's length after that awful day, it was because I didn't ever want to feel that way again. I was *so* afraid of losing you—"

The words hung in the air. My chest felt raw and full at the same time, but on some level, I didn't know whether to believe what she was saying. My mother was a politician, a wordsmith, a master debater. She knew how to play a crowd to get what she wanted. And I'd never seen her like this before. Ever. Was this for real, or was she manipulating me?

"And then, a couple of weeks ago, you were gone again and my worst fear was realized."

The accusation was unspoken. That it was my fault. That I had made her nightmare come true for my own selfish purposes. This was the part where she told me what I owed her for that infraction.

"There's something I want to give you."

My mother reached into her purse and pulled out a red velvet jewelry case. My grandmother's pearls. I knew before she even opened the box. My mother had always kept them in the top drawer of her vanity and I'd snuck in countless times to try them on when I was little.

"Open it," my mother prompted gently.

I cracked the lid. The creak was still familiar, as was the

slightly stale scent of ingrained dust that wafted off the velvet. I touched the pearls with my fingertips.

"You're not really giving these to me," I stated. "This is a loan, right?"

My mother looked exasperated. "Of course it's not a loan. My mother gave them to me the day I graduated college and her mother gave them to her when she graduated high school. They've been passed down for generations on significant occasions, and I'd say this one counts."

"Wow, Mom. Thanks."

She held my gaze for at least ten seconds and then looked away, as if embarrassed. "Here."

She tugged the necklace out of the box and clasped it around my neck. The pearls felt cool and slick against my skin. My mother leaned back to admire the effect and smiled. It was a small smile, a real smile. Not a politician's smile.

"They really suit you," she said, and then she did squeeze my knee. It was quick, but it happened.

"Thanks, Mom. Really. I . . . they're perfect."

"You're welcome," she said.

Then she stood up and straightened her skirt.

"Well, then. I'll let you and your team get back to work. Alexis will escort you down to breakfast at seven thirty."

Without another word, she turned and swept out the door. As it shut behind her, I heard her issuing orders to the people in the hallway and I felt, suddenly, like I'd just been through a wrestling match. My mother and I had barely spent more than an hour at a time together for the past ten years. I'd seen her more in this last week than I had since I was eight years old, but in all that time she hadn't really looked at me. Not even when she was busy reading me the riot act for what I'd done. There were always ten other things going on, half a dozen other people in the room.

So that . . . that alone time . . . that bonding moment—whether it was real or not—that was new.

I got up and checked my reflection in the mirror, but I barely glanced at the pearls. Instead I found myself staring into my own eyes, trying to figure out what the heck was going on. And more important, how I felt about it.

I had to be the single most unpopular person in my graduating class. Everyone around me had friends to talk to, group selfies to pose for, yearbooks to sign, but I just sat there at my table, alone, trying to make a crab cake appetizer last long enough for my parents to return to the table. They were currently across the room, schmoozing with a group of old money, and every once in a while I'd hear my father's deep belly laugh accompanied by my mother's polite and not-too-girlie chuckle. Hovering behind me, Alexis barely seemed to breathe. The woman had her statue impression down.

"Are you hungry?" I asked, glancing over my shoulder.

"I'm fine, miss."

"But I haven't seen you eat all day," I replied. "Do you want one of the rolls? They're really good. Or are you one of those no-carb people?"

I swear I saw the very corner of her mouth twitch—a blink-and-you'll-miss-it movement. Maybe she was warming up to me. But she still didn't look my way.

"No, miss. I am not one of those people." There was a long pause during which I stared down at my plate. "Those people scare me."

I laughed, but this time she didn't betray a hint of a smile. You wouldn't even have known she'd spoken. But I knew what I heard. If I'd ever been on Twitter in my life, I'd be announcing to the world that Alexis had a personality. #bodyguardhumor

"Can I take those for you, Lia?"

Every hair on my body stiffened. That was not my name. At least, not anymore.

Starched cotton brushed my bare arm as Britta Tanaka leaned over me wearing a black-and-white waiter's uniform. Her black hair was slicked back from her face and she wasn't wearing her fake eyeglass frames or her colorful jewelry, but it was her. I almost screeched in excitement but she gave me such a tight-lipped, wide-eyed warning, I clamped my teeth down on my tongue.

Of course. Right. No one could know that I knew her. But what. The hell. Was she doing here?

"Bathroom," she whispered under her breath.

Then she slipped my plate from the table and hustled off. It took every ounce of my willpower not to get up and chase after her. Instead, I clasped my now-sweaty palms together in my lap and ever so slowly counted to one hundred Mississippis.

Somewhere around the sixties, Frieda Christova, who lived on my floor, stopped by and asked me to sign her yearbook. "Since you're the valedictorian and all," she said. Real nice. But I did it anyway. When I was done, I finished the count, then got up.

"Can I help you, miss?" Alexis asked.

"Bathroom," I said calmly. "I need to use the bathroom."

I started across the wide, gleaming wood floor of the Worthington School's boathouse and instantly felt my mother's eyes on me. I swear it was like she had radar on her irises. Alexis followed me at a distance of about three feet every step of the way, until we'd made it to the hall. There, she pushed open the door of the bathroom and glanced inside.

"All clear."

At least she hadn't gone in to check every last stall—which she probably would have done if we weren't already on the campus of a school with some of the tightest security of any in the nation.

"Thank you." I slipped inside, the tulle skirt of the deeply purple dress Matilda had chosen for me swishing against the doorjamb. The door closed behind me and goose bumps prickled my skin. "Britta?" I whispered.

"Back here!"

Britta jumped down from the last toilet, her boots hitting the floor hard, and peeked out from the wheelchair-accessible stall. I raced over to her and grabbed her into a hug. She started to talk, but I clamped my hand over her mouth and dragged her into the stall.

"Bodyguard," I whispered, releasing her. "What are you doing here?"

"I came to take you home," Britta replied, a phrase that nearly stopped my heart. "Jasper and Fiona are here too. We're gonna bust you out."

"Jasper's here?" The words were more like a gasp. "He doesn't hate me?"

"What? No!" Britta paused and considered. "Shelby does, though, so I could see how you'd think that. Getting arrested by the feds is apparently a pretty scary deal."

"I know. I was there," I replied. I didn't think I'd ever stop seeing those men running into Jasper's house with guns drawn, one of them pointing his weapon at Jasper's heart.

"But it's not like it was your fault the FBI thought he kidnapped you."

No. It wasn't my fault. But it was my mother's, which felt close enough. It *was* close enough. Did Shelby and Jasper not know that my mother was the one who had sent the feds after them? But then again, why would they? It wasn't like it was the habit of federal interrogators to give information to their suspects. At least, I assumed it wasn't.

It must have been terrifying. I had to talk to Jasper. I had to apologize.

"So where is he?" I asked.

Britta crossed her arms over her chest. She looked almost like a stranger without the dozens of rubber bracelets she always wore on her wrists.

"You know, I went out of my way to land this job so I could be the inside man—went through the background checks, the lie detector test, peed in a cup and everything—and still I'm the chopped liver."

"Oh my God, Britta, I'm sorry. Honestly. I'm so grateful you're here and it is *so* good to see you," I said. "I just . . . I texted him last night and he hasn't texted me back. I thought he was never going to talk to me again."

"Well, I'm guessing you guys have a lot to talk about. But if he's mad, he's not mad enough to leave you with the wicked witch of Washington."

I giggled, which was not something I did very often. "So what's the plan? Is there a plan?"

"We're going to create a distraction and then Jasper's going to sneak you out through the kitchen. Just try to stay as close to those swinging doors as you can for the rest of the night and then wait for my signal."

"What's the signal?"

"Oh, you'll know it when it happens."

The door to the bathroom creaked open. Britta instantly jumped up, landing with her feet on the toilet seat. Since when was she Spider-Man?

"You all right, miss?" Alexis called out.

"Um . . . I'm okay," I said. "It's just . . . really hard to pee in this dress!"

There was a pause. "Interesting. Do you need . . . my assistance?"

Britta slapped her hand over her mouth to keep from laughing out loud.

"Uh, no thanks! I'll be right out!"

The door closed. I could just imagine Alexis out there thanking her lucky stars that I'd said no.

"Holy crap, Lia. You have people offering to help you *pee*!"

I smacked Britta's arm and we both laughed as silently as possible.

"Okay wait. Stop. Stop laughing!" I demanded, bracing myself against the wall. "We need to think this through. If I leave, my mother will know exactly where I am. She'll just come back and get me again."

"We have a plan for that too. You know how Fiona and Duncan's mom is a civil rights lawyer?"

I blinked. "Actually, I didn't know that." In the two weeks I'd been in Sweetbriar, I'd never met the twins' mom, Caitlin. Only their father, Hal, who owned the Little Tree Diner, where the twins worked, and where I'd worked for about ten days before moving on to Second Chances.

"Oh. Well, that's why she's never around. Anyway, she's totally ready to defend you. She's got it all worked out." Britta smiled and raised her palms. "Who's working for you, babe?"

"Wow." I leaned back against the wall of the stall, flinching as my shoulder blades hit the cold metal. I felt overwhelmed suddenly that anyone cared about me enough to go to all this trouble. "Britta, this is amazing."

"So, is Operation Free Lia a go?"

They'd even given their mission a code name.

"All right," I said, biting my bottom lip. "I'm in."

For the first time in my life, I asked a guy to dance. I kind of had to. It was the only way to get Alexis to keep even a slight distance and make sure I stayed relatively close to the kitchen doors, which were just down a short hall behind the bandstand. Luckily, I found Frederick Valois, a native Frenchman for whom I'd written basically every assignment during American Lit, leaning against a wall looking bored. No big surprise there. Compact, lithe, and handsome in a swarthy, *Pirates of the Caribbean* kind of way, the guy pretty much always looked bored. It made me wonder what it would take to entertain him.

"Bonjour, Frederick," I began, sliding up next to his right shoulder. *"Voulez-vous danser avec moi?"*

Frederick's eyes lit up for half a second before he rearranged his face into its ever-present mask of indifference. Honestly, I felt honored to have elicited a reaction. He sighed.

"Pourquoi pas?"

And with two tons of enthusiasm, we took the floor. It was a slow song, so all I had to do was wrap my arms around his skinny neck and step side to side. Frederick, who was wearing a pinstripe suit, an open-collar shirt, and a silk pocket square, gazed past my shoulder, not bothering to look me in the eye or attempt conversation, which was fine by me. I was too busy guesstimating how many steps it would take me to get to the kitchen, my heart pounding an erratic rhythm in my chest.

Somewhere on campus was Jasper. I was about to see him again. I just hoped Frederick couldn't tell how keyed up I was, and that if he could, he didn't think it was about him.

"So," he said finally, "you have been on the news lately, no?"

I blinked. Part of Frederick's mystique was that he cared about nothing and no one other than himself. I couldn't imagine him watching any sort of news program, whether it was on CNN or MTV. "You know about that?"

Frederick gave a short laugh. His breath smelled salty somehow. "Everybody knows about that. You are the new celebrity. The party girl no one knew about. Do you like the parties, Cecilia?"

He had this sort of mischievous and challenging look in his eyes that set off instinctive alarm bells. Oh no. Next thing you knew this kid was going to whip out a tiny bag of something I definitely didn't want to get involved in. Was this my reputation now? That I was just off the rails? The music swelled, the lights seemed to dim, and my hands got seriously sweaty. I was opening my mouth to tell him off, when suddenly, there was an epic crash.

I stepped back. Glass and chocolate mousse splattered across the floor like a culinary nuclear blast zone—and Alexis was covered in it.

"Oh my God! I am *so* sorry!" Britta cried.

She must have been slightly behind me, because I couldn't see her. But the second I heard her voice, I ran. This was my distraction.

37

My heart was in my throat as I burst into the brightly lit white-and-chrome kitchen. No Jasper. All I saw were cooks in chef's hats and men wiping sweat from their brows with bandanas. Plus there was steam. Lots of steam. Then someone grabbed my wrist and pulled me around a corner.

"Jasper!"

He looked a little pale, but otherwise just the same. Blond hair sticking out from behind his ears, blue eyes searching mine. He wore a black T-shirt and jeans with his favorite black cowboy boots tucked under the cuffs, and he smelled like mint and fresh air.

He smelled like freedom.

"Are you okay?" he asked me.

The simple sound of his voice sent shivers right through me. I nodded, overwhelmed. "Are you?"

"Aces." And then he smiled. And then he kissed me. And even though I knew we didn't have the time, I wouldn't have pulled out of that embrace for anything. So it was probably a good thing he broke away first.

"We have to go," he said.

I nodded again and he grabbed my hand, leading me down a hall and out into the open air. We ran over to his white convertible, tulle bouncing around my thighs. It was so weird, seeing his car on this campus. Two worlds colliding in the most surreal way possible. Jasper skidded to a stop and grabbed a trench coat and baseball cap out of the backseat.

"Put these on."

I did as I was told, covering my hair and then my dress and cinching the coat tight.

"You're not mad?" I asked. "I mean . . . I lied to you. You didn't know who I really was. You didn't know we'd met before. You didn't even know my real name."

He glanced past me at the boathouse. Inside were dozens of security guards, police, and probably even Secret Service.

"We can talk about all that later. Right now, we have to get the hell out of here."

It didn't escape my attention that he hadn't exactly answered my question. A hard stone of dread settled in my stomach as I jumped in the car. "What about Britta?"

"Fiona's waiting at the hotel for her. I'm assuming that she's currently getting fired."

Jasper slammed his car door, dropped the car into gear, and swung out of the space, one hand maneuvering the wheel while the other expertly worked the stick shift. He took off down a service road I'd never been on in my life and didn't even know existed on campus. I glanced over my shoulder, half expecting to see flashing lights, but there was no one and nothing. I imagined my mother's face when she realized I was gone and, oddly, felt a pang of guilt.

Alexis was probably getting fired too. The second bodyguard I'd gotten canned in less than a month. What was I doing? This was insane. I was totally living up to the public's opinion of me. Acting like a spoiled brat. Or even worse, I was acting like my mother—only caring about myself and what

I wanted. And she'd been so different this morning. So . . . human. Most of the day, really. She'd let me pick out my own graduation gift—I'd talked her into a new laptop instead of a tennis bracelet—had barely cringed when I'd ordered the hamburger at lunch, and hadn't even forced me to sit next to Chet Westinghouse at the table. What if doing this meant I'd never see that side of her again?

But then I looked at Jasper as he concentrated on the road, and I realized it didn't matter. I was eighteen and I'd never had the opportunity to choose anything for myself. It was time for me to live my life and if I was going to do that, it should be the life I wanted, shouldn't it? It was either this, or jump squarely onto the Rebecca Montgomery for President parade float.

"What is it?" Jasper asked, glancing over at me as the wind played with his hair. "What's wrong?"

We were coming to the end of the road. Up ahead, one guard manned an entry gate, but the exit was wide open.

"Nothing," I said. "Not one little thing."

Then I leaned back in my seat and smiled.

"Floor it."

And that's exactly what Jasper did.

"So tell me," Jasper said quietly, holding my hand between us. "Why did you run?"

We were sitting on the hood of his convertible, looking out over the sheer surface of a random fishing pond alongside the highway somewhere in the middle of Virginia, the water reflecting the light of a zillion stars. This wasn't the first question I thought he'd ask. I thought he'd ask why I lied. I thought he'd make it about him. That's what any normal guy would want to know. But Jasper, as I was constantly rediscovering, was not a normal guy.

"Honestly? Because I finally had the chance. I'd been thinking about running for so long, but I never got up the guts and they were always keeping such a close watch on me." I paused and looked down at our fingers, the contrast of his light skin against mine. A cool breeze tickled the back of my bare neck. I knew Jasper wanted to ask questions, could practically feel them crowding the air between us, but he held back. "I just felt so trapped, that's the thing," I continued. "Ever since I was little, I was never allowed to go anywhere other than school or do anything other than what my mother told me to do. I had no friends, no life. Even when I went places with the family, I was always surrounded by bodyguards. It was like I could never see any farther than the one-by-one-foot block of sky above my head."

We both tilted our faces up automatically, and the expanse of the star-filled canopy overwhelmed me. Everything seemed so much bigger since I ran. The world, the future, everything.

"And then Gigi died and I . . . I guess I kind of snapped. We were supposed to go away together after I graduated. At least, that was our crazy plan. And I was stupid enough to believe it would actually happen."

My throat tightened unexpectedly. That was how it was

with memories of Gigi. They came on hard, fast, and out of nowhere, and I'd suddenly go from fine to basket case at the speed of a moving train. Just like that, I found myself blinking back tears.

Jasper released my hand, put his warm, strong arm around me, and pulled me close. A few tears squeezed out, but I managed to hold the rest in. I didn't want him to think I was getting weepy about my cloistered, yet admittedly over-privileged-in-other-ways life. I could cry about Gigi later. I *would* cry about Gigi later, I knew from experience. I had a feeling I'd be crying about her for a long time.

"I'm so sorry that you were made to feel that way." Jasper kissed the side of my forehead. "You're not stupid, and you are definitely not trapped. Not anymore."

I smiled, savoring the rumble of his voice as my ear pressed into his chest. But I couldn't have confidence in his words. Because my mother was still out there. And if there was one thing I knew for sure, it was that she was going to do everything in her power to bring me back.

"The thing I don't get is, why did you lie?" Jasper asked, breaking the silence. "Why didn't you tell me who you really were?"

There it was. Question number two. I lifted my head and looked him in the eye.

"I didn't want to go back, and I knew that if anyone found out where I was, they'd sell my story to the highest-paying tabloid."

Jasper's brow creased beneath that flop of blond hair. "I would never—"

"I know. I know *you* wouldn't, but I mean, *I* almost slipped up, like, a dozen times and gave it away. So if I couldn't trust myself not to spill, how could I trust anyone else? Do you really think that if you'd mistakenly blurted something to Shelby that first week, that I would have lasted as long as I did?"

Jasper sighed. "True. I wish you had trusted me, though. Especially after I told you I loved you."

There was a lump of something hard and cold wedged between my windpipe and my heart. "I know. I wish I had too." Overhead a shooting star streaked by, but it winked out so fast I didn't have the time to tell him. Which made me inexplicably sad. "By that point I felt like I was in too deep. I knew in the back of my mind that it couldn't last much longer and I think . . . I think I just wanted things to stay the way they were. I was living the dream, you know? This dream I'd had for ten years to get the hell out of there and away from them. To have friends. To have a hot boyfriend."

I shot him a wet smile and he cracked a grin.

"That would be me?" he joked.

"That would be you," I said with a laugh. Then I sighed. "I didn't want to wake up."

Jasper leaned back on his elbows, the car hood popping beneath his shifting weight. He looked so handsome in the starlight. A tiny bit of glossy stubble peppered his perfect cheekbones. He tilted his head as he looked at me.

"I do love you, you know."

Why did I sense a "but" coming?

"I love you too," I said, trying not to sound desperate.

"But here's the thing." He reached over and took my hand again. His palm was big, warm, dry, familiar. My heart pounded a mile a minute. "No more lying, okay? From here on out, you and me, we're honest with each other."

"I promise. No more lying."

"Good." He lifted our hands and kissed the back of mine. Crisis averted. Only now did my body start to calm its freaked-out self down. "And I never want to meet this crazy family of yours, I'll tell ya that right now."

Something shifted in my gut as an image of my father—gaunt from two weeks of worrying—flickered through my mind. "Well, it's mostly my mom. . . ."

"Your mother then. She sounds like a real winner," he said sarcastically. "If she ever comes within two feet of you again, she's gonna have to deal with me."

I smirked and Jasper's eyes widened.

"What? You don't think I can take her?"

Now I laughed out loud. "Yes, of course you can take her," I said, patting his back. "If you could get past the constant army of bodyguards, state police, FBI. . . ."

I was exaggerating. My mother was never surrounded by FBI. Unless she was busy sending them to arrest my boyfriend, like she had just a few days ago. I slid off the hood of the car and stretched my arms over my head. Now that I knew I wasn't being dumped, I felt light on my feet.

"Don't even get me started on the FBI. I'm as patriotic as the next guy, but I'd love to know what brainiac inside that stellar organization decided to arrest me and Shelby without a shred of evidence that we'd done anything wrong."

My heart thunked. "What?"

"I'm serious!" he exclaimed, walking around to the driver's side door. "Kidnapping? Where did they get that from? It's like they're making up theories out of thin air."

I leaned both hands on the car and took a breath. And there it was. He didn't know. He didn't know my mother had been behind his arrest.

"I mean, do you have any idea how many phone calls I've had trying to explain everything to the people at the record company?" he said, opening the door and flopping down behind the wheel. "Thank the good lord Evan convinced them that all publicity is good publicity, but I still gotta do damage control or whatever—convince the general public I'm not some kind of maniac. This whole thing coulda cost me my career." He ran a hand lightly along the steering wheel. "Still could, really, if the next few days don't go right. Least that's what they tell me. But do those jerks care? No. *Just doing our job, sir.* That was what they told us after two days of nonstop questioning. Like that made it all okay."

Shit. What was I supposed to do here? We'd *just* promised not to lie to each other, but he also already mistrusted my mother.

My mother, who, no matter what I did, would always be part of my life. My mother, who, in all likelihood, was going to show up in Sweetbriar to squire me home again within the next twenty-four hours. If he ever found out she was the real reason his dream had almost crashed and burned . . . he'd hate me forever.

Okay, but did he really need to know? It *was* the FBI who had arrested them. Wasn't it better for him to focus his ire on one faceless organization than on my mom and, by extension, me? Not telling him wasn't really a lie. Who's to say I even knew my mother was behind it?

Awesome. Now I was thinking like a politician. Like . . . my mother.

Slowly, I pulled open the door and sat down next to him. "It's going to be okay, Jasper."

"Yeah?" he said, revving the engine. "What makes you say that?"

"You're a star," I told him. "You were born to be a star."

He grinned and my heart all but stopped.

"And besides, I've already been all over the news apologizing for taking off. Everyone knows I wasn't kidnapped."

"True," he said. "But I'm still the guy who corrupted America's sweetheart."

I grabbed his black cowboy hat from the backseat and placed it on my own head. "Maybe, but that just makes you sexier," I said, improvising

Jasper's smile turned wolfish. "You know what? I think I'm gonna keep you around."

"Sounds like a plan to me," I said.

He leaned over to kiss me, revved the engine one more time, and took off down the road. A while later, we crossed the state line and left Virginia behind. If only I could've left my guilt there too.

3

"HOME SWEET HOME!"

I collapsed face-first onto my bed and nuzzled my nose into the soft striped pillowcase. Fiona Taylor hovered in the doorway, laughing, while out in the living room, Britta checked Twitter for any mention of my escape. Fi had bags under her brown eyes but still seemed energized—lit from within by adrenaline, same as me. She was wearing baggy jeans and a comfy-looking T-shirt, her blond hair pulled back in a low ponytail as she sipped from a paper coffee cup. The whole "team" had pulled an all-nighter, driving from D.C. to Sweetbriar, but it was well worth it.

"Anything?" I called out.

"Nothing!" Britta shouted back. "Not one hashtag!"

Fiona and I locked eyes. "Weird," we said in unison.

I sat up and grabbed my violin case from the corner next to my bed, then hugged it to my chest.

"I never thought I'd see you again," I whispered.

"Okay, is that normal? You talking to inanimate objects?" Fiona asked. "Or do I need to get you to sleep, stat?"

"I'm fine," I said with a laugh. "It's just so good to be back. And I really did think I'd never see this again. Or anything else here. You included."

I got up and hugged her for the fourth or fifth time. Fiona groaned in a good-natured way and hugged me back. She was going to have to humor me, because who knew how long we were going to be together? My mother might have gone dormant for now, but there was no chance in hell she was going to stay that way.

I hadn't been able to believe it when we'd pulled up in front Hadley's Drugs, the storefront on the first floor of the apartment I shared with Britta, and no one was there. Not one black sedan, not one cop car. Not even a reporter with a crappy digital camera. Jasper and I had driven all the way down from D.C, with Britta and Fiona an hour behind us, giving my mother plenty of time to scramble an FBI team out of Nashville to be waiting for us when we arrived. But there had been nothing other than the glowing streetlamps and the birds singing in the town square as the sun came up.

Honestly, I was almost disappointed.

"What do you think she's planning?" Britta asked, appearing behind Fiona's shoulder. She was back in true Britta form—skull and crossbones T-shirt, red ribbons in her hair, and fishnets under a purple pleated skirt. Apparently she'd changed back at the hotel and Fiona had been forced to talk her out of burning her boring waitress uniform.

I hadn't even considered that—the possibility that the

reason I'd yet to be dragged home again was that my mother was busy planning something bigger for me. Something worse. But what could possibly be worse?

"I . . . I don't know."

At that moment the front door banged open and we all jumped. Fiona actually screamed.

"The conquering heroes return!"

"Duncan! You scared the crap out of us!" Fiona shouted at her brother.

Duncan Taylor pushed his way between the girls to enter my room, carrying a piece of white poster board with the words WELCOME HOME! spelled out in red marker. He also had a cake box and my stomach growled at the site of it. He dropped both items on my bed and tackled me backward onto the mattress in a huge bear hug. Our legs entwined and our chests mashed up against each other until we both realized how awkward it was and disentangled.

"It's really good to see you," Duncan said, pushing his dark hair out of his now ruby-red face. He wore a clean USA SOCCER T-shirt, athletic shorts, and sandals, and smelled as if he'd just showered. "And my mom's on speed dial just waiting for your call."

"Thanks." I shrugged. "But so far it's been pretty quiet."

"Cool. Then let's bust open this cake."

"Cake for breakfast!" Fiona cheered. "It's anarchy!"

Duncan grabbed the box and sign and we followed him to

the small kitchen, where he sliced the red twine with a knife and revealed a scrumptious-looking, buttercream-covered monstrosity. The cake read WE MISSED YOU CECILIA, with the *LIA* underlined.

"Yeah, that's a good question," Fiona said, grabbing the knife from her brother to cut the cake. "What are we supposed to call you now?"

"Cecilia, I guess," I replied, though the idea didn't sit well.

"What's wrong?" Britta asked, holding out a plate while Fiona flopped a slice of cake onto it. Fiona handed me the plate and dug a fork out of a drawer. Duncan dipped his finger in a glob of pink frosting.

"I really liked Lia," I said. "She was kind of everything I always wanted to be."

They all stared at me.

"But she *was* you," Duncan said, pointing at me with the frosting glob. "And you were her. It's not like she died. I mean, like it's not like *you* died. You're standing right here."

"I know. It's crazy," I said. "But being Lia Washington in name kind of freed me up to not act like myself. To, I don't know, be brave or something." I blushed. "I know it sounds stupid."

"No it doesn't," Fiona said. "I totally get it. In fact, I'm kind of jealous you got the chance. I can't imagine everything I would do if I got to go be someone else."

"Well, why don't you both stop being whoever it is you

don't want to be and start being the people you want to be?" Britta suggested.

"Yeah, like it's that simple," Fiona groused, cutting another piece of cake.

Britt and Duncan looked at each other as if Fiona and I were speaking another, incomprehensible language. Which wasn't surprising. It was pretty clear the two of them owned their identities in ways that were totally natural. To them, at least.

"Maybe it is," I said. "I mean, I did do it. For a while. Just because everyone knows who I am now doesn't mean I have to go back to acting like a timid little recluse." I thought of the way I'd asked Frederick to dance—how it hadn't intimidated me in the slightest. "I'll do it if you'll do it," I said to Fiona.

She paused mid-chew, one cheek full of cake. "Do what, exactly?"

"Be brave," I suggested. "Do one brave thing that you'd never thought you'd do. Something unexpected. Something that makes everyone you know go, *no way, really?*"

Fiona laughed. "You're crazy."

"Just one?" Duncan challenged.

"One's a start," I replied. "Whaddaya say, Taylor? You up for it?"

Fiona swallowed. "You know what? Yes. I'm in. One brave thing."

"It's a deal." I dipped a finger in the cake's thick icing and held it out. "I suggest a frosting toast—to being who you want to be, not what everyone else expects you to be."

Duncan touched his pink fingertip to mine. Then Fiona scooped up a bit of green from a leaf and Britta took a whole chunk of buttercream.

"To being who you want to be."

We touched fingers, then sucked the frosting off, smiles all around. The door opened again, and this time it was Jasper. He'd changed into clean jeans and a plaid shirt.

"Did I interrupt something?" he drawled.

"Just the first-ever frosting toast," I replied.

"Well, I'm sorry I missed that," he said, pushing his hands into the front pockets of his jeans. He left the door open, which made me wonder what was coming—whether it was good or bad. Was he leaving the door open because the FBI was right behind him? Or worse, my mother?

"You guys mind if I steal Cecilia here away for some alone time?" he asked.

So it was good then. Very, very good.

Then he looked me in the eye, and his expression grew serious. "We have a lot to talk about."

"So I have something to tell you."

Jasper held my hand as we emerged onto the sidewalk on Main Street, pausing to let a group of elderly power walkers stride by. They each greeted us with a friendly "Morning!" until one of them narrowed her eyes and whispered something to the woman next to her. By the time they reached the corner, they were all looking back over their shoulders at us, their arms still pumping away.

What was that about? People in this town had to know that Jasper hadn't actually done anything wrong, right? He was one of their own. They knew him.

"Well, like I told you last night, I gotta do some damage control," Jasper continued, apparently not noticing the staring ladies, who finally rounded a corner out of sight. "The label's a little concerned, now that there's all this footage of me being led out of my house at gunpoint and in handcuffs."

I pulled my fingers from his and hid my face behind my hands. Suddenly all I wanted to do was crawl into a hole somewhere and die. "What a nightmare. I'm so sorry, Jasper."

"No. No, it's okay. I don't blame you. It's not about that."

We crossed Main toward the park at the center of town, where a few people were jogging or walking their dogs. The sun rose steadily, casting long shadows across the dewy grass. Nearby, a church bell rang, inviting parishioners to Sunday services. Jasper slung his arm over my shoulders and I settled in against him as we walked.

"But he's lined up all these interviews over the next couple of weeks and I have a few concert dates in Nashville and Austin coming up—"

"Austin? That's great!" I said. Not that I'd ever been there or knew anything about it firsthand, but Jasper had mentioned a few times how huge the music scene was there.

"And I'm also going to start recording my album."

"Wow." I paused in the middle of the brick walkway. "So you're gonna be pretty busy then."

"Looks that way." Jasper smiled. He was excited about this. "I just wanted to make sure I was clear about it up front so you don't think I'm, well, avoiding you or anything. It's just . . . bad timing. We won't be seeing much of each other."

"But for such a great reason!" I said, hugging him. Well, mostly a great reason. If I hadn't gotten him arrested, he wouldn't be half as busy. But I decided not to hammer home that point. I turned and walked over to a bench underneath the full branches of a magnolia tree. Suddenly I felt utterly exhausted. The adrenaline of the past twelve hours had finally worn off, but I sat up straight, trying to hide it. "Anything I can do to help, Jasper. Really."

It was the least I could offer, considering what my mother had done to him.

"Thanks. I sure do appreciate that." He sat next to me and kissed my cheek. He'd shaved since he'd been home and his skin felt smooth and clean. "The good news is, my agent worked it out so that I can record the album in Gary Benson's private studio, which is up at his house here in Sweetbriar. So at least I can stay here. I mean, when I'm not on the road."

"That's great!" I leaned against his shoulder and looked out across the green grass of the park. A huge banner was strung across the gazebo advertising the Sweetbriar Summer Fest, coming up in three weeks. I had no idea what Summer Fest was, but it sounded like fun. It sounded like some good, normal, fun.

What if my mother really never came after me? What if my escape made her realize I was actually a lost cause? Was she even capable of giving up? If she left me alone, then in a few weeks I'd be at Summer Fest with Jasper and my friends, laughing, eating, dancing (I imagined). Being free. I wondered if there were going to be carnival rides at this thing. I hadn't sat my butt inside so much as a Ferris wheel car since I was eight years old. Did I even like carnival rides?

A tiny flutter of hope sprang up inside my chest, and I realized it was about time for me to start figuring out my life. Finding out who I was and planning my actual future. Maybe it was a good thing that Jasper was going to be busy. I had a lot to do.

On the far side of the park, a man dressed in black smoked a cigarette, leaning back against the side of his dark gray pickup truck. He suddenly lifted a camera, trained the lens right on us, and snapped off a few pictures. My heart hammered painfully in my chest and I sat up straight.

"What?" Jasper said. "What's wrong?"

The man jumped into his truck and pulled out, the engine rumbling. He was probably working for my mother—confirming I was here so she could send in her flying monkeys.

"Lia? Are you okay?"

"I'm fine," I said, not wanting to concern him and spoil the moment. I put my head on his shoulder again. "Sorry. It was nothing."

Jasper was quiet for a moment, and I tensed, waiting for more questions, but they never came.

"I'm glad you're home," Jasper said softly, kissing the side of my head.

I took a deep breath and sighed. "Me too."

Now all I had to do was figure out a way to stay here.

4

I SAT UP IN BED, CLUTCHING THE SHEETS AT MY sides. Sunlight streamed through the windows, an early-morning kind of glare. When the hell had I fallen asleep? I could have sworn it was never going to happen. Every time I'd started to doze off, I'd flinch awake seconds later, expecting a bang on the door or the screech of tires outside my window. I grabbed the watch Britta had loaned me the night before and squinted at the numbers. Even then, the thing was blurry—I didn't have my glasses with me and my contacts were in two cups of water on the nightstand—but it looked like it was after ten. I'd disappeared from my post-graduation party almost twelve hours ago. There could be no confusion as to where I'd gone. Something was seriously wrong.

I stepped tentatively into the living room, half expecting to see a camera crew setting up there, but found only Britta, hair pushed back in a purple headband, eating a huge stack of scrumptious-looking pancakes at the kitchen island. She had her phone in one hand, a fork in the other, and a drop of maple syrup on her lip. Her thumb moved up and down the phone's screen as she scrolled through messages or feeds.

"Good morning," I said, sounding wary.

"Hey. Sleep okay?" she asked. Then she looked at me and her nose scrunched. "Ugh. Apparently not."

"Thanks." I slid onto a stool across from her. "Is that Twitter?"

"Yeah, and there's nothing." She turned her phone in its pineapple-shaped case to face me. "No mention of you or your mom or your family or your daring escape. Not that I did it for the accolades, but one mention would be nice."

"Is there anything about the school?" I asked, making a pocket out of the front of my T-shirt and pushing my hands deep inside.

"Why? You think someone blew up the boathouse after we left?" she joked.

I leveled her with a stare.

"Oh. That stuff actually happens in your world. Sorry." She paled and typed into the phone. "Some people tweeted pictures from the post-graduation parties, but that's it."

"This is so strange. I mean, the silence is almost scarier than anything. It's like she's trying to make me sweat."

And it was totally working.

I reached up and touched my grandmother's pearls. I'd slept in them all night, not wanting to take them off when I changed my clothes. They were the only sentimental gift my mother had ever given me. The only one that hadn't been selected by one of her assistants. Maybe that's what this was about. She was hoping I'd start to feel guilty for bailing again. Trying to manipulate me into coming home on my own.

Britta got up from her stool, went to the oven, and took out a plate of pancakes that she'd clearly put in there to warm.

"Carb therapy?" she asked, arching one eyebrow.

Normally, I'd never eat something that heavy first thing in the morning. The detriments of a heavy breakfast had been hammered into my brain from a very early age. Breakfast was supposed to be light. Lean protein. Fruit. Maybe a little yogurt and flaxseed. Certainly not carbs and sugar. Yes, I'd dabbled in Tammy Tanaka's homemade muffins over the past couple of weeks, but pancakes and syrup? I mean, my mother's brain would explode.

But my mother wasn't here. And apparently, she wasn't going to be. I reached back and unclasped the necklace.

"Sure," I said, forcing a smile. "Bring it on."

"So what's it like on Martha's Vineyard, Fiddler?" Tammy Tanaka asked me, leaning back against the counter at Second Chances, sipping a cup of tea. Her dark curls were shiny as they tumbled over her shoulders. She was wearing a fringed silk shawl over a flowy white sundress and was looking at me with this kind of weird awe in her eyes.

I didn't like it.

"Do you know any celebrities?" she asked. "Wait. What am I talking about? You *are* a celebrity! We should get your picture framed for the wall. And you could autograph it!"

"Mom! You're embarrassing yourself," Shelby hissed.

"Oh please, Binky. She doesn't mind, do you, hon?" Tammy took another sip of her tea. "We're like family."

We *had* been like family, which was exactly why I did mind. Fame did strange things to people—even the proximity to fame. I knew this, not from personal experience, but because I'd spent my entire life hearing stories spun by my uncles, aunts, and cousins about boyfriends who craved the spotlight more than they craved a relationship, and girlfriends who thought dating a Montgomery meant getting free clothes and trips and invites to cool events. But of all the people in town, I never would have expected Tammy to treat me differently once she found out who I really was. Unfortunately, if the last ten minutes of conversation were any indication, it turned out that Tammy was a Montgomery family fan. A big one. She even knew the dates my mother and her four brothers were born, plus some of her cousins. She knew the date *I* was born. And the date of my almost-kidnapping.

"Um . . . do you want me to sweep the sidewalk?" I offered, already reaching into the broom closet. I'd been rearranging the scarves to mimic the gradations of a rainbow, but was starting to feel like fresh air was in order. And silence. "It was looking a little dusty when I came in."

I didn't wait for an answer, but hoofed it outside with the broom. Shelby came out after me and I turned to face her. She hadn't actually looked me in the eye all morning.

"I'm really sorry, Shelby. Honestly," I said, lifting one hand to shield my face from the sun. "I figured my mother would eventually find me, but I never thought she'd—"

Shelby held up one delicate hand, her scowl so intimidating that I actually took a step back. "I have a mug shot, Cecilia. A *mug shot*. And it's atrocious. It's all over the Internet! Do you really think this town is going to elect me Sweetbriar Summer Princess when I have a *mug shot*!?"

She whipped out her phone and showed it to me. The lights reflected off her forehead, making it look like a greasy movie screen, and her eyes were half closed, her mouth slightly open. It was not attractive.

"Um . . . what's Sweetbriar Summer Princess?"

Shelby groaned and flicked her long hair behind her shoulders. "Don't talk to me for the rest of the day. Don't even look at me."

She stormed back inside, letting the door slam, and I started to sweep. My mother really did ruin everything. Just when Shelby and I had started to sort of become friends, she swooped in and destroyed it. Not that it was intentional, of course. My mother hadn't even known that Shelby existed when she descended on Sweetbriar to arrest the love of my life in a desperate effort to save face. Shelby was simply collateral damage. Something my mom had left a trail of throughout her career without ever taking a second to look back.

Across the park, two shiny pickup trucks and a couple of sedans pulled up in front of an old brick building. The doors popped open and people poured out.

For a second, I thought this was it—that they'd finally come for me—but then I saw that the men and women who emerged were wearing jeans and baseball caps and one of them carried a yellow hard hat. They gathered on the sidewalk and a man with white hair pointed up at the building. There was some chatting, some nodding, some gesturing, and then they dispersed, a couple of people going inside while others stepped along the sidewalk as if inspecting the walls and windows.

Tammy walked out and handed me a glossy brochure. "I almost forgot. I got this for you."

I tucked the broom handle under one arm and looked at the cover. Tennessee School of Design. The illustration was a needle through a button with thread spooling out into an explosion of colors.

"What's this for?" I asked.

"I think you should apply. You'd make a great designer, Cecilia," she said, putting a warm hand on my back. "But they also have classes in merchandising, accessories, styling, branding. I imagine there'd be a lot there that would interest you. And they're taking applications for the spring semester."

Pride welled up inside of me. Tammy thought I was good at my job. She thought I had talent.

"Wow, Tammy. Thank you! This is . . . this is amazing."

I gave her a one-armed hug, deciding not to tell her I had already been accepted at Harvard for the fall. In only eight weeks, I was expected to attend orientation in the same hallowed halls my parents had graced with their presence all those years ago. Of course, when I'd run, I'd thought I was giving up on all that. I'd never really wanted to go anyway, but I hadn't been able to come up with a viable alternative, and I knew what my mother expected of me. If she had anything to say about it, I'd be in Cambridge, Massachusetts, in September, and I'd never step foot in Tennessee again.

But then . . . she hadn't shown up here yet. Hadn't tried to contact me. Maybe . . . maybe design school was a possibility.

"Thank you," I said again, leaning the broom against the wall now so I could flip through the brochure. Someone on the far side of the park shouted, catching our attention, and I saw that the man in the hard hat was leaning out a third-story window to talk to the people on the sidewalk.

"What's going on over there?" I asked.

Tammy narrowed her eyes. "I don't know. That's the old primary school. I've been begging Mayor Wilson to let me lease it for years. I had this idea to turn it into artists' studios and maybe open a bigger store. But it's historical and so there's all kinds of hoops you gotta jump through. He didn't think my business plan was up to snuff."

Another car pulled up and this time the driver got out to open the back door. The man who emerged was tall, black, clean-shaven, and already buttoning one button on the front of his sport jacket. The brochure slipped from my grasp and hit the pavement with a thwap.

Tammy let out a gasp. "Is that—"

"My dad," I said.

"Cecilia? Cecilia Montgomery?"

A young woman with a sleek auburn ponytail approached, jogging across the street toward us. She was already pulling a digital recorder out of her bag. I grabbed the college brochure off the ground and automatically started walking in the opposite direction, keeping my head down and my face turned away. My brain raced a mile a minute as my fingers went automatically to the silver bird pendant Tammy had given me my first week here. It felt much lighter around my neck than those emotionally loaded pearls. What was my dad doing in Sweetbriar? Why was he currently shaking hands with the mayor and not looking for me? Where was my mother?

And who the hell was this stalker person?

"You okay, Fiddler?" Tammy shouted after me as the woman speed-walked to keep up.

"Fine!" I shouted back, my voice strained. "I'll just be back in a sec!" I yelled, because I had to yell something and technically, I was still on the clock.

I crossed the street, hugging the brochure to my chest like a lifeline, and a man stood up from the bench outside Hadley's. He pointed an iPad at me. My heart all but stopped. It was the same man who'd snapped Jasper's and my picture in the park yesterday morning.

"Cecilia. Why did you choose Sweetbriar? What is it about this place that your family loves so much?"

I put up a hand to block his video feed and upped my pace, jogging toward the corner. Part of me wanted to run down the alley and into my apartment, but then I realized I didn't want these people to know where I lived. They'd find out soon enough, but it didn't have to be now. I saw the diner sign up ahead and started to run.

"Cecilia! Come on! Just one comment!" the woman called. When I glanced over my shoulder, they'd been joined by a third reporter, this one tall, lanky, and hungry-looking. I shoved open the door of the Little Tree Diner and Duncan looked up with a bright smile.

"Hey, Lia!" When he saw my panic, his face fell. "What's—"

"Don't let them follow me!" I ran right past him into the kitchen just as the reporters came in through the front door.

The cooks seemed surprised to see me, and Hal stood up from his desk with a crease of concern on his forehead. His mostly bald head shone under the hot lights and he looked like a fighter in his tight black T-shirt and jeans. Maybe he and Duncan could hold these people off until I figured out what to do.

"What is it?" He glanced toward the doors and registered the shouting. "Do you need me to call Caitlin?"

Caitlin, his wife. The civil rights lawyer who was supposed to step in when my mother tried to kidnap me home again. That was the crisis we'd all been preparing for. Not this.

But of course there were reporters here. Of course there were. This was the town where I'd been found. Where Jasper and Shelby had been arrested. They'd probably started trolling the place from the second the news had hit the wire.

Fiona slid through the double doors, keeping them as close to closed as possible. Her half apron was stained with coffee and she wiped her hands on it as she approached.

"Are you okay?" she asked.

"I don't . . . did you know there were reporters in town?" I asked.

She bit her lip. "They showed up right after you left and started asking questions about you. How long you'd been here, what you'd been doing, who you hung out with. My mom told us all to say 'no comment,' so that was what we did, but some people—some other people—talked."

Of course they did. How else would the newscasters have gotten that video of me at The Mixer? I held my head in my hands and tried to think. How could I get out of here without them following me?

"Why didn't you tell me?" I asked.

"We wanted you to come home," Fiona said, lifting her slight shoulders. "And my mom said they'd go away once the story got cold."

"Well, the story's officially cold," I replied, sounding a tad whinier than I intended. "My own mother doesn't even care where I am. Why do they?"

"Cecilia! Come back!" someone shouted. "We just have a few questions!"

"Who did you wear to your high school graduation?"

"Are you really bound for Harvard in the fall?"

"We hear your mother is announcing her bid for president

today. How do you feel about her setting up her campaign headquarters here in Sweetbriar?"

"*What?*" I blurted.

I looked at Fiona. Her eyes had gone wide. "Your mother . . . in Sweetbriar?" she stammered. "She's . . . president?"

I sank into the nearest chair. Suddenly, my mother's silence made perfect sense. She'd needed time to regroup. Time to plan. Time to change the narrative in her favor. And that was exactly what she was doing—right in my new backyard.

5

THE TV THAT HUNG IN THE BACK CORNER OF THE
kitchen was on, as always, and a breaking news report flashed
onto the screen.

"Could we turn that up, please?" I said, my voice shaky.

Hal glanced around for the remote, found it under a pile
of papers on his desk, and pointed it at the screen. Everyone in
the kitchen stopped working and we all turned to watch as my
mother stepped up to a gleaming oak podium. Behind her was
the primary school across the park.

"Is that—" Hal said, then looked at me. "Is she . . . ?"

I pulled his desk chair out and sat down in it, my brain
filled with fuzz.

"Yep," I said. "That's her. She's here."

The podium had been placed at the foot of the wide brick
stairs leading up to the school. Standing on those steps was my
father—backing up my mom as always—as well as Tash, and
a few other support people who were always flitting around
my mother. Her publicist, her political strategist, her chief of

staff. The mayor was there, too, as well as a handful of other men and women I recognized from town. My mother wore a red suit with an American flag pinned to the lapel and when she smiled, the world must have blinked. Her teeth were even whiter than they'd been two days ago.

"Thank you all so much for coming," Rebecca Montgomery said to her audience. The camera panned out a bit and I saw that the park had filled with people. In the five minutes since I'd been chased off the street, they'd managed to pack them in by the dozens and hand out MONTGOMERY FOR PRESIDENT signs to half the onlookers.

"Where the hell did all those people come from?" Fiona asked.

"She bused them in," I said. "That's what she does."

Hal narrowed his eyes, then grabbed Felix, one of the cooks, and disappeared into the walk-in refrigerator.

"You know, nothing means more to me than the people of this great nation," my mother said, her voice echoing across the square. "Except, of course, for my family. Family is the backbone of our country. Families are the foundation on which this republic was built. Communities like this one, the lovely town of Sweetbriar, Tennessee, could not exist without its families. So I thought, what better way to get to know my fellow Americans than to set up shop in a small town? And what better way to stay close to my own daughter than to make my home where Cecilia has decided to make hers?"

"I think I'm gonna be sick," I muttered.

Fiona pushed back into the diner and returned seconds later with a cold ginger ale for me to sip.

"Thanks to the extraordinary accommodations of Sweetbriar's own Mayor Virgil Wilson, I've just recently purchased this gorgeous historical building behind me, which I intend to renovate to its former glory and turn into offices for my upcoming campaign. Once the election cycle is over, I'll return the deed to the town so that the people of Sweetbriar can put their former primary school to good use once again."

There was a huge cheer from the monster crowd, which was probably made up of only about 10 percent Sweetbriar residents.

"Campaign for what, you ask?" my mother said slyly. "Well, I'm sure you've already guessed, but I don't want to make the official announcement without my daughter by my side." My mother looked directly into the camera. "Cecilia? I know you're out there, sweetie. Why don't you come on up here and join me?"

"Sweetie?" I said. "Did she just call me sweetie?"

The people in the crowd looked around as if they expected me to emerge from their ranks and go striding up to the stage, waving my hand beauty-queen style. When I didn't appear, a murmur broke out. My mother's smile didn't flinch, but I knew she was sweating. This was live television. The longer I waited to go out there, the more dead air there would be, and it would be on her to fill it.

"Are you gonna go?" Fiona asked.

Part of me wanted to say no. Part of me wanted to walk out the back door of the diner, steal someone's car, drive off, and never look back. It's not like I hadn't done it before. But then I saw my dad standing there. And the mayor, looking a tad green. And all those people. I knew what I had to do. It had been ingrained into my very marrow since the day I was born. The Montgomerys don't let the people down.

I handed Fiona the glass, cleared my throat, and rolled my shoulders back. "Thanks, Fiona."

The reporters in the diner had thinned out, but auburn ponytail and the hungry-looking dude still lurked, and they shouted questions at me as I walked through the eatery. The throngs outside were thick as molasses, and I almost chickened out, but then I felt Duncan at my shoulder.

"I'm coming with you," he said quietly.

"Yes, please," I squeaked, and together we stepped into the sun.

Duncan parted the crowd for me, starting out with a polite "Excuse us," and eventually escalating to a shouted, "Get out of the way!" About halfway across the square, my mother's security guys intercepted us and escorted me toward the school. My heart pounding as the faces blurred by, I lost Duncan and could only hope he was okay. Before I knew it, I was practically lifted up onto the stage next to my mother, and she'd taken my hand. My father stepped up on her other side, as if she'd scripted the whole thing. Which, let's face it, she had.

Her gaze flicked to my neck and she noticed that I was

wearing my bird pendant and not her pearls. It was the first time I saw so much as a pockmark in her veneer.

"Citizens of America, I'm Rebecca Montgomery," she shouted into the microphone, "and I'm running for president of the United States!"

My mother thrust our hands into the air, and the crowd went wild.

"What the hell are you doing here?"

This was said through my teeth as I plastered on the widest, most painful smile I'd ever managed in my life. My parents and I were now on a happy family stroll through Sweetbriar, just like any other family unit on a bright and sunny day. Except for the fact that we were being trailed by a camera crew, four bodyguards, two assistants, a publicist, and a motley crowd of random gawkers. My palms were clammy from the proximity of so many cameras, and it was all I could do to keep from bolting at every turn.

"Well, Cecilia, I thought that if you wanted to live in this place so badly, it must have something going for it." My mother paused to shake the hand of a woman in a gingham dress, carrying a baby on her hip. The Montgomery for President campaign photographer snapped their picture. "So I thought I'd come see for myself."

She paused at the corner of the square, about a block and a half from Jasper's house, where just a few days ago she'd had FBI units in riot gear swarming.

"It really is quite lovely." She put her bony arm around me and squeezed. "And now the whole family can be together. We don't have to worry about you running off again," she added under her breath.

"Yeah, right," I said. "You're just using me to paint the perfect picture of yourself. And now you're using the people of Sweetbriar, too."

My mother shot me a blink-and-you-might-miss-it silencing glare before turning around to shake a few more hands. She let out her throaty laugh when someone cracked a joke, throwing her head back. As always, her short blond hair didn't move. Not one strand.

"This is where Daria Case lives, correct?" my father said under his breath as my mom continued to schmooze. "Mom's best friend. She's still here?"

My palms prickled. "Yeah. She is." I looked up at him, squinting against the sun. "You should go see her, Dad. I bet she'd love to catch up with you."

My father sniffed and looked across his shoulder toward Main Street. The sun glinted off his mirrored sunglasses. "She probably hates me."

Before I could respond, my mother had returned, linking her arm around mine and steering me down the north side of the park toward Main. My dad fell into step at my side.

"As for your accusation, I don't think you have to worry about the citizens of Sweetbriar," she said quietly. "These small-towners are going to eat this up. The attention, the notoriety, the business we'll bring in."

"I hate to point out the obvious, Mom, but these small-towners like their small town. They don't want to be overrun with press and your politicos and your legions of drooling fans."

I couldn't believe I was actually standing up for myself, but something had come over me when I'd seen her on the television, smiling smugly out over this town—*my* town. I couldn't let her come in here and take over this place, these people, my life. I was practically vibrating from the rage simmering inside my veins.

"They like things quiet around here," I added.

"Sweet tea!" a voice shouted nearby. "Get your authentic Southern sweet tea here! Only two bucks a cup!"

My jaw dropped. Hal had set up a table near the sidewalk, complete with a handmade sign, and he and Felix were serving plastic cups of tea out of three huge glass jugs. There was already a line to the corner, packed with patrons in red, white, and blue. I even saw the gangly reporter waiting impatiently on his toes.

"Oh, I think they're going to eat it up," my mother said with a wry laugh. She released my arm and stepped forward—cutting the line, of course—and lifted a finger. "We'll take three."

"With pleasure, Senator Montgomery," Hal said, winking at me.

My face burned. I couldn't believe this was happening.

"I'm always happy to support small local businesses," my mother said, raising her voice as she looked around at the people—and the cameras. "Our small-business men and women are what make this country great."

Gag. Barf. Barf. Gag.

"Pay the man, Tash," my mother said, handing me and my father our teas. Ugh. She didn't even realize how awful she sounded. She wasn't a woman of the people. She needed a freaking assistant to pay for something in cash. And she hadn't even included said assistant in her order. Tash jumped forward, fumbling a few dollars out of her bag—dollars that were probably her own, no less—and forked them over to Hal.

My mother turned to her team and the camera crew and smiled. "Would you all mind giving me and my family a minute alone to chat?" she asked. The cameraman stopped filming and lowered his lens, while everyone around him looked confused and bereft. Tash took charge, ushering them into a little klatch underneath the shade of a nearby magnolia. My mother, meanwhile, led my father and me deeper into the park, where she perched on one of the shaded benches.

"It really is unbearably hot here, isn't it?" she said, taking a sip of her tea. "I can see why this is a popular drink."

I sat down next to her with my father at my other side, holding the sweating cup in both hands between my legs.

"What're we doing here, Mom?" I asked tiredly. "Really. Are you seriously going to run your campaign from here? All your people are based in Boston. All your offices and your home and your . . . clothes are in Boston."

"One of the first things you learn to do as a politician is adjust, Cecilia," my mother said. "Anything I need can be shipped. And we're only here because of you."

I scoffed. "Right, because you want to be where I want to be."

"Cecilia, would you just hear her out?" my father asked.

He took off his sunglasses to look me in the eye, and I sighed. After everything I'd put him through, I owed him one. Or ten. Or twenty.

"Sorry, Dad," I said, wishing I could cover everything with that one word. "Fine, Mom. Go ahead."

My mother blinked, half surprised I was acquiescing, half annoyed I thought I could *allow* her to speak.

"Yes, I was angry at you for running off again," she said. "And yes, I had to find a way to spin it. That's just the reality of the situation."

My mother straightened her posture and shook her hair back. Which was pointless because it still didn't move.

"But, Cecilia, I could have had you brought home again. I could have hired a whole team of security to keep you by my side." She laughed shortly. "Hell, I could have had you committed if I really wanted to."

My mouth fell open. The very fact that she'd just said that out loud meant she'd actually considered it. I wondered which one of her trusted advisors had floated *that* idea. Tash, probably.

"Instead I came here," my mother continued. "For you. I'm sorry if that's hard for you to believe, but I *am* trying." She sighed and placed the almost full cup of tea on the pathway near her feet. "You have to meet me halfway."

I felt myself start to cave, just a little. I suppose, with all the options available to her, she *had* chosen the least selfish. Which was a first. But what did she expect me to do, exactly? Go live with her in whatever mansion they were probably going to rent? Attend all her events? Make speeches? Do photo ops?

"What does halfway mean?" I asked. "Because I have my own apartment and a roommate who depends on my rent money. I can't give that up."

"Fair enough. I won't ask you to," my mother replied. "But we will of course be hiring you a new bodyguard. Someone a bit more competent than Alexis."

"I don't want a bodyguard," I said. "The whole point of this . . . of everything . . . was that I want a normal life."

"Cecilia," my mother said in a warning tone.

"No. If I have to meet you halfway, then you have to meet me, too," I said, looking at my father instead of her. "Please, Dad. I can't be babysat anymore."

My father shot my mother a look behind my back. My mother sighed.

"Fine. But the first sign of trouble, and you're getting a full detail," she said.

Whoa. Had I just won an actual battle with Rebecca Montgomery? This day was full of surprises.

From the corner of my eye, I saw someone emerge from the crowd that had so far kept a respectful distance. Jasper. My whole body inflated at the sight of him. I put my cup down on the bench and stood up as he strode over to us, wearing jeans and a white button-down. He glanced warily around his town square as if he'd just crashed on an alien planet.

"Hey, Lia. I saw you on the news. This is pretty crazy." He reached for my hand and glared past me at my parents. "You okay? You need me to get you out of here?"

"No. I'm fine. At least, I am now," I replied, and he smiled. "But there *is* something you can do for me. Are you free for the next hour or so?"

"Yeah, actually I am."

"Great." I turned to my parents and smiled. "You want to be a part of my life? How about we start with lunch with my boyfriend?"

"So, Jasper, tell me . . . is being a famous country musician your only plan?"

"Dad!" I blurted.

But Jasper laughed. "It's okay, Lia. I—"

"Her name is Cecilia," my mother said, polite but firm.

I toyed with the salt shaker on the table in front of me. Jasper had been polite but cold to her ever since I'd introduced him. Apparently, when he'd told me he never wanted to be near her, he wasn't kidding around.

"What? It took your father and me a good many weeks to

choose your name," my mother said. "It would be nice if the people in your life used it."

At that moment, Fiona appeared to take our order. This was just way too awkward for polite society. I introduced her to my parents, with whom she could barely make eye contact, and we all placed our orders quickly. Burger for Jasper, sliced steak for my dad, salads for me and my mom.

"Want some fried green tomatoes to start?" Fiona asked.

I opened my mouth to say yes, but my mother cut me off. "We don't eat fried food."

Both Jasper and Fiona looked ready to crack up laughing, but instead Fiona took off and Jasper cleared his throat. They'd seen me scarf more fried food in the past two weeks than I'd had in the rest of my life combined.

"Anyway, as I was saying, Mr. Phillips."

I blinked, surprised that he knew my father's actual last name. Someone had done his research. Most people ended up calling him Mr. Montgomery, which drove him crazy, although he'd never let on. I could only tell because he always licked his lips when it happened, and licking his lips was not something he ever did otherwise. Not even when he was eating.

My parents had decided before I was born to give me the Montgomery name so there would never be any question that I was part of the vaunted Montgomery family—America's royalty.

"I realize that 'country music star' isn't the most stable career field to choose, so I'm also getting my teaching certificate,"

Jasper told my father. "I've been assistant teaching in the music program at the middle school here in town for the last couple of years."

"Teaching. A noble profession," my father said. "And will the two of you stay together when Cecilia starts Harvard in the fall?"

"Actually—"

"Harvard?" Jasper shifted in his seat and put his arm along the back of the bench behind me. My mother's gaze shifted ever so slightly, resting on his hand. "You never said anything about Harvard."

I thought of the brochure Tammy had given me earlier, which I'd left back in Hal's office in my help-my-mom-is-here daze. I'd barely had a second to flip through it before insanity had descended. I hoped Fiona or Duncan had picked it up and saved it for me. And then I realized with a start that I'd never gone back to work at Second Chances. I'd only been there for an hour of my six-hour shift.

I hoped Tammy would understand. She definitely knew the reason for my absence. You couldn't look sideways without seeing another MONTGOMERY FOR PRESIDENT sign.

"Well, that's where she's going," my mother replied. "It's where her father and I both went to school."

"Yes, but is that where Lia wants to go?" Jasper said, his words clipped.

"Of course it is," my mother replied, staring him down.

"Well, that's funny, because last I heard she—"

"Actually, I haven't decided yet. What I'm going to do in the fall," I blurted awkwardly.

My mother and I locked eyes. Me going to her alma mater had always been her plan. And I knew she was not happy about the fact that Jasper was standing up to her. At that moment Fiona put a basket of bread on the table.

"Perhaps we should talk about something else," my father suggested, taking a sip from his water glass.

"Yes. Perhaps we should." My mother's helmet of hair vibrated around her cheekbones, which was never a good sign. "Jasper, why don't you tell us about this Sweetbriar Summer Festival. There are posters and flyers all over town."

Jasper reached for the bread, ripped off a chunk, and spread some honey butter over it. "We have it every summer and it's something everyone round here looks forward to," he said. "The fest takes over the whole park with rides and baking competitions and dancing, plus there's all kinds of great food. Oh, and we elect a Sweetbriar Summer Princess—someone from the graduating class. Which means Fiona will be up for it."

He looked up and grinned at Fiona as she placed four sweet teas on the table.

"Right, but I have no chance at winning," she said, wiping her hands on her apron.

"Why not? Lovely girl like you," my mother said. "I'm sure you'll get plenty of votes."

Fiona grinned. From the look on her face you'd think she'd just won a trip around the world. "Thank you, Mrs.

Montgomery. But I don't think I could run. I've never run for anything in my life." She paused and blanched. "And considering who you are, you probably think that's incredibly lame."

"Not at all. But there's a first time for everything. You should try it," my mother said. "You never know what might happen."

"She's right. One thing that scares you, remember, Fi?" I added. "Something unexpected?"

My mother held my gaze over the table and I held hers. Neither one of us was able to believe I'd just agreed with her.

"Right . . . well . . . maybe. Thanks!" Fiona wiped her palms on her apron. "Anyway. Your order should be up any minute."

And then she scurried off.

"Well, I think the night of the festival would be the perfect night to officially open my new headquarters," my mother said, deftly changing the subject back to herself. "We can hold a gala inside the old gymnasium and spilling out onto the stone patio behind the school."

Jasper's brow creased. "There's no stone patio behind the school."

"There will be," my mother informed him. "We'll invite all our friends from Washington and some of the bigger Hollywood donors, and all of the townspeople will be welcome, of course. They can start their evening at the festival and end it at the gala."

Jasper let out a short, derisive laugh. "Galas aren't really a thing around here, ma'am." He managed to say the word "ma'am" sarcastically. "I'm not even sure people would know what to wear."

"Seriously, Mom. You expect them to go from tilt-a-whirls and cotton candy to ball gowns and waltzing?" Not to mention that these "gala events" usually cost the attendees upwards of a thousand dollars a plate.

"Honestly, people usually end their night half drunk or in a food coma," Jasper put in.

My mother laughed, and it might have just been the sweet tea and the heat, but I'm pretty sure it was genuine. "But wouldn't they be excited by the opportunity to hobnob with celebrities? The people they see on the cover of *People* magazine? Of course they will," she added, before anyone could answer. "It will be a night to remember. And I'm going to put the two of you in charge of local relations."

"What?" I blurted.

"What?" Tash asked from the next table over. She was always the next table over.

"Sorry," Jasper said, "but what does that even mean?"

"It means you two will be in charge of getting the community excited about the event, as well as helping the planning committee bring a little local culture into the décor . . . the food . . . the music," my mother said, beaming. "You've made it fairly clear that this is your home now, Cecilia. If you love it so much, you should be the one to make sure the party is up to Sweetbriar's standards."

My jaw hung open. I couldn't believe she was giving me

any sort of responsibility, let alone a responsibility I might actually . . . enjoy. But at the same time, was this really what I wanted to be doing right now? I had a job, I had friends, a busy-ass boyfriend. Not to mention the fact that I needed to figure out my future.

"And you're a musician, correct?" my mother added, eyeing Jasper. "So you'll be in charge of the music."

Jasper and I exchanged an incredulous look.

"Mom. This party is in less than three weeks."

"It's a gala, Cecilia," she corrected. "And people have planned larger events in less time. Why, Tash pulled off this announcement rally in the space of two days," my mother informed me, and Tash beamed with pride. "Plus you'll have the assistance of the entire planning committee, as well as any friends you might like to enlist."

"Mrs. Montgomery," Jasper began, leaning in to the table. "I don't know if I—"

"Find me a great country band," she interrupted. "Someone up and coming, but with name recognition."

"Actually, I don't know that many people yet," Jasper protested, clearly uncomfortable. "And I'm gonna be kinda busy with—"

"You'll make time. Everyone can make time. This is important."

A cell phone rang and Tash picked it up from the table in front of her. "It's the majority leader, Senator."

"I have to take this."

My mother grabbed the phone, got up from the table, and headed to the rear of the restaurant, where she pushed into the small alcove in front of the restrooms.

"Excuse me, I see someone outside that I need to talk to," my father said, sliding out as well.

As he walked away, Fiona appeared with two arms full of food, which she placed down on a now half-deserted table.

"What happened?" she asked.

"I have no idea," Jasper replied, gobsmacked.

"Congratulations, Jasper," I said, reaching up to pat him on the back. "You've officially been Montgomeried."

6

"I DEFINITELY MISSED THIS."

Jasper cupped my face with both hands, walking me backward toward my bed. The sun was just starting to set on what had to be one of the most bizarro days of my life, but none of that mattered. Not here. Not now. Not when I was alone with Jasper. My butt hit the side of the mattress and I fell back, Jasper toppling over me with a laugh. I scooted over so we both had room, but it wasn't like we needed it. He pulled me against him so tightly, we took up the space of one person.

"Missed me, or missed the kissing?" I joked, coming up for a breath.

"Missed it all," Jasper replied, and touched his lips to my earlobe. "Every. Last. Bit." He punctuated his words by kissing my cheek and then my neck and then my collarbone. He was just inching my tank top strap off my shoulder when the downstairs buzzer buzzed. We both froze.

"Don't move," I whispered. "Maybe they'll go away."

I didn't know why I was whispering. If someone was in the

alley downstairs, they definitely couldn't hear us. We both held our breath. After a minute or so, Jasper leaned in to kiss me again— and the buzzer went off. This time, whoever it was just laid on the thing and didn't let up. The noise was seriously grating.

"Dang it!" I said, swinging my legs over the side of the bed.

"Did you just say 'dang it,' Red Sox?" Jasper joked, pushing himself up in the bed and settling back against the pillows, comfy as can be.

I grinned. "I think I did."

I ran to the door and pressed the talk button on our old-school intercom.

"Hello! Please stop buzzing! I'm here!"

"Cecilia, it's Tash."

I groaned inwardly. "Tash, I'm really busy right now. Can you come back tomorrow?"

"No. I can't. I'm here with the movers and we have all your stuff. Just let me up!" she barked.

This time I groaned audibly, then pressed the unlock button. I wasn't sure what she meant by "all your stuff," but I knew she wasn't going to go away until she did what my mother had sent her here to do. Tash was reliable that way. I heard footsteps stomping up the stairs and opened the door. Tash swept into my apartment, carrying a white box with my new laptop, and she was followed by five men with armloads of cardboard crates.

"Where's your room?" Tash asked.

I pointed, and she led the charge.

"Whoa! Hey!" Jasper bleated as his cozy time was interrupted. I was about to explain when Max and Matilda brought up the rear.

"What are you two doing here?" I asked.

"Pleasure to see you too!" Max air-kissed me as he breezed by.

"Hi, Cecilia!" Matilda greeted me. "Oooh, great dress. Vintage?"

"Um, yeah."

She had a few outfits on hangers slung over her shoulder. "Your mother asked me to come over and organize your closet—you know, color-code by seasons and make notes of what you might need."

She followed Max into my room. When I got there I saw that the five men were unpacking my boxes onto the bed, the dresser, and any other available surface. Tash was booting up my new computer at the desk, and Jasper had been backed into a corner, where he stood with his arms crossed over his chest, trying to make himself as small as possible.

"Ooh, Tennessee School of Design?" Matilda said, noticing the catalog—which I'd retrieved on my way out of the diner—at the foot of my bed. "Great program. You going there?"

"Um . . . I'm not sure yet."

"But she's definitely applying, right, Red Sox?" Jasper said hopefully. We'd leafed through the application materials when we'd first gotten back and he was 100 percent psyched about the idea of me sticking around.

"We'll see," I said with a laugh.

"Where's the closet?" Matilda asked.

"Right there."

I pointed at the Johnny Cash shower curtain that served as a closet door. To her credit, Matilda didn't even hesitate. She just shoved the curtain aside and yanked down on the string that turned on the one hanging light bulb.

"Where're all your clothes!?" she gasped.

"I was . . . on a budget when I moved here," I replied. "Most of my stuff from school is out here being unpacked."

I launched myself at a large, neckless man who was currently manhandling my underwear, and grabbed them to my chest. Jasper stifled a laugh.

"Max, get your cute butt in here, and bring your iPad!" Matilda shouted.

"Gladly," Max replied, sliding sideways to get past me and out of the mayhem.

"Okay, I connected you to the wifi. Your mom's having the whole building upgraded to the highest speed connection they get in this backward town," Tash said, turning to look at me.

"Hey!" Jasper protested.

She shot him a silencing look.

"If I were you, I'd check my e-mail. I've already sent you lists of items we'll need to address at Wednesday's budgetary meeting for the gala, and I've started to compile the catalogs and menus of local vendors, such as they are," she added with a sneer.

"I reiterate my 'hey,'" Jasper said more firmly, stepping away from the wall.

"Wait. Wednesday's budgetary meeting?" I asked.

Tash poked at her iPad. "At HQ, ten a.m. I've uploaded the meeting schedule and all your deadlines onto your iCal. You're welcome."

"I have to work from nine to two on Wednesday," I told her.

Tash rolled her eyes. "Fine then, I'll reschedule for . . . three p.m. Will that suit you?"

Her tone was so condescending, it made me want to drop-kick her out the window. I could tell Jasper wanted me to say "no," just to put her in her place, but the gala was less than three weeks away and there was no way I was squirming my way out of this. My responsible, deadline-hitting, straight-A side kicked in.

"Fine. Three o'clock."

"Good. I'll just have everyone else rearrange their schedules around yours."

Tash hit the screen a few more times for emphasis.

"You do realize you have only five T-shirts and two pairs of shoes?" Matilda said, emerging from the closet. "Two pairs. Two pairs of shoes."

"Breathe, Matty. Breathe," Max said, kneading her shoulders from behind.

Matilda saw the piles of sweaters and dresses and sensible corduroys that had been unpacked on my bed and deflated in relief. "Oh, thank God!"

She and Max started to sort through everything and new piles quickly emerged.

"Well, we're done here. I'll leave Matilda and Max to do their job." Tash snapped her fingers at the movers and they all filed out. "See you Wednesday at three, Cecilia," she said. "In the meantime, if I were you, I'd start reading the information I sent you."

And then she was, mercifully, gone.

"Um . . . Jasper, this is Matilda and Max," I said, gesturing weakly at the pair. "They're my stylist and . . . what was your preferred job title again, Max?"

"Transformation specialist. Pleasure to meet you," Max said, leaning across the bed to shake Jasper's hand.

Matilda barely looked up from the dress she was inspecting. "Hi."

"Nice to meet y'all too," Jasper said. He turned to check out the new computer and the piles of papers and notebooks stacked next to it. "Wow. Your mother *really* wants you to go to Harvard."

"What? Why?"

I joined him and saw that atop a bunch of my high school notebooks was the Harvard course catalog, my acceptance letter, and the instructions for choosing dorm preferences and meal plans online. Then there was another stack of clean Harvard notebooks, a Harvard iPad cover, and a bag full of Harvard clothing.

"Yeah, she really does," I said with a sigh.

"But you're not going to, are you?" Jasper asked. "Not

now that you have other options. I mean, Boston's pretty far away."

"No," I answered automatically. "I mean . . . I don't really know."

"Oh."

My heart squeezed. "I just haven't had time to think about it. There's a lot going on and it's a little overwhelming," I told him. "I need some time to figure it all out."

What I didn't tell him was that when we'd looked over the application for the Tennessee School of Design earlier, my heart had been steadily sinking. Not because it didn't sound great. It sounded, in fact, amazing. Students were allowed to create their own major, choosing which courses were related to their personal creative vision for their career. And the courses were incredible. Everything from basic clothing construction to interior design to merchandising for children. The heart-sinking part came from the requirements for admission. On top of the general application, interview, and personal essay, I'd need to provide two letters of recommendation from teachers or other authority figures who could attest to my unique creative style *and* I'd have to submit a portfolio of my work in a tactile creative medium.

What was I supposed to hand in? Photos of the window at Second Chances?

Harvard was looking more and more like the only viable option.

My new computer dinged loudly. Another e-mail arriving from Tash. Was she writing them on her way down the stairs?

"Doesn't look like your mom's gonna be giving you that time," Jasper said wryly.

The back of my neck prickled. It was bad enough that I had to deal with all this stuff, but him rubbing it in didn't help. In fact, it made me feel even worse. At that moment, Jasper's phone let out a little trumpet blare and he yanked it from his jeans pocket.

"Do you want to help me go through these e-mails?" I asked, as Matilda and Max began hanging up my clothes. "We could take it in the living room?"

It wasn't exactly the night I had planned, but maybe after Max and Matilda left we could get back to the smooching.

"Holy buckets, Lia! I just got invited to Blue Peak's twenty-fifth anniversary party tomorrow night," Jasper announced, scrolling through the e-mail. "And they want me to perform!"

"Jasper! That's amazing!"

"Evan says I have a plus one." He looked up at me, his eyes bright with excitement. "You have to come! You'll come, right?"

"Of course! Are you kidding?" I threw my arms around him. "I'm totally in!"

"Aw!" Max and Matilda trilled in unison.

Embarrassed, I went to pull away, but Jasper gave me a

long, closed-mouthed kiss, then released me and headed for the door.

"Wait. Where're you going?"

"I have to go figure out what I'm gonna sing!" he said excitedly. "And *my* stylist is sending over some outfits to choose from." He laughed and shoved the phone away. "Who woulda thought we'd both have stylists. I'll call you later, okay?"

"Sure. Love you!" I called out as he opened the door.

"Love you too!"

And then the door slammed behind him.

"Cecilia, my friend, your man is *fine*," Max said.

"Yeah," I said dreamily. "He kind of is."

Then my computer dinged again and I sighed. Jasper may have been dreamy, but he'd also just left me to deal with Tash's e-mail deluge on my own.

"Oh come on, Lia, you have to apply to this school." Fiona plopped down atop a stack of unpacked boxes of books in the Book Nook's back room as she flipped through the TSoD catalog. "They have a minor in silk screening!"

"Do you have some secret passion for silk screening that I don't know about?" Britta asked, leveling a stare over her eyeglass frames as she hauled a few books out of a box and shelved them.

"No, but maybe Cecilia does. Maybe she does and she doesn't even know it and if she went to this school she'd find out she did!"

"Wow. Someone's had too much coffee this morning," I said, leaning back against the brick wall.

It was Tuesday morning, and Britta was helping out her boss, Maisy Freiss, with inventory. Fiona and I had come along to hang, because stockrooms and bathrooms and broom closets were some of the few places we could go anymore without being bothered by the press.

"I don't know, guys. It's just a lot," I said as the grain of the brick tugged at my curls. "My mom wants me to work on this gala, I have my job at Second Chances. And honestly, I don't even know what I would submit for the creative portion. Maybe I should just go to Harvard."

"No. You can't go to Harvard," Fiona said.

"Why not? You guys are both going away to school in the fall. It's not like you'll miss me."

"We *will* miss you no matter where we all go, but that's not the point," Fiona said. "The point is, I don't think you want to go to Harvard."

"What makes you say that?" I asked.

"Because most people would kill to get into Harvard and be chewing their own arms off in anticipation of going," Britta said in her bland tone. "You? Not so much."

"Ugh! But my mother will murder me if I don't go." I groaned and bent forward at the waist. "You guys, what am I gonna do?"

Fiona slid off her pile of boxes and her feet smacked the floor. "I've got it!"

"What?" Britta and I said in unison.

Fiona turned the catalog around to face me, bending it back so that only one page was visible—the list of acceptable media for the application's creative portion. "Event design!"

"Wait . . . what?" I said, pushing myself forward.

"It says it right here. Event design is on the list." I snatched the catalog from Fiona and stared at the words, my skin prickling. "You design your mom's gala with local flair or whatever and then send all the amazing pictures in as your portfolio!"

"That might actually work," Britta said, dusting her hands off on her jeans shorts.

"I don't know, you guys. I have almost no time to pull this off."

"So we'll help!" Fiona offered. "Won't we, Britta?"

"Sure. I'm in." Britta shrugged.

"Come on, Lia! What do you have to lose?" Fiona asked. "One brave thing, right?"

I chewed my bottom lip. Could I really do this? Could I pull off a portfolio-worthy event with basically zero experience? I supposed it was possible, if my friends were here to help and I had my mom's staff on my side. How great would that be? Using the event my mother was forcing me to work on to get out of going to Harvard? Her brain would explode.

"If you do this, I'll run for Sweetbriar Princess," Fiona offered, mistaking my silence for hesitation.

"What? You hate this town," Britta stated. "You can't be princess of a town you hate."

Fiona lifted one shoulder. "I don't know. I think it could maybe be fun. And unexpected. And brave, right?" She looked at us hopefully. "Also, it would probably look good on my resume, doing something outside the box."

"Totally!" I said. "And you'd be an amazing princess."

Though I still had no idea exactly what the requirements were for the position, or what the responsibilities were once it was won. At that moment, I felt like I could do anything. And if I could, so could Fiona.

"So we have a deal?" Fiona asked.

"We have a deal."

And suddenly, I had a ton of work to do.

"So I spent the entire afternoon in the library looking through all these gorgeous books about Southern style and Tennessee architecture through the ages, and I think I've come up with some really cool ideas."

"That's great," Jasper said, his warm hand cupping mine on the seat between us as our limousine turned onto a wide boulevard in downtown Nashville. "I'm so psyched you decided to apply. It's just too bad part of the process involves helping out a person that you hate."

"It's not that I *hate* her," I said. "We just never really had a relationship."

I took a breath as I scrolled through another twenty-four

e-mails from Tash, setting up meetings and tastings and phone calls for later in the week. Now that I'd decided to focus on the design of the event, it all seemed pretty superfluous. Did I really have to be in on cake tastings?

"I just wish I had more time. Party planning is way more complicated than you'd think."

"I'm sure you're gonna do great." Jasper leaned over to kiss my nose.

"Thank you," I said with a smile.

But the back of my neck was beginning to prickle with sweat. And not just because my brain was running a mile a minute in ten different directions. The straps on the white eyelet lace dress I'd chosen from the stockroom at Second Chances were itching my shoulders something awful, and I'd allowed Britta to do my makeup, which meant false eyelashes that kept sticking together. Matilda and Max had wanted to help, but this was Jasper's night, and they were being paid by my mom to make me presentable for *her* events. Besides, it wasn't like I can't dress myself.

Or can I? I thought, reaching up to scratch my shoulder.

"Do you think you'll be all right, though? Working with your mom every day?" he asked.

"I don't know. It's complicated."

"So then uncomplicate it." Jasper shrugged. He looked so adorable in his black cowboy hat and a light blue plaid shirt with a dark gray jacket over it. And when he said things like that, with that level of assuredness and just a twist of naiveté, I could so easily remember what he'd looked like when we'd first met as little kids. It made me feel closer to him, because I could say I knew him even back then. When the biggest challenge between us was who could clamber to the top of the monkey bars faster.

"And how do I do that, exactly?"

"Don't let her push you around. Just keep reminding yourself you're an adult now. You don't have to do anything you don't want to do."

I attempted a smile, but only one corner of my mouth twitched. It was so easy for Jasper to say something like that. He'd never had parental expectations. Jasper had been raised by his grandmother, Daria Case—Gigi's best friend—and even though she was pretty strict, she'd made it clear that all she ever expected from him was to find something he loved to do and do it. I would have sold my left foot for someone to say that to me.

"I don't know. The gala's only three weeks away. I feel like it's easier to just do what she wants, get it over with, and move on."

"If you say so," Jasper said under his breath.

His tone bothered me. It was dismissive. Almost condescending. Did he think *I* was being naive?

"What's that supposed to mean?" I asked.

"Nothing! I just . . . Are you sure you can't find something else to do for the application? Something with Tammy? Or maybe your stylist! She seemed pretty gung ho about the whole thing." He looked me in the eye. "I don't want your mom taking advantage of you, that's all."

I squirmed a bit in my seat, and the straps cut into my skin. "That's not what this is," I told him. "This is just me killing two birds with one stone. Make my mother happy and get into college. It's a win-win."

"If you say so."

Okay, I was going to have to put an end to this conversational thread before I screamed.

"Have you thought of anyone we could ask to play at the gala?" I ventured. "Maybe Blake Ralston? You're playing a lot of dates with him."

Jasper laughed. "I can barely get up the guts to talk to that man, let alone ask him for a favor."

"It's not necessarily a favor," I ventured. "It could be good PR for him too."

"True, I guess," Jasper said, and took a sip from a bottle of water. "But I don't know, Lia. Your mom said someone up-and-coming. Blake Ralston's a superstar."

"But I—"

"We're pulling up to the venue now, Mr. Case," the driver interjected, glancing in the rearview mirror.

"Thank you kindly, sir," Jasper replied. He smiled, buttoned his jacket, and looked at me. "We'll figure it out. I promise. You good to go, beautiful?"

"Fine," I said, forcing a smile. "We can talk about it later."

Outside the windows, a smattering of people quickly

turned into a crowd as the car paused outside the Vanderbilt Hotel. I gazed down the red carpet, which was surrounded by paparazzi and reporters and fans, twenty people deep. My vision swam. All those faces. All those bodies. All those hands.

The door opened.

"Let's do this!"

Jasper got out of the car and the already-shouting crowd grew louder. I slid to the edge of the seat and peered out. Too many people. Way too many people. And flash pops. And microphones. And screaming—oh, the screaming. My heart felt like a moth caught inside an outdoor lamp, trying to bust its way out in every direction.

"You coming?"

Jasper smiled his wide, comforting, beautiful smile and offered his hand. I put my fingers into his and he tugged me out of the car, then slipped his arm around my waist. I felt marginally better with my side pressed against his solid body.

"All right, you two!" Evan Meyer was there in his signature scarf and T-shirt ensemble. He had to bellow to be heard. "The first twenty feet or so you just stop to pose for pictures. Answer questions if you like, but make it quick. We've given priorities to TNN, E!, and *Today*. They're near the entrance and will each get two minutes."

"Cecilia! Cecilia! Over here!"

"Jasper! Can we get a smile! One smile? Come on?"

"Or a kiss maybe? Show us a kiss!"

"Now remember, key number one to ridding the public's memory of the sight of Jasper in handcuffs is replacing it with images of the hot new couple on the scene!" Evan shouted.

Key number one? That was key number one? Nobody had told me that. My pulse vibrated inside my veins and my mouth had gone gummy. I couldn't do this. All those cameras. All those lenses.

"All right!" Evan rubbed his hands together. "Let's premiere Jasilia!"

Ja-what-now?

Jasper started to follow Evan, his foot landing on the red carpet, but I froze. He moved until our arms were stretched out between us, then looked behind him with concern. He was back at my side in half a second.

"What's wrong?" he whispered in my ear.

"All those people," I said. "I don't think I can do this."

"Do you want to go home? We can go home right now," Jasper said.

Evan bit his lip. "Um . . . actually . . ."

I looked up into Jasper's blue eyes. He had no idea. He couldn't just go home. He had responsibilities now. And one of those responsibilities was feeding the fame machine. If there had been a Montgomery Family Handbook, that would have been on page one. I might not have been allowed to live it, but I had certainly witnessed it. There was no way I was going to ruin this for him. Not after the damage my mother and the FBI had already done. I'd promised to do whatever I could to help.

"You are the greatest boyfriend in the history of the world for offering that," I said. Then I slid my hand into his and smiled. "Come on. Your public awaits."

"You sure?" he asked, touching my face with his fingers. My skin tingled.

I so wasn't. "I'm sure," I said.

I just really hoped I didn't throw up on some poor reporter's shoes.

7

EXHAUSTED. NEVER IN MY LIFE HAD I BEEN SO
exhausted. As I walked down Main Street toward Second
Chances, past all the colorful signs for Summer Fest, I prayed
that Tammy would have some coffee on. Clearly, partying in
Nashville until two a.m., then driving the two hours home,
only to get up at eight for a nine o'clock shift, was not a good
plan.

"Hey, Cecilia!"

Fiona jogged up from behind and fell into step with me.
She looked way too awake and perky in her wide-legged jeans
and gauzy top. And was it just me, or was she wearing her
ponytail a bit higher these days?

"Did you have fun last night? What was it like? Was Blake
Ralston there?"

I yawned hugely, doing a very bad job of hiding it behind
my hand. "He was, but I didn't meet him."

"Oh my God, still! You were in the same room with him!?
That's insane!"

We crossed Peach and I glanced at the message painted on the wall of the Book Nook. Ever since my first day in Sweetbriar, I'd felt as if the daily words of wisdom—painted over each night and replaced with a new inspiration by a mysterious, anonymous artist—were speaking directly to me. Today's missive read:

YOU GOTTA DO WHAT YOU GOTTA DO, UNTIL YOU DECIDE YOU DON'T GOTTA DO IT ANYMORE.

Huh. Wasn't quite sure what to do with that one.

"Anyway, here. Could you hand these out to some people today? Whenever you have a chance."

She handed me a stack of rainbow-colored flyers. Across the top of each was the headline "Fiona Taylor for Sweetbriar Summer Princess!"

"Oh my gosh! It's actually happening! This is so great, Fiona."

"Thanks. It's all about the unexpected, right? And no one I know would expect me to do this."

Printed underneath the headline was a full-color picture of a smiling Fiona . . . and me. I vaguely remembered Britta taking it the night we'd gone to see the Firebrand Three a couple of weeks ago and I'd had a panic attack right after, worried she'd post it on Instagram or something and my mother would find me. But both Britta and Fiona had promised it would never leave their phones—thinking I was totally wasted, because why else would I be begging them to keep a perfectly fine photo under wraps. And now, here it was.

And it was weird. At least, it seemed weird to me.

Campaign posters normally featured a picture of the candidate. Alone. Unless he or she had a running mate.

Huh. I wondered who my mother was going to choose as her running mate. If she made it past the primaries, anyway. Thinking of my mom made me realize I'd yet to check my phone this morning, and when I did I had four missed calls—two from Tash and two from my mother. All from the last ten minutes.

I adjusted my bag on my shoulder, making sure the mood boards I'd thrown together for the gala yesterday afternoon weren't getting smushed. I was both excited and terrified to show them at the meeting later today.

"Great picture, huh?" Fiona said, leaning her chin on my shoulder.

"It is, actually," I said. "But—"

The door to Second Chances opened and Tammy stuck her head out. "Cecilia! There you are! I have to talk to you, hon!"

In the window of the shop, blocking out our latest display of summer dresses, was a huge poster of a smiling Shelby, her hair back in a tortoiseshell headband as she smiled prettily out at the world. SHELBY TANAKA! YOUR SWEETBRIAR SUMMER PRINCESS!

"Sheesh. Jumping the gun a little, isn't she?" Fiona griped, and crossed her arms over her stomach.

"Power of suggestion," I told her. "Girl knows her psychology."

Fiona looked crestfallen.

"Sorry. I'll definitely hand these out," I promised her,

shoving the flyers in my bag along with my phone, which was currently vibrating. "I gotta get to work. See you later."

"You bet! Come by the diner for lunch!"

Fiona pulled me into a quick hug, then bounded off down the street, handing out flyers to everyone in her path. I'd never seen her so peppy, and I was happy for her. She was trying something new. And so was I. Or I would be once I attended the gala meeting this afternoon. I hoped our new opportunities worked out for the both of us.

The bells tinkled overhead as I walked into Second Chances, and the scent of fresh coffee hit me square in the face. I placed my bag carefully inside the door of the back room and trudged past a beaming Tammy, directly into the office to fill my favorite cup—the one that read PERFECT TENNESSEE.

"You okay there, Fiddler?" Tammy asked me.

"Just in need of caffeine," I told her.

She leaned up against the office doorjamb. "Well, when you're out partying like a rock star all night . . . ," she joked lightly.

"You heard about that, huh?" I asked, and took a sip of my coffee, black.

"Oh, hon, the whole world has heard about it."

Tammy fished her phone out of the pocket of her colorful muumuu-style dress and hit the screen a few times before showing it to me. On it was a perfectly posed, beautifully lit photo of me and Jasper from last night's epic red-carpet walk. It must have been taken somewhere near the theater, after I'd gotten a bit used to all the lights and the screaming, because my smile didn't appear to be particularly strained. If one looked closely, however, they would have been able to see how tightly I was clutching Jasper's jacket.

Still, I had to say, we looked pretty cute together.

"Where was that posted?" I asked.

"This one? This is on the record company's Instagram. It already has two hundred and fifty thousand likes."

"What!?" I shrieked as I set down the coffee mug and grabbed the phone. I scrolled down and saw that she was right—250K and counting. Unfortunately, I also saw some of the comments.

He is so effing hot! I would take him home to meet mama.

Why would he tie himself down when he could get so much play right now? And to that uptight bitch? For serious?

Jasilia? Horrible. Who came up with that crap?

There's no way these two last.

Ugh! How big is this girl's forehead? Is that where she keeps her ego?

My stomach turned. I handed back the phone and turned away from Tammy.

It doesn't mean anything, I told myself. *They don't know you. They don't know him. And they never will.*

I picked up my coffee again and slowly took a long, bolstering sip.

"So, what did you want to talk to me about?" I asked.

Tammy's eyes lit up. "Well! Come take a look at this!"

I followed her through the door and saw that she had several blueprints stacked up on the counter, their edges curling under. Curiosity officially piqued.

"What are these for?" I asked.

"These are my original plans for the Tanner Street School," Tammy said, beaming. "Remember I told you? How I was going to turn it into studio space?"

My curiosity was suddenly tainted by suspicion. And maybe a smidge of dread.

"Well, I was thinking maybe you could introduce me to your mother and I could show her the blueprints!" Tammy announced, lifting a palm. "If she likes what she sees, we could come up with a plan for when she returns the school to the town. She could put in a good word for me with the mayor and the planning board."

Right. So dread it was.

"What do you think?"

"Maybe . . . ," I said.

"Maybe? You don't think she'd like them?"

"No! I mean, I don't know. I don't really know anything about blueprints, so . . ."

Tammy's face registered confusion and then disappointment. What was wrong with me? Tammy was my friend. She gave me a job when I needed one and helped me discover my talent for styling clothes. She'd even gone out of her way to get me that information on TSoD. Shouldn't helping her be my knee-jerk response?

It was just . . . I didn't like this feeling. This feeling that she was using me to get to my mother—to get something she wanted. Our friendship now felt tainted somehow.

But then, I had gotten her daughter arrested, so maybe I owed her one.

Ugh. Why was this all so hard?

"If you don't feel comfortable . . ." Tammy began to roll up the plans.

"No!" I blurted. "I mean, yes. Of course I'll show them to my mother."

My face felt hot, and somewhere inside I felt angry at Tammy for putting me in this position. Because yes, it did make me feel uncomfortable. And honestly, knowing my mother, she'd probably brush the whole thing off as something she couldn't focus on right now. And I'd be the one who had to break the news to Tammy. But page two of the Montgomery Family Handbook, if it existed, would have read, *Make sure to repay every favor with a favor.*

"You will?" Tammy asked.

"Of course I will." I took the plans from her and placed them next to my bag in the stockroom, ignoring the fact that my phone was—yet again—vibrating. Then I turned to Tammy and tried to smile. "That's what friends are for."

"Oh, hey! I'm glad you're here," I said as I walked into my mother's conference room that afternoon. My heart was pounding in my throat, but I pushed through, thanks to a whopping dose of adrenaline. "I wanted to show you some ideas I came up with for the décor."

I placed my bag down at the end of the gleaming oak table and started to pull out my mood boards. My mother was typing on her phone while a minion I'd never met placed folders, legal pads, and pens at each of eight places.

"Put those away, Cecilia. You won't be needing them today," my mother said with a sniff.

I paused with my favorite color scheme in my hands. It was all oranges, purples, and golds to represent the Tennessee sunrise. I had photos, swatches of fabrics I'd grabbed from the discard bin at Second Chances, and even a few choices of font style for the menus and place cards.

"But I spent half my day yesterday working on this."

"Perhaps you did, but this is a budgetary meeting. No one is going to want to look at your little art project here."

I sat down hard in one of the leather chairs around the table, and suddenly I felt exhausted all over again—maybe even worse than I'd felt that morning. The room we were in had once been the teacher's lounge. It had been cleared of most of its furniture, but there was still an old tin NO SMOKING sign in the corner and the Tanner Street School Code of Conduct hung on the wall near the door. It went out of focus as I stared at it. After the awkward blueprint question, I had spent most of the day fielding more questions from Tammy about my childhood—and fudging the truth all over the place so she wouldn't think I felt sorry for myself (she was so starry-eyed about the Montgomerys, I just couldn't do that to her). When we weren't talking about what the Montgomerys ate for Sunday brunch or where we summered or who had the best clothes, we were dealing with "customers" who were clearly just tourists who had somehow found out where I worked. I couldn't get used to people staring at me while trying to look like they weren't staring at me, and all morning I'd felt on edge. At least some of them had made actual purchases, so it wasn't all for naught.

And in between all of this, I'd been sneaking little moments to add to my mood boards, to perfect them, to make them so dazzling, my mother couldn't deny me. Except that she just had. Without even looking at them.

"So . . . what does one do at a budgetary meeting?" I asked quietly.

"You're going to set the budget, so that you can hire some vendors right away," my mother said.

"Wait," I said, my brain suddenly catching up. "*I'm* going to set the budget?"

"You and your team." My mother moved over to the window to look out at the workers in the courtyard, who were flattening the ground using a machine that made enough noise to wake the dead.

"You're not staying?" I asked.

And since when am I in charge of the budget? I wondered. *I thought I was just coming up with suggestions to make the gala "more Sweetbriar." Thus the Tennessee-inspired mood boards.*

"I have meetings, Cecilia," my mother replied, in a tone that made it clear that *her* meetings were *real* meetings, unlike *this* meeting she was forcing me to attend. "Where's Jasper? I thought he was coming today with some suggestions for musical acts."

Yeah. I thought he was coming too, I thought. *But it's probably a good thing he's not, since I don't think he* has *any suggestions for musical acts.* And also, the last five minutes would just have given him more fuel for his Anti-Rebecca Montgomery campaign. What had he said again? Don't let her push me around? So far, no good.

Jasper had been called in to the studio to rework one of his tracks. He'd told me he'd be here as soon as he could, but Gary Benson's house was at least fifteen minutes outside of town. Once he got there, did what he needed to do, and drove back, we'd be done. At least I was seeing him tonight. We had plans to watch a mindless action movie and stuff our faces with Jimmy's dim sum. What I wouldn't give to be there right now.

"I told you, he's not going to be able to come to every meeting. He's busy making appearances and recording his album." I checked my phone and saw he'd texted me a photo. He was standing in front of a mic with a pair of huge headphones on and an expression of giddy disbelief on his face. "He has a life."

Unlike me.

"Right. And isn't that life meant to include you?"

Ouch. Was your mother really supposed to *try* to hit you where it hurt?

"Well, he wouldn't have to be doing as much as he is if you hadn't had him arrested for no reason," I said, my face burning from the effort of talking back to her.

The door opened, and in filed Tash, followed by the six other people on the planning committee. They were all chatting in low tones, looking chipper and ready after what had probably been a short work lunch of kale and flaxseed salads. These people were all about the superfoods.

"You know, Cecilia," my mother said, as if no one else was there, "you're going to have to get over that eventually. I only did what I did in direct response to your actions. If you want to act like a child, you should be ready to accept the consequences."

The happy chatter died. One of the men had paused with his butt halfway to his chair, and when he saw me looking at him, he fell into it, making the springs squeak. Tash smirked as she opened her folder on the table.

If you don't want me to act like a child, maybe you should stop treating me like one, I thought, but of course didn't say.

"Oh, and one other thing," she said, as she slipped her suit jacket off the chair behind her desk. "We all saw the photos of you two from that event last night. If you're going to parade yourself around like that, I expect you to make use of your makeup artist and stylist. We want to make sure you project the *proper* image."

"I *told* them to work with her last night, but she sent them away," Tash tattled like a toddler.

My fingers curled around the edges of my legal pad. If I karate chopped her with it, would my mother's bodyguards barrel in here and tackle me to the ground?

"Well, now that you're all here, I'll let you get down to work," my mother said, checking her watch. "Cecilia, I want to see all of your plans by midday tomorrow. Don't overspend."

She patted Tash on the back, letting everyone know who was *really* in charge, and swept out of the room. Just when I thought she was gone, she was standing in the doorway again, looking almost regal as she tugged at the sleeves of her jacket.

"And I do find it interesting, Cecilia, that you were there for your boyfriend's event last night, but he can't be bothered to show up here for you."

I opened my mouth to respond, but she was gone before I could. Not that I had any idea what to say anyway. All eyes turned to gaze at me, some disdainful, others sympathetic. One woman looked downright pitying.

"Well, Cecilia," Tash said finally, "why don't you go ahead and let us know how you'd like to proceed?"

I had not one tiny clue. And I'd never felt like more of a child in my life.

Jasper was late. He'd never made it to campaign HQ, and now he was late for our chill dinner plans. That budget meeting had taken the life right out of me. All those facts and details and discounts and calling in favors. The lists and lists of potential local vendors. The twenty-minute-long debate over whether we should fly seafood in and if the benefits would merit the cost. Was this really what these people talked about all day?

Meanwhile, I'd barely been able to keep myself awake and had only survived by looking forward to seeing Jasper tonight. But clearly he had not been looking forward to seeing me. Otherwise, he would have been on time.

My foot bounced and my legs crossed tightly as I sat on his couch and pointed the remote at his flatscreen TV. The takeout from Jimmy's was laid out on the coffee table, the sauces congealing, and there was nothing to watch. At least, I was pretty sure there was nothing to watch. My brain hadn't registered much as I scrolled through the channels again and again and again.

I knew I should be on my computer, answering e-mails from Tash and going over the list of potential musical acts she'd compiled for me and Jasper, or sifting through the roughly twenty-five sample menus she'd sent from local caterers so that I could at least have it narrowed down for my meeting with my mom tomorrow, but I just didn't feel like it. I knew I wouldn't be able to concentrate, and trying to decide between bison and regular old beef was just not something that interested me. Especially not when I was starving and trying very hard not to eat the delectable food that was right in front of me.

The digital clock clicked off another minute and I blew out a sigh.

He told you he was going to be busy, I reminded myself. *Right now his life is not his own.*

But did he really not have five seconds to shoot off a text?

Finally, I heard a heavy footfall on the porch and a second later, his key in the lock. Part of me wanted to stand up to greet him, but the angry part of me—the larger part of me—kept me rooted to the spot. The TV landed on a cooking show and I left it there, glaring at the screen.

Immature, I know. But I was exhausted. And annoyed. And between Tammy, and my mother, and Tash, and three hours of fighting over how much to spend on décor versus music versus food versus bathroom attendants and always being voted down, I was feeling used and unappreciated.

"Hey! There's my girl!"

Jasper launched himself over the back of the couch and basically tackled me into it, my head coming to rest on the arm. He laid a big closed-mouth kiss on me, then cupped the top of his hat with his hand, tossed it across the room, and deepened the kiss.

Wow. Someone was in a good mood. I pressed my hands into his chest and pushed him back. He grinned. This boy was really not picking up on my body language.

"Guess what?" he said, sitting up. "I got over a thousand new Twitter followers *today*!"

He flashed his phone's screen at me so quickly, I didn't see a thing.

"And the record label Instagram told their followers to follow me, so now my Instagram is blowing up too. It's ridiculous!"

He leaned into me and held out the phone for a selfie. "Smile!"

I did not smile. Jasper did not notice.

He sat up again and started typing. "What's your screen name? I'll tag you!"

His thumbs paused and he looked over at me, the picture of blue-eyed obliviousness.

"Um, I'm not on Instagram. Up until a month ago no one was allowed to know what I looked like, remember?"

A tiny shadow passed through Jasper's eyes, at a blink-and-you-might-miss-it speed. "Right. Sorry. Forgot about that for a second."

He tapped the phone a couple more times and then, apparently satisfied with whatever he'd posted, shoved it into his back pocket.

"You should join. Now that you're out as the real you, I mean." Jasper reached forward for a wonton noodle and crunched into it. "You'd probably get, like, a million followers."

"Not even a little bit interested."

I pushed myself up off the couch and walked into the kitchen, needing to put some distance between me and the social media maven. It was like he'd forgotten who I was—why I was even here. I realized his career might make him famous, but I never thought he'd get so excited about fame itself. I'd thought he was about the music, not about the followers.

I, for one, didn't want followers. I didn't need a million more people tracking my every move more than they already did. I just wanted friends. People I could trust. And I'd thought I found that here. But now, I was starting to wonder.

"Everything okay, Red Sox?"

I yanked open the fridge and studied the contents, as if that was the reason for my getting up in the first place. His use of my nickname had melted my armor—just a touch.

"I'm fine. It's just been a long day." I popped open a seltzer and took a swig. "And the only thing that got me through it was looking forward to tonight, but I've been sitting here for half an hour. Alone."

Jasper's shoulders slumped. "Right. Dang it. I'm sorry. I tried to leave on time, but they kept calling me back in to finish this or sign that. By the time I got out of there, I didn't even realize how much time had gotten away from me."

He took a step closer to me and I stared at the top of the can I was holding, unable to meet his eye.

"You could have texted," I said.

"You're right. I will. Next time I promise I will."

I gave him a semi-sarcastic look and he raised his palms.

"Not that there's gonna be a next time! No siree. I'll never neglect my woman again, I swear!"

"Your woman? Wow! I feel so special."

Jasper grinned, took the can from my hand, and put it aside before pulling me to him, waist to waist. "Do you now?" he said, lowering his voice.

"Well . . . almost," I replied.

And then he kissed me. And this time, there was no mistaking my body language.

The following afternoon, while Jasper was boarding a plane from Nashville to Austin, I was facedown on my bed, passed out. I had thought about going with him, but we'd been up half the night, and I was so tired, and he'd told me there was no point since he'd really just be performing and then coming home, so I'd been happy to have the night off. After a tense meeting with my mother during which she'd made it clear how unimpressed she was by the fact that I'd whittled a list of caterers down from twenty-two to ten—and didn't have any clue which musical acts might be available to play—I'd come home to take a nap.

I woke up when my phone rang at exactly ten p.m., groggy, disheveled, and feeling like something only distantly related to human. As I looked around for my phone, I caught a glance in the mirror, which was new and hung above the rows of beauty products Max had left for me. There was a deep sleep crease in my face and my right eyeball felt dry, while my left was tearing. When I finally found my phone beneath my pillow, I noticed that the pillowcase was dotted with drool. If my mother could see me now.

And speaking of whom . . . guess whose face was on my phone? My heart skipped a double beat as I answered. Earlier that day I'd left my mood boards with my mother and she'd promised to take a look.

"Hi, Mom!" I said brightly.

"Hello, Cecilia." She paused. "You sound funny. Are you coming down with something? Because Doctor Chen is on staff now, so if you need to see someone—"

"I'm fine, Mom," I said. "What's up? Did you have a chance to look at the materials I left for you?"

There was a sigh. A not-good sigh. "I did, and Cecilia, I have to say, these color schemes are not going to work."

Blunt as always.

"What? But they're so beautiful and . . . and outside the box," I replied, sitting up straight. "No one is going to expect—"

"And that's exactly the problem. This is a patriotic event, Cecilia. I'm running for president, not prom queen."

I felt like I was going to be sick. I had already envisioned the entire event in my mind—the swaths of colorful fabric, the soft pink lighting, the elegant champagne glasses and gold flatware. I'd practically had my portfolio laid out already.

"I know, Mom, but you said you wanted some local flair and I—"

"So throw some Tennessee purple irises in the centerpiece, get me some traditional bunting, and call it a day. I'm not asking you to reinvent the wheel here."

My grip on the phone tightened as I saw all my hopes and dreams crumble before me. I couldn't submit a bunch of pictures of red, white, and blue bunting and substandard flower arrangements to the Tennessee School of Design. They'd dump me right into the reject pile. So much for killing two birds with one stone.

"I just . . . I thought you'd want something a little different. A little more sophisticated?" I still clung to the hope that I could turn this in my favor.

There was a long pause. "Cecilia, please just do as I ask."

I swallowed hard. "Fine," I said. "Whatever you say."

Then I hung up without saying good-bye.

The apartment was silent. Tears pricked my eyes. I forced myself up and shuffled out of my room, because if I didn't move I was going to scream. There was a note on the kitchen counter.

We're at The Roadhouse if you want to join us! B & F

The Roadhouse? How many bars did this town have? I glanced at my distorted reflection in the refrigerator door, irritated that my eyes were now rimmed in red. But getting the hell out of here suddenly seemed like a good plan—the only plan. I was full of pent-up anger and I needed to do something before I exploded. Could I possibly make myself look human again?

But then, I had so much to do, and I'd just napped six hours, so I did have some energy.

I should really try to work on my essay for the application.

Except that seemed sort of pointless now. Or look through the Harvard materials? Ugh, no thank you. Work on this new, boring, entirely *inside*-the-box concept for the gala? I'd rather bang my head against the wall.

A fist pounded on my door. I was so startled, I yelped.

"Cecilia? You okay?"

It was Duncan. I opened the door and he strode in, wearing a polo shirt and khaki shorts, his dark hair flopping over one eye.

"What's up? You look like the walking dead."

"Thanks," I said, rolling my eyes.

"Sorry . . . did you just wake up?"

"Kind of." I sat at the island and pulled out my phone again. One text from Jasper letting me know he'd arrived okay. It had come in four hours ago.

"So, listen, I'm headed out to this party and I thought you might want to come," Duncan said.

"Party?" I asked, my interest piqued.

"Yeah, the soccer league I play in? We have this big party every summer to welcome new recruits. It's out at the old mill and it's kind of a big deal."

I bit my lip and tried to hide the sleep crease behind my hand. "I don't know, Duncan. I'm kind of tired. . . ."

But even as I said it, I could feel myself warming to the plan. It would take me five minutes to throw together ideas for the party my mom wanted—staid and traditional and bland. And everything else could wait until tomorrow. It was ten o'clock, after all. Way past time to have a life.

"Come on, Lia! I've barely seen you since you've been back. And we definitely haven't done anything fun," Duncan argued. "Unless you count me pretending to be your security escort for five minutes *fun*."

I looked at him from the corner of my eye. "You are a very talented bringer of guilt, you know that?"

Duncan grinned. "I try. But seriously, why else did you run away from home if it wasn't to sow some wild oats or whatever? When was the last time you actually had a good time?"

I narrowed my eyes. He was right. I honestly couldn't remember. Between my mom and the gala and Tash and her e-mails and almost having a panic attack on the red carpet the other night, I really hadn't relaxed. At all.

"I'm in," I said, standing up.

Duncan's eyebrows shot up. "You are?"

I tossed my phone into my bag, which was sitting on the couch where I'd dropped it earlier, then headed off for my freshly organized and color-coded closet.

"Yeah. Just give me ten minutes."

8

THE OLD MILL TURNED OUT TO BE A BROKEN-DOWN, ancient structure on the outskirts of town that sat between a burbling brook and a small lake. There was a dilapidated water-wheel, its paddles rotted and crumbling, and a number of gables that seemed to be inhabited by an army of bats and owls. Basically it looked like a horror movie or a lawsuit waiting to happen, but the partiers surrounding it didn't seem to care.

By the time Duncan and I arrived, things were already going full tilt. Girls in bikinis danced on tables, boulders, and any other surface raised up off the ground—including a rusted, wheelless tractor—hoisting red cups in the air. A man about the size of a small planet worked a barbecue pit, roasting huge racks of ribs over the open flame. Someone had set up a bar on top of a half-collapsed wagon—a haphazard collection of bottles, some full, some with an inch of alcohol in the bottom. Duncan added a couple of bottles of vodka to the array and then dragged me over to the makeshift dance floor—a patch of dirt near the water.

"You guys do this every year?" I shouted over the music, which was pumping through speakers hidden from view.

"Yeah! It's gotten bigger the last couple of seasons. When it first started, it was really just the guys hanging out, getting to know the kids who were trying out for the teams." He looked around and raised his palms. "Now, it's . . . this."

It was too bad my mother and Tash couldn't see this. Talk about local flavor. Maybe the next time I saw them I'd suggest barbecued ribs as the main dish for the gala. They'd run back to Boston so fast they'd be nothing but a blur.

We danced for a while, Duncan slapping hands with friends, and the crowd growing louder and more intense. At some point people began scaling the building, using old ladders and a questionable-looking staircase to get close to the top, then launching themselves into the lake, making tremendous splashes. Everywhere I looked people were taking dares, doing shots and keg-stands, sneaking off into the woods to do God knew what. This was the kind of party I'd always dreamed about. The kind of party where people let loose, got a little dangerous. I felt like an actual kid—the kind who grew up with normal parents and went to a normal school and did normal-kid things.

"I'm so glad you brought me here, Duncan," I told him. "This is exactly what I needed."

And it was true. For the first time in days, I didn't feel tense. Aside from the fact that I was missing Jasper, I was perfectly content. At least, I was if I managed not to think about the butt-load of work waiting for me back at my apartment, which I did for a few minutes here and there.

"To freedom!" Duncan shouted, raising his cup over his head.

"To freedom!" I shouted back, along with a dozen other random people.

Right about then, a familiar figure emerged from the crowd, though it was so unexpected it took me a few seconds to place him. Also contributing to my confusion was his shirtlessness. His *ripped-abbed* shirtlessness.

"Frederick?" I blurted as he sauntered toward me with a smile. "What the hell are you doing here?"

And did you apply some kind of oil to those stomach muscles? Because, shiny.

"I have been looking for you, Cecilia Montgomery. You are harder to find than I thought you would be."

He took a sip from his cup and grinned again, his dark green eyes alight.

"Um, Lia?" Duncan asked.

"Right. Sorry. Duncan Taylor this is Frederick Valois. We went to school together. He's from France."

"Pleasure to meet you," Duncan said, extending a hand.

"The pleasure is mine," Frederick said as they shook. He took another sip and smiled again. I'd never seen this guy form an emotional expression in my life, and here he was, grinning like a schoolkid.

And did I mention shirtless?

"You play soccer?" Duncan asked.

"I dabble," Frederick said. "But I am very interested in trying out for this league. It seems as if you all know how to have a good time."

"That we do," Duncan said, and they slapped hands. What was it with boys? How could they make friends that easily?

"I'm sorry, what are you doing here?" I asked Frederick.

"I saw your mother's speech and came down to volunteer," Frederick replied. "My parents are very interested in politics for me, but I did not want to go home yet, so this seemed like a way to gain the experience without leaving the States. Your mother is a very kind woman."

"You met her?" I blurted.

"Certainly. She and my father are very old friends," he replied, taking another sip. "So I am here now, and we are friends, yes?"

"Uh . . . yeah. Sure," I replied.

"Good, then you let me do this . . . belly shot?"

I laughed so hard it might have been a guffaw. "Um, no."

Frederick's handsome brow creased. "Why not? It looks like it is fun."

Duncan turned to me, an amused look in his eye. "Yeah, Lia. Why not?"

His Southern drawl right on the heels of Frederick's thick French accent was somehow making me giddy. "Because it's gross!"

Over at the picnic table, some scrawny, tattoo-covered

guy had just finished licking what I hoped was his girlfriend's tummy. The crowd cheered so loudly, it was as if they were trying to specifically contradict me.

Frederick and Duncan looked at me with matching cocked eyebrows. I laughed again. And then a familiar song came on the radio—one Jasper and I had heard on the street down in Nashville and sung along to. Jasper. My heart panged at the mere thought of him. I checked my phone again. Nothing.

On a whim, I clicked on the Instagram icon he'd installed on my phone so I could follow him. The first picture I saw was a selfie of Jasper, grinning, with his arm around three gorgeous female fans.

"Whoa. They're hot," Duncan said, looking over my shoulder.

"It's just for publicity," I said through gritted teeth. But I shoved the phone away. Whatever. Jasper was off living his life. I may as well live mine.

I downed the dregs of the beer I'd been nursing and grabbed Frederick's hand. "Let's do this!"

Duncan cheered as I pulled Frederick over to the table. We cut through the crowd and I climbed up onto the table as Duncan started everyone chanting, "Lia! Lia! Lia! Lia!"

What the hell was I doing? What. The hell. Was I *doing*?

I put my head back and tugged up my shirt, but lifted my head again the second the cold liquid hit my stomach. Then all I saw was Frederick's tongue coming at me. Then all I *felt* was Frederick's tongue *licking* me. And it was disgusting, but it also kind of tickled and I couldn't help laughing, mostly because I was embarrassed and mortified and also kind of proud all at once. Frederick raised his hands in triumph, the crowd cheered, and I jumped up. The next girl started to climb up onto the table, and I looked at Frederick. I must have had fourteen gallons of adrenaline coursing through me, because I didn't even think about it before shouting, "Oh no! Stop right there!"

Because why should the girls be the only ones who were getting their bellies licked? I was nothing if not a feminist. It was the way I'd been raised as a Montgomery. My mother would be so proud. The girl froze with one pink cowboy boot on the picnic table bench. I gestured from Frederick to the table and grinned.

"Your turn."

And that's how I ended up sucking tequila out of Frederick Valois's belly button.

"Are you friggin kidding me?"

"Jasper!" I blurted, half asleep. "What the hell?"

Jasper stood at the door of my apartment and shoved his phone at my face. I hadn't put my contacts in yet, so I fumbled across the kitchen island for my glasses and put them on. The phone was open to some gossip website, specifically an image. And when the image came into focus, I understood. It was me, on my back, shirt up, laughing, while Frederick licked my bare stomach.

Well, at least it wasn't *me* licking *his* stomach. I had a feeling somehow the image of that would have been harder to explain. I could still taste the mixture of alcohol and male sweat in the back of my throat. It wasn't yum.

"Ugh! I should have known someone would sell their pictures," I said, snatching the paper from his hands.

Jasper laughed a short, sarcastic laugh. "Of course they're going to sell their pictures. You're famous, Cecilia, remember?"

He slammed the door and I whirled around, my shoulder muscles coiling. "I'm not used to having my picture taken, okay? I'm not used to going to parties. I didn't even think about it."

Which, okay, was maybe pretty naive. But I was just trying to have a little fun.

"Who the hell took them, anyway?" I asked.

Jasper groaned and shoved both hands through his hair above his ears. "Forget about the photographer. Who *is* this guy and why is he not wearing any clothes while he *licks* my girlfriend?"

I swallowed against a dry throat. "He's a friend. From school," I lied. Frederick and I had never been actual friends. We'd only ever done business together and had that one dance at the graduation party. "He came down to volunteer for my mother's campaign."

"Well, that's awesome. Now I *really* don't like the guy."

The comment stung more than it should have. I already knew he didn't like my mother. But he didn't have to keep reminding me.

"And he had pants on, just . . . not a shirt."

"That's comforting," Jasper snapped. The heat of his anger startled me—and scared me too.

"Look, it just happened," I said, speaking calmly. I put his phone on the counter with the piles of Britta's other rag mags, not wanting to look at the image anymore. It looked a whole lot more lewd than it had seemed at the time. "Duncan stopped by and asked me to this party and I had nothing else to do so I—"

"Oh, so you went out last night with *two* random guys," Jasper spat.

"Duncan is not random! And neither is Frederick, just because you don't know him. Besides, if you want to start throwing around accusations about half-dressed members of the opposite sex, what the heck did you get up to last night? I can play show-and-tell too, you know."

For the first time since his arrival, Jasper fell silent.

I went into my room, retrieved my phone, and pulled up Instagram. When I showed Jasper his feed, he turned red, but barely looked at the dozens of pictures of him with tanned, taut female fans. I swear, the theme of his feed could have been "cleavage." When he spoke again, his voice was a lot calmer. Chagrined even.

"Yeah, I could see how that might rattle you a bit."

There was a sarcastic retort on the tip of my tongue, but I bit down on it. Jasper was retreating. At least a little. I didn't want to press my luck. I tossed the phone onto the plaid couch and we stood there for a moment, silent. Finally, Jasper blew out a sigh. He sat down next to my phone and blanked the screen, which had still been glowing with a pic of him and some busty brunette with sideboob. He looked me in the eye for a second before speaking.

"Unfortunately, my publicist tells me that kind of thing is part of my job." He lifted his shoulders. "If you'd come with me . . ."

"Oh, so now this is my fault?" I crossed my arms over my chest and held on tight.

"No! No, I'm not saying that," Jasper rubbed his face with both hands. "Can we maybe call a truce here?"

Jasper held out his hand to me, but I didn't move. I was still smarting.

"Hey, you're the one who barged into my house and attacked me," I said quietly. "I didn't even know that picture had been taken, let alone put on the front page."

"I'm sorry, okay? I should have gotten the story first," he replied. "But put yourself in my shoes and imagine how you'd feel if you woke up and found *that* on your screen."

I glanced at the phone and cringed, then shook his hand. "Truce. But only if you promise to forget you ever saw that photo."

"It's a deal."

Jasper grasped my hand tighter and pulled me toward him, nearly yanking me off my feet. Not that I minded. He'd just shaved and smelled like peppermint and soap. His lips were just about to touch mine when my phone rang and vibrated its way across the couch. I looked down and saw my mother's campaign headshot. What the hell? I hadn't programmed that in there.

But then, my phone *had* been left with her minions for a few days. Ugh. I hoped they hadn't read all my texts.

I grabbed the phone, even as Jasper was saying, "Don't answer that."

I shot him an apologetic look as I hit talk. "Hello? Mom?"

"Cecilia, I'd like to see you in my office," my mother said. *"Now."*

"What were you thinking!?" my mother shouted, gesturing at Tash to close her office door. Tash jumped up to do my mother's bidding.

"It was just a party, Mom," I said, glancing helplessly at Jasper. He'd come with me for moral support, but there wasn't much he could do or say. It wasn't as if he'd been there. "We were just blowing off steam."

"Oh, because your life is so stressful?" she demanded, her face going pink. "You can't even decide on a caterer, Cecilia. It's not as if you're stretching yourself."

"I'm sorry, I—"

"This sort of thing will *not* happen again, do you hear me? I've been on the phone all morning doing damage control. No more parties." She tossed her Blackberry down, open on the image of me and Frederick.

My jaw dropped. "You can't *ground* me."

From the corner of my eye, I saw Tash go pale. I suppose she wasn't expecting me to contradict my mother. I wasn't really expecting it either.

"It's not a grounding, it's a direct order," my mother said, walking stiffly around her desk to go toe-to-toe with me. "You are a member of this campaign and, as my daughter, a purveyor of the Montgomery image. I'm running for president of the United States, Cecilia. I can't have my daughter parading around like a common whore!"

"Hey, now! Watch what you say," Jasper snapped, stepping in.

It felt nice, him defending me, but it didn't entirely take away the sting. Had my own mother really just called me a common whore?

"And you! Where the hell were you while your girlfriend was getting mauled by a stranger?" my mother demanded.

"Now you're going to turn this around on him?" I cried, my voice breaking. "Jasper has nothing to do with this. He was *working*. And the guy is not a stranger. He's Frederick Valois, your *old friend's* son. You're the one who hired him to work on your campaign."

"Yes, to work on my campaign, not fraternize with my daughter," my mother snapped.

"Mother, I promise I will not be photographed in a compromising position again," I said, throwing my hands out. "But you can't blame Frederick and you can't blame Jasper."

There was a quick rap on the door and one of my mother's

PR staffers walked in with an iPad. "I'm so sorry to interrupt, Senator, but I thought you'd want to see this right away."

"What is it, Victoria?" my mother said, rolling her eyes closed as if she was *so* put upon.

Victoria hustled over and hit play on the iPad screen. "You might want to see this too," she said, glancing at me in an apologetic, almost sheepish way.

My stomach sank. Dear God, please don't let them have video of last night as well. I stepped up to look over her shoulder, feeling like I was walking to the guillotine. But the video wasn't of me. Instead, two women sitting on a park bench appeared on the screen. One of the women wore a pink pantsuit and had seriously teased blond hair. The other woman, I realized after a double take, was Fiona. My friend Fiona. Except she didn't look like herself. She was wearing a chic little yellow dress with a pleated skirt, and her brown hair had been straightened and shined until it almost looked lacquered. Plus she was wearing eyeliner. Blue eyeliner.

"What is this?" I asked.

"Just watch," Victoria said.

"Thanks so much for joining us today on Music Now, the biggest and best Nashville music vlog on the net," the blond woman said.

"Thanks for having me, Christa," Fiona replied.

Suddenly, a box appeared underneath Fiona's face. It read: "Fiona Taylor, Best Friend of Cecilia Montgomery, America's Sweetheart."

"What the—?"

"Oh, lord help us," my mother put in.

"So tell me, Fiona, what's Cecilia Montgomery really like? She's been out of the spotlight for so long that no one really knows."

"Is that Fiona Taylor?" Jasper asked, unable to see the screen. I nodded, but couldn't tear my eyes away. Heat gradually travelled from my toes, up my legs, across my chest, and into my neck.

"Well, she's awesome," Fiona said. "She's one of the nicest people I know."

"Good to hear, but come on. She can't be perfect."

"Well, nobody's *perfect*," Fiona said with a laugh.

My mother shot me a scathing look, as if this was somehow my doing. I clenched my teeth to keep from grabbing the device and throwing it through the plate-glass window, Frisbee-style.

"So in what ways is Cecilia *not* perfect?"

Jasper sat down on the arm of a chair and folded his hands over his nose and mouth, just waiting. There was a beat as the camera closed in on Fiona's face. I held my breath. I could see a tiny flicker of uncertainty cross her eyes.

Please don't let her start talking about the time I drank myself into oblivion and threw up in the back of the bar. Or about how I went after the guy she was crushing on the second I arrived in town. Or how I sort of maybe broke her brother's heart too, I begged silently.

"Well," Fiona said.

What the hell was she even doing with this woman? Why had she agreed to do an interview about me in the first place? Who had set this up?

"Honestly? I can't say one bad thing about her," Fiona answered finally. "She even saved me once when I was attacked by this loser I went out on a date with."

Jasper bowed his head in silent thanks. I let out a breath of relief as the vlogger's eyebrows popped upward. "Saved you?"

"Yeah, she totally leveled the guy. You should have seen it!" Fiona replied. "Did you know she's trained in three different styles of martial arts?"

"Really? That's an accomplishment."

"Right? I guess once you're almost kidnapped, you learn how to fight back."

My mother hooked one finger over her lips. Fiona and the interviewer laughed and bile rose up my throat. Laughing over the most traumatizing event of my life. That's cool.

"Do we really need to keep watching this?" I asked under my breath.

Victoria paused the video. "She doesn't say anything incriminating, or even off-color," she assured my mother. "But you know that if she's talking now, she's not going to stop talking. And eventually . . ."

"Eventually she'll slip up," Tash supplied, staring me down.

This woman really wished I had never been born.

"Call her in for a meeting," my mother said finally.

"What?" I blurted, feeling protective and defensive all at

once. "What are you gonna do, have her thrown in jail too?"

Jasper's head snapped up and I realized what I'd just said. My heart began to slam against my ribcage. He looked like he was going to puke as his eyes traveled from mine to my mother's face—which was utterly clueless. He stood and grabbed his hat off the table.

"Cecilia, I'm gonna wait for you outside. I suddenly need some air."

I wanted to run after him, but I couldn't seem to make my feet move.

"I already did call Fiona Taylor, Senator," Victoria said. "She should be here any minute." She gathered her iPad up against her chest with one arm. "Sorry," she said under her breath as she passed by me, oblivious to my internal nervous breakdown. "But I'd want to know if my best friend was going around talking about me online."

She swept out, leaving me, Tash, and my mother alone again.

"You may go too, Cecilia," my mother said as she sat down behind her desk. "As long as we understand each other."

"No. We don't understand each other," I replied, shaking from head to toe. Jasper was going to break up with me. There was no doubt in my mind. "What are you going to do to Fiona?"

"I'm not going to *do* anything to her," my mother replied. "Don't be so Machiavellian."

The door to the office opened and Fiona timidly stuck her head into the room.

"Oh good! You're here," she said to me, letting out a sigh of relief. "What the heck is going on? One second I'm drinking a smoothie on my front porch, making Sweetbriar Summer Princess signs, and the next second a black town car is coming to whisk me away."

She had on another stylish, body-conscious dress, this one in a deep pink, and a pair of nude-colored heels. Fiona never wore heels. And she really didn't look as if she'd just been sipping a yogurt-based drink and messing with glitter glue.

"Actually, Cecilia was just leaving," my mother said. "I want to speak to you alone, Miss Taylor."

Fiona shot me an alarmed look. I stepped past her toward the door. "Why did you do that interview?" I hissed.

"Is that what this is about?" she whispered, wide-eyed. "I just—"

"*Now*, Cecilia," my mother said.

And Tash practically shoved me into the hallway. Fiona wore a look of dread as the door closed on her. But there was nothing I could do to help her now. Honestly, I wasn't even sure I wanted to.

"What the hell did *that* mean?"

I nearly yelped out loud as Jasper came up behind me.

"I thought you were getting air!" I whispered.

"What did that mean? Lia, did your *mother* somehow have me and Shelby thrown in jail?"

I swallowed a pocket of air that had gotten jammed inside my throat, and pulled him out into the courtyard. The workers had laid the paver stones and there were a half dozen landscapers putting in lush floral plantings all around the edges of the patio. None of them looked up or seemed to care that we were there.

"Jasper, listen, I was going to tell you—"

"Tell me what? That your own mother was the one behind me spending two days scared shitless in a metal chair?" he demanded. "What the hell, Lia? Did she really think I kidnapped you?"

My eyes burned. "No. That's what she does. She couldn't let America think I'd run off, so her big plan was to make them think I'd been kidnapped. Again."

Jasper covered his mouth with one hand. "She's truly evil. She cares more about her image than people's lives?"

"You don't understand," I said. "That's just who she is. In her mind, she did what she did to survive."

"And you're making excuses for her?" Jasper demanded.

"No! No!" I grabbed his arm, and was surprised when he let me hold on to his wrist. I could feel his pulse thrumming beneath my fingertips and it was almost as fast as mine. "Please, Jasper. I'm sorry. If you'll just let me explain—"

But before I could finish, Jasper pulled away. "I can't. I just . . . I can't. I have to get out of here."

"Jasper, please," I whispered.

"I'm sorry, Lia. I just need to be alone right now. . . . I'll talk to you later."

And before I could say anything else, Jasper stormed down the short hallway and shoved open the metal door into the sunlight.

* * *

A few hours later, I sat on the patio outside my mom's office, scrolling through a zillion images of campaign parties and conventions. Supposedly, I was coming up with new ideas for the gala décor. Really, I was listlessly clicking the mouse, obsessing about whether Jasper would ever talk to me again. The sun blared down on the back of my neck and my T-shirt clung to my spine with sweat. I was hungry—hadn't eaten anything all day—but I couldn't seem to move. Heartache really sucked.

The buzz of my mom's intercom sounded. I'd been hearing it all damn day and had gotten used to the sound. What was surprising was what came next.

"Senator Montgomery, Jasper Case is here to see you."

My pulse began to thrum and I slapped my laptop closed.

"Send him in."

I stood up and slunk away from the open window, pressing my back against the brick wall where he wouldn't be able to see me. What was he doing here? Looking for me? Or had my mother summoned him, too?

"Hello, Mr. Case."

She sounded cold as ever, but did I detect some curiosity in her tone?

"Senator Montgomery."

His voice was clipped. No mistaking the anger there.

"Please, have a seat."

"No thanks. I won't be here long."

There was a pause. He'd thrown her. I imagined them

standing on equal ground—facing off—except that Jasper was significantly taller than my mother, which she would not appreciate.

"I just came here to tell you that what you did to myself and Shelby Tanaka was unacceptable."

"Mr. Case—"

"I'm not finished."

My heart thunked. No one spoke to my mom that way. Ever.

"You can't just go around messing with people's lives like that. You have a problem with your daughter, ma'am, all due respect, you should take it up with your daughter. Not drag innocent people off to jail because it makes you feel better."

"I did not do what I did to make myself feel better," my mother said.

"No? Well, then, why did you? I'm standing right here in front of you, hat in my hands. Why don't you tell me why I needed to spend a couple of nights in federal custody for doing absolutely nothing wrong?"

"Mr. Case, there are factors at play here that are beyond the scope of your comprehension."

"Oh, really? Is that what you're going to tell the American people once you're president and they don't like the way you handle something? So much for being a woman of the people."

I bit my lip. Part of me wanted to go in there and hug Jasper for saying everything I was thinking. Another part of me wanted to smack him upside the head. What was he thinking?

Making an enemy of my mother was not a good idea.

"Mr. Case, why did you come here today?" my mother asked. "Because if it was simply to insult me or throw accusations—"

"I'm not throwing accusations, I'm stating fact. We both know what you did." Jasper sounded incredibly calm. "I came here for some answers. But, clearly, I'm not going to get them. Thanks for your time, ma'am."

I heard a door close, and only after counting to twenty did I hazard a glance through the window. My mother was shaking her head incredulously as she sat back down in her chair. At first I thought it was all for nothing. She looked completely unfazed. But as she reached for a pen, I saw her hand was shaking.

I turned and walked into the hallway, then raced toward the front of the building where the outer door slowly swung closed. Outside, Jasper was just placing his black cowboy hat atop his head as he stormed off.

"Jasper, wait!" I called.

He turned, his expression unreadable.

"That was amazing!" I said, hugging my laptop as I jogged up to him.

"Amazing? Are you kidding me? That woman is infuriating."

"This is not news."

He blinked. "Wait. How did you even hear what I said?"

"I was outside," I admitted. "I didn't mean to eavesdrop. I'm sorry."

"It's okay. I just—"

"No, I mean, I'm *really* sorry. About everything. I wish I could have stopped her before she sent the FBI to Sweetbriar, but I had no idea what she was planning, Jasper, I swear. And then, afterward, I did everything I could to get you and Shelby out of there." My voice cracked. "Please . . . just . . . don't hate me. I couldn't take it if you hated me for something she'd done."

Jasper sighed. "I don't hate you, Lia. I wish you'd told me, but I don't hate you."

He reached out and took my hand, and I stepped in to him. I was relieved when he put his arms around me—and my laptop.

"I do hate her, though."

There was a lump in my throat the size of Texas. "I know."

He kissed the top of my head and pulled back, holding me at arm's length. "You have to promise me something."

"What?"

"Promise me you won't let that crazy person run your life. Not ever again."

I wiped under my eyes and nodded. "I promise."

But even as I said it, I knew it was going to be a difficult promise to keep.

9

"SHE'S GOING TO GROOM HER. MY MOTHER IS GOING to groom Fiona to be my best friend."

I couldn't believe it. Honestly. Just when I'd decided to break free from under my mom's thumb, my best friend had agreed to put herself squarely beneath it.

"What does that even mean?" Jasper asked, taking a sip of champagne.

We were standing in the lobby of a theater in Nashville on Saturday night, having just sat through the Young Nashville awards, during which Jasper had presented a guitar-shaped trophy to Vivi Timmons, the winner of the Young Vocalist of the Year. We were now waiting to be escorted along a red carpet outside, where more salivating photogs and fans awaited us, and into the party venue next door. Because we hadn't had enough pictures taken of us on our way *into* the awards.

You're doing this for Jasper, Cecilia, I told myself whenever I started to panic. *After everything he's done for you, and all he's forgiven, it's the least you can do.*

I took a deep breath, followed by a gulp of champagne.

"She's getting Fiona her own stylist and setting her up with interview lessons and a poise specialist or something. Plus Pilates classes. It's good for the posture."

I rolled my eyes and took another swig, this one too fast. The bubbles tickled my nose and I sneezed quietly.

"Are you okay?" Jasper asked, whipping out his pocket square. He was all fancy tonight in a pinstripe suit with a deep red tie and matching square. As always, a pair of cowboy boots adorned his feet, but these were new, shiny, black, and silver-toed.

"I'm fine." I touched the pocket square to my nose. "Thank you. It's just . . . why didn't my mother tell her to stay the hell off camera? How about that as a solution?"

But I knew why. It was because Fiona was a good girl. An honest-to-goodness, country-raised, pure specimen of American values. My mother wanted Fiona to represent me, because she thought it would help clean up my now-tarnished image. She was using Fiona, which was bad enough. What really hurt was that Fiona was allowing herself to be used.

I held out Jasper's pocket square, but he raised a hand and I shoved it in my tiny beaded purse instead.

"I'm sorry. That sucks." Jasper took another sip from his crystal flute and stared past me at the wall of windows. Every time someone opened the glass door near the far end, the roar of the crowd traveled inside, enveloping us along with a warm breath of summer air. "Maybe you should just talk to Fiona yourself. If she sees how upset you are, she'll back off."

"I doubt it," I said, refusing to be placated. "She's been Montgomeried. There's no coming back from that."

"Well, I'm sure it'll be fine. It's not like Fiona's gonna be on the news every night, right?" He straightened up and nodded at someone behind me. I turned to see Evan Meyer approaching, a white scarf tossed artfully around his neck. "It's not like she's a fame hound or anything," Jasper concluded.

"True," I said. "I wonder if she thinks all of this will help her win Sweetbriar Princess. She's pretty obsessed with that all of a sudden."

"Maybe," Jasper said. "If she gets herself on TV, it'll definitely up her profile around town."

"Jasper, Cecilia, you two are up," Evan said, gesturing toward the door to the red carpet.

"All right. Let's do this thing." Jasper's grin was the widest I'd seen it all night as he held out his arm to me. I hooked my own arm around his elbow and sighed as we pushed out into the humid evening. Jasper's free hand immediately raised up into a wave and the crowd behind the red ropes went wild. Jasper laughed.

"Jasper! Cecilia! Over here!"

"Jasper! Put your arm around her a little more tightly!"

"Could you pose chest to chest?"

"Let's see a smile, Cecilia! Pretend you're happy to be here!"

That one got a laugh from the other photographers and I grinned back even as my face burned. Where did these people get off telling us how to pose, telling me what to feel? They didn't even know me. They didn't know what was going on in my life or in Jasper's. They only knew the image they wanted to present to the world.

All anyone in my life seemed to care about was image. *But at least it hasn't gone to Jasper's head,* I thought, as he leaned in to tell me how beautiful I looked.

We made our way along the red carpet slowly, stopping every two feet or so, me trying not to gush buckets of nervous sweat.

"Oh, hey. Is that the Firebrand Three?" I asked, checking out the group of bright haired, scantily clad musicians posing just ahead of us.

"Yep. Lanie, Margie, and Marissa," he said.

"You're on a first-name basis?" I said, impressed. "Maybe they'd like to play the gala."

Jasper somehow managed to groan even as he smiled for a photo. "Lia, I'm sorry, but there's no way I'm helping your mom out with that party. Not after what she did to me and Shelby."

He moved away from me, headed for the next *X* taped onto the red carpet, but I didn't follow. I was that stunned.

"Cecilia," Evan hissed, prompting me, while photogs snapped off a few shots of Jasper alone.

I slowly walked over and put my arm around Jasper, not quite as tightly. "Don't think of it as helping her. Think of it as helping me."

"You're gonna do a great job with the decorations. That's your job, right? So what does me getting a band to play have to do with that?"

Okay, he had a point. But the more successful the party, the better the press, and the more photos I'd have for my portfolio. I was about to point this out, but Jasper spoke first.

"I don't really see why you feel the need to go above and beyond for her." He looked me in the eye. "I mean, she totally blew me off when I tried to get her to just tell the truth, and now she's appropriated your best friend, for God's sake. How much crap are you going to take?"

I swallowed hard, feeling as if I'd just been scolded for dumping over my glass of milk. What was it with everyone making me feel like a child lately?

"Big smile, Cecilia!"

"Over here!"

I managed to pose for a few more photos, and before I knew it, I was back inside the air-conditioning, the sounds of the insanity once again muted. I turned to Jasper, hoping to pull him off into a secluded corner to talk about this. But before I could suggest it, a hand came down on his arm.

"All right, buddy. Ready for those meetings we talked about?" Evan asked.

"What meetings?" I interjected.

Jasper turned to me with apologetic eyes. "I gotta meet some of the execs from Blue Peak. They have a private room in the back. I promised Evan. Still have some feathers to smooth, apparently."

"I'll come with you," I offered.

"No, this is solo Jasper stuff," Evan said, holding up a hand. "There's gonna be some business talk. You'd be bored anyway."

"Really?" I snapped, irritated. "You know me so well that you know what does and doesn't bore me?"

Jasper's smile grew strained. "It'll just be a few minutes, Lia. I swear."

I could tell he didn't want me to make a scene. Hell, I didn't want to make a scene. Scenes were so not my thing. So instead, I took a deep breath and told him to go. I told him I'd be fine. He kissed my cheek, whispered in my ear that he loved me, and was gone.

And there I was, alone in a crowded party of perfect strangers with no one to talk to. I turned toward the bar and ordered a bottle of water, then backed myself up against the nearest wall. I still wasn't used to being anywhere on my own, followed as I'd been by a bodyguard my entire life. I wanted my independence for sure, but thanks to my sheltered upbringing, I felt totally exposed in a situation like this. I unscrewed the cap on my water and took a sip, trying to look natural.

"Cecilia? I *thought* it was you!"

I was so surprised, I choked and spit water onto the floor.

"Oh my God! I'm *so* sorry!"

"No problem."

I touched the back of my hand to my chin to dry it and looked into the eyes of Morrisey Blue, one of my classmates from the Worthington School. She looked stunning in a red sequined dress, her kinky black curls surrounding her face like a truly chic mane. Morrisey was the daughter of Jasmine Blue, a classic country singer, and Rodney P, a rap mogul. Morrisey herself was an amazing singer; I'd seen her front the school choir at every concert.

"Morrisey!" I said, once I'd dried myself off. "What're you doing here?"

She lifted one shoulder and leaned back next to me. "My parents are invited to all these things."

"Where are they?" I asked.

"Oh . . . somewhere schmoozing with . . . someone." She rolled her hand around in a carefree, airy way. "That's how it is with these things. They drag me along so the world can get a family picture, and then they disappear."

My stomach tightened. Sounded familiar.

"Where's Jasper?" she asked. "My mom says he's pretty much all anyone can talk about around town."

I blinked. It was hard to get used to people I'd never spoken to knowing everything about my life.

"Really? How nice for him," I said, sounding more sarcastic than I'd intended. "He's around here somewhere, schmoozing with someone," I repeated back to her.

"Not surprising. These parties aren't about hanging out with your guests. They're about climbing the ladder." Morrisey laughed and pushed her curls away from her face. They fell right back where they'd been a second ago. "Get used to being on your own, Cecilia," she said, tilting her head and clicking her tongue. "And good luck."

There was absolutely nothing hopeful or supportive in her tone, and though I wanted to say thank you as she sauntered away—to let her know that I was confident Jasper was nothing like her parents—I somehow couldn't find my voice.

"I don't think they're coming."

As always, Britta was brief and to the point. We were sitting in a booth at the Little Tree Diner, and had been for the last half hour. Britta was busily scrolling through my new Pinterest pages, full of traditional American decorations and ideas for not-entirely-blah centerpieces. Meanwhile, spread out across the table were five sample menus—I'd reduced the list to five!—on which I was hoping to get my friends' opinions. Britta and I had already started to make notes on a few, crossing out things we didn't want (foie gras on toast points?) or couldn't get (it wasn't apple season in Tennessee), but we were waiting for Jasper and Fiona. Jasper and Fiona, who had promised they'd be here.

"Maybe they're just running late?" I ventured.

"Fifteen minutes is late. Half an hour is a no-show." Britta took a slug of coffee, draining the cup, and signaled for Jessie, our waitress.

I couldn't believe Jasper was going to just skip out on me. After he'd finally come back from his meetings at the party last night, he'd promised to at least help me out with the decorations for the gala—since it meant so much to me and my future. I'd shown up for him last night, and now it was his turn to show up for me.

I was about to check my phone for the millionth time when Hal appeared at the end of the table, holding the steaming carafe.

"I have a fantastic idea!" he said by way of greeting. "You should serve my sweet tea at the gala! Add a little local flavor. I can provide the five-gallon jugs at a great price."

As he reached past Britta to refill her cup, one of her eyebrows rose, trained across his hairy wrist at me. There was a squirmy feeling in my gut—the same one I'd had when Tammy had shown me those blueprints at Second Chances.

"Um . . . yeah. That's a great idea," I said.

Hal snapped his fingers. "Or what about my fried green tomatoes? You could even put on the menu, 'Little Tree Diner's Famous Fried Green Tomatoes.' They make a great app."

Britta cleared her throat. I felt totally trapped and put on the spot as Hal watched me expectantly, waiting for an answer. Was there anyone left in this town who didn't want to use me?

"Um . . . I'll think about it," I said. And when Hal got that quizzical dent between his eyebrows I added, "I have to run everything past my mom and her assistant."

Britta stared me down from across the table, and I felt like a jerk for deflecting blame, but not everyone could be as blunt as her. Hal looked as if he was about to follow up with another suggestion, when suddenly the TV caught his eye.

"There she is!" he blurted. "There's Fiona! Crank up the volume, Matt."

I turned fully around to see the television hanging from the ceiling in the corner. The *Entertainment Tomorrow* logo flashed blue and silver across the screen and then I was looking at Fiona's smiling face. She'd gotten her hair cut into a stylish, wispy, below-the-chin bob and was wearing a sophisticated black-and-white sleeveless dress. Her makeup was perfectly contoured and her eyes looked double their normal size with all the eyeliner and mascara the makeup artist had applied.

"What is Fiona doing on *Entertainment Tomorrow*?" Britta asked.

"You don't want to know," I said, rolling my eyes. Even *I* didn't know—not for sure. But I had my suspicions.

I got up on my knees and leaned my arms on the back of the vinyl bench. Britta walked around to join me. We must have looked like two little girls waiting impatiently for our ice cream to come out of the kitchen. I only wished that was what I was waiting for. Instead, I held my breath.

"Thank you so much for joining us, Fiona." The brunette interviewer had the shimmeriest lips I'd ever seen.

"Maria Morocco. Fiona is sitting two feet away from Maria Morocco," Britta breathed.

She was transfixed. Of course she was. These gossip reporters were her idols. The girl probably knew more about Maria Morocco than Maria Morocco did.

A hard rock sank through my chest and settled in my gut, hoping this appearance of Fiona's wouldn't give Britta any ideas about getting her mug on television. I needed someone to remain normal around here.

"So tell me, what are Cecilia Montgomery and Jasper Case really like . . . as a couple?"

Britta looked at me, alarmed. I didn't look back. I couldn't. I was too busy burning with barely containable rage. This was what Fiona was going to be talking about now? My relationship?

"Well, Maria, they are *so* cute," Fiona said, her voice sounding a bit lower and smoother than usual. This from the girl who had been bitching me out for stealing him from her less than two weeks ago. "They're the classic case of opposites attract. Jasper, with his manly, rugged, down-home thing, and Cecilia with her mannered, polite, New England attitude. I just love them together."

"My attitude?" I hissed to Britta under my breath. "Did she just use the word 'attitude'?"

"She didn't mean it that way," Britta said, placing her hand on my back.

"That's my daughter, everyone! My daughter's on TV!" Hal crowed. A few of his clientele scattered around the diner clapped.

"Do you have any intimate details you can give us about America's couple?"

America's couple? Now we were *America's* couple?

On the screen, Fiona's eyes lit up. "Well. I *was* there for their first kiss. . . ."

My fingers gripped the back of the bench so tightly, one of my fingernails pierced the vinyl.

"I think it's time to go outside." Britta grabbed my arm and tugged me across the bench.

"But I—"

"No. Outside. You need air. Now."

Hal shot us a curious look as we barreled toward the door, leaving my laptop and paperwork and backpack behind. Outside, the evening air was warm but clear, and I took a deep breath, trying to calm myself. Unfortunately, I couldn't seem to do it, so instead I brought my hands to my head and screamed as loud as I could. It came out more like a growl, and it made my throat hurt. Over in the park, someone's head swiveled, and I just hoped it wasn't a reporter.

"Cecilia, you must chill," Britta said. Behind her, tacked to a lamppost, was Fiona's Sweetbriar Summer Princess flyer, but the only smiling face I could see was mine. Ugh. Another reminder that she was using me—and our friendship—to win.

"Chill!? Are you kidding me? One of my best friends is telling secrets about me on national television!"

"Okay, but your first kiss with Jasper wasn't exactly a secret," Britta pointed out. "He kissed you in front of a concert hall packed with people."

"I know. I know that, okay? But not everyone there knew it was our first kiss. And also, did you see her face? She was so excited! It was like she couldn't wait to blab every single thing she knows about me!"

And my mother set her up with that interview, I realized. That was the only way Fiona could have shot from a local vlog to a national broadcast in less than twenty-four hours. What was Rebecca Montgomery's end game here? Why did she suddenly want everyone in the universe to know everything about me?

"Hey! Did you guys see me!?"

I whipped around and there was Fiona, getting out of a black town car. She was wearing a red dress and a cute leather jacket as the driver ran around to get her bags out of the trunk.

"Just in from LA?" I snapped.

"New York, actually. So sorry I'm late for the meeting." Fiona's face fell. "Why are you looking at me like that? I texted you. My flight had to circle the airport for a while, so I—"

"I love how you have enough time to go on TV and gossip about me, but you can't manage to be here on time when I really need you. When you *said* you'd be here."

Fiona darted a wary glance at Britta. It was clear that it had never occurred to her she was doing anything remotely wrong. I wasn't sure whether to be relieved or appalled.

"But your mom said this was more important," Fiona replied, looking shaken. "And I wasn't gossiping. Everything I said was the truth."

Of course my mother had said that. Whatever suited her agenda at the moment was always more important. And Fiona had *known* I was irritated after the vlog interview. Did she really think I wouldn't care when she then went on national television?

"It's still gossip! If it's on a gossip show, it's gossip! Everyone's going to think that I don't have any real friends because a real friend wouldn't sell my story to the highest bidder!" I yelled.

"Cecilia," Britta said placatingly.

"That's not what I did!" Fiona screeched.

"Yeah, you just keep telling yourself that," I said, and turned on my heel. "I'm done."

I stalked away, leaving all my crap behind in the diner. There was no way I was getting any work done tonight anyway. Not after that. And clearly Jasper wasn't going to show up to help.

As I crossed the street I realized that I was vibrating with anger. Why had I ever come back here in the first place? Clearly the friends I'd put so much faith in weren't as great as I'd thought they were. They were either using me to try to meet my mom or to make a buck or to get on TV or to get more coverage on the red carpet and then ditch me. Was any one of the relationships I'd made here real? Would any of these people still care about me if I wasn't famous?

"Cecilia! Cecilia Montgomery! I just have a few questions."

I glanced over my shoulder. Great. That person in the park *was* a reporter and now he was coming after me.

"No comment!" I shouted, picking up the pace.

"Come on! I'm on deadline!"

"No comment!" I shouted again, turning to look at him. He snapped a picture, of course. I groaned and started to run.

"Fine! Whatever! Be a bitch!" he called after me.

I slowed at the corner of Peach, the wind knocked out of me by the slur. All I could think was that if Fiona and Jasper had met us at the diner when they said they would, I wouldn't be out here now. I wouldn't be getting called awful names by total strangers. I looked up at the message painted on the wall across the street and almost laughed.

HARD TIMES WILL ALWAYS REVEAL TRUE FRIENDS.

10

BY THE NEXT MORNING, I WAS WIRED. JASPER HAD finally called around midnight to tell me that some other artists from his label had showed up to surprise him with a night out on the town, and he couldn't say no. He'd tried to text me a few times, but "the boys," as he called them, confiscated his phone to free him up for fun. Luckily, he hadn't posted any pictures online, so I had no clue what said "fun" had entailed—I didn't think I wanted to know. We'd talked for at least an hour, and I'd felt somewhat better, but Morrisey Blue's sarcastic *good luck* kept echoing in my mind. Why did it feel like Jasper only wanted to be around me if it could result in a photo op?

I'd tried to sleep, but there was too much in my head. On top of everything else, I'd realized that Jasper was living his dream. Right here, right now, he was living his dream. And I wanted that for myself, too. So around two a.m., I'd flung off the covers and decided I was not going to give up. No matter what boring-ass decorations my mother wanted, no matter who was or was not willing to help, I was going to apply to the Tennessee School of Design and I was going to get in. Somehow. So after a frenetic work session that had kept me up nearly until dawn, I had a plan for the décor for the gala and a checklist of all the things I needed to finish for my application.

First on the list were recommendations. I had fired off an e-mail to my favorite English teacher at Worthington early this morning—Mr. Frangipane, who had taught poetry and said I was a talented writer. Poetry counted as a creative pursuit, right? It was a stretch, but it was the best I could do. Next up was Tammy—the only person who could reasonably speak to my abilities in a visually creative field. I walked into Second Chances at nine a.m., head held high, and she looked up from the morning paper.

"Hey there, Fiddler! You look like you've got a bee in your bonnet this morning."

"Tammy, would you write a letter of recommendation for my design school application?" I asked. My heart pounded as if I'd just downed a gallon of espresso. "Please?"

Tammy's face lit up. "Of course! Are you kidding? I'd be honored!"

She got up from her stool and headed for the back room.

"Where're you going?" I asked.

"To get a pen! I already have some ideas and I don't want to forget them."

"Thank you!" I called after her.

Suddenly I felt guilty for questioning our friendship last

week. Of course she'd write a letter for me. She was one of my biggest fans. We weren't using each other, we were helping each other, and it felt nice to have a friend who was there for me, no hesitation. I walked around the counter and picked up one of the freshly baked blueberry muffins. It was halfway to my mouth when my mother walked through the door with Tash. For a second, I thought I was hallucinating.

"Good morning, Cecilia!" my mother said cheerily. Her eyes twitched almost imperceptibly and she pointed at my muffin. "So we're doing this now, are we?"

I dropped the pastry onto a paper plate and shoved it away. My brain was refusing to process the fact that my mother was visiting me at my tiny little place of work. I'd told her my boss wanted to meet her—that Tammy was a big fan and that she had some ideas to share with the senator, but I hadn't thought she'd been listening, let alone that she'd show. Outside, her bodyguards dealt with a few hovering fans and photographers.

"You work here?" Tash asked, wrinkling her nose. She touched the sleeve of a sheer chiffon blouse, then retracted her hand as if stung.

"Oh, Tash, I think it's charming. And I love the name—Second Chances. It's so . . . hopeful."

My mother looked me right in the eye as she said it, her expression pointed.

"I'm glad you chose to take a position here, Cecilia. I like that you're working in a quality establishment."

"Um . . . thanks," I said, trying to figure out what was going on and how I felt about it.

"Senator Montgomery!"

Tammy walked out of the storage room and almost tripped backward when she laid eyes on my mother. Her hand fluttered to her chest, covering the huge shell that centered her arts-and-crafts necklace.

"It is *such* an honor to have you in my store."

Tammy dropped the pen she was holding and offered her trembling hand, which my mother shook warmly, clasping her other hand over the top of their joined fingers. If there was one thing my mother had down, it was the politician's handshake.

"The honor is mine," my mother said. "There's nothing I love more than to see the small businesses of America thriving."

"Well. Thank you, ma'am."

"There's no need for that," my mother said. "Call me Rebecca."

Tammy snorted a laugh. "I couldn't."

"You're going to have to," my mother replied, walking along the wall of vintage dresses, touching a collar here, checking out a price tag there, "if we're going to be friends."

Tammy looked at me as if I'd just handed her the personal number for Coco Chanel in heaven.

"Mom, Tammy had some plans she wanted to show you," I said. "Remember? For the school?"

"Yes! Right!"

My mother walked over and waited at the counter while

Tammy fumbled out the plans and flattened them, using jewelry trays to hold down the corners.

"I've always wanted to turn it into artists' studios," Tammy explained, running her finger along the blueprint. "But the first floor would be occupied by businesses, with Second Chances as the anchor store."

"Will you be calling it *Third* Chances, then?" Tash asked.

Tammy laughed, but my mother didn't look amused.

"Tash, kindly keep your commentary to yourself," my mother said.

Tash's skin reddened and it was all I could do to hide my smile behind my hand.

"I think this is a fantastic idea," my mother proclaimed, slapping a hand atop the plans. "Bring this by my office tomorrow at four, and Tash, have the mayor meet us there. We'll get this whole thing sorted out. Provided you don't mind me using the building for the next year and a half or so."

My mother gave Tammy a wink, and I swear, I thought she was going to faint. Tash, meanwhile, typed furiously into her iPad.

"Of course. Are you kidding? It will be an honor to take it over after such an esteemed tenant," Tammy replied, breathless.

"Fantastic. Now, show me what you've got when it comes to wide-brimmed hats," my mother ordered. "The sun down here is wreaking havoc on my delicate New England skin."

"Of course!" Tammy swept around the counter, showing my mother to the back of the store, where the hats were displayed on two tall racks. Within fifteen minutes, my mother had amassed a collection of hats, along with a black pearl brooch and a chunky wool cable-knit sweater. I knew she'd never wear any of it—that she was just throwing my boss a bone—and I felt oddly proud of her for it.

"Please come again," Tammy said as she handed my mother's packages to Tash.

"I will," my mother said confidently. "And I'll see you tomorrow at four."

"You sure will!" Tammy replied.

I followed my mother as she and Tash made their way down the stairs to the sidewalk. My mother slipped on her sunglasses and, much to my surprise, placed one of the big straw hats over her hair. It looked perfect on her. How did she *do* that?

"Mom, I just wanted to say thanks," I told her. "That was really . . . kind of you."

"Kind? Are you kidding? That's the only worthwhile clothing shop in this town. And the woman's plans for the building are not only sound, but smart."

My mother adjusted her bag on her shoulder and held up a hand to the paparazzi, who were keeping a respectful distance across the street now. Probably a zillion pictures were snapped in that millisecond.

"I'm not the fake you think I am, Cecilia," she told me. "Nor am I the monster you make me out to be."

Then she turned and strode off toward her offices, Tash keeping pace just off her right shoulder.

* * *

When Jasper showed up at my door at four o'clock that afternoon, I was in my pajamas. I'd just shot off an e-mail to my mother and Tash with a huge zip file full of new, simple, and understated but also lame and expected patriotic ideas for the gala décor, and I felt spent. Britta had left early that morning for a flight to Dallas. She was covering the Blake Ralston concert for her blog, and Jasper had gotten her backstage access, but he hadn't been able to score her a seat on the private jet he was taking to get there—his plus one was all mine. She was crashing on a friend's couch afterward, so I had the entire place to myself. Which was nice. I'd spent most of my life alone, so now, every once in a while, it was a relief to have some peace.

"I realize the lounge look is in, but that's kinda taking it to the extreme," Jasper commented, taking in my pink plaid ensemble.

He was wearing distressed jeans, a white shirt, and a black suit jacket. The collar was popped to reveal a red paisley pattern underneath. He looked hot. And for the first time since I'd remet him, I didn't care.

"I'm not going," I told him, sitting down in front of the TV and drawing a pillow into my lap. "I need a night off. I'm sorry, I should have texted you, but I only just decided."

This wasn't technically true. I'd been 95 percent decided up until about ten minutes ago, but I hadn't texted him. I was still smarting over being stood up at the diner and Morrisey's warning.

"What do you mean you're not coming?" Jasper asked.

"We had a plan. Everyone knows you're going to be there."

I shot him a glare. I didn't even mean to. It just happened. Because, really? He was going to start lecturing me about plans and saying you'd be somewhere and then not showing? I mean, hell, even my mother had shown up somewhere for me when she said she'd be there, but he couldn't?

"What?" he asked, looking baffled.

"Nothing," I lied. I didn't want to get into a fight, even though my body temperature was skyrocketing. "I just sent some new gala plans to my mom and I'm sure she'll call me to go over them soon. Besides, you don't need me."

"Yeah, I do," Jasper said, putting his hands on his hips. "I told Evan you were gonna be there and he set up all these interviews for us and—"

"Oh, so it's not that you want me to be there, it's that Evan needs me to be there," I blurted, standing up. "You know what, Jasper? If you only want me around to attend events with you, then we might as well end this right now!"

Dead silence. I couldn't believe those words had just come out of my mouth. From the look on his face, neither could Jasper.

"I don't only want you around to attend events with me," he replied evenly. "Are you out of your mind?"

"I don't know, am I?" My voice was kind of veering into shriek territory, but I couldn't help it.

Jasper shifted his weight from one foot to the other. "Look, Lia, I told you I was gonna be busy—"

"Yeah, too busy to show up for me, but I'm expected to be there for you whenever you snap your fingers?"

"I did *not* snap my fingers!" Jasper shot back. "You've known about this concert for a week!"

"Whatever," I said. "I've been in a relationship like that with my mother my entire life, and I don't want to be part of another one."

I sat down again and crossed my arms over my chest, staring pointedly away from him.

"Oh, really? So instead of coming out with me, you're gonna sit around and wait for her to call? How does that make any sense?" he shouted.

I flinched and my eyes stung. Jasper had never raised his voice to me like that before. But I didn't give him the satisfaction of looking over at him.

"Well, at least she seems to be taking an interest in my life right now," I muttered.

"What life?" Jasper cried.

My jaw dropped, and I looked up at him. One tear spilled over and I wiped it indignantly away. "Excuse me?"

His face went white. "I didn't mean it like that. Not like it sounded. I mean it. I . . . I really want to know what's going on with you. I only said it because . . . because we've barely had a chance to talk lately."

"Yeah, well. That's not my fault."

I returned my attention to the TV—or at least pretended to. I couldn't have concentrated on anything right then if I'd tried. My whole body vibrated, and a little voice in my head screamed at me, asking what I was doing, telling me to take back what I'd said. But I was too angry, too hurt, and too stubborn.

"Lia . . ."

"You can go. I wouldn't want you to miss your private plane."

"Lia—"

"I'm serious, Jasper. Just go."

He stood there for maybe another minute, the air between us charged with unsaid words, and then he turned around and walked out, slamming the door behind him.

11

"HELLO, MOTHER."

My heart had jumped when my phone rang, then plummeted when I saw my mother's picture on the screen. A few hours had gone by since Jasper had stormed out, and I hadn't heard from him. No text. No call. But he hadn't posted any pictures of himself living it up on the private jet, either, so maybe he was just as miserable and pensive as I was.

Also, I really had to give him and my mom their own ringtones. That was, if Jasper ever intended to call me again.

Now I held my breath, hoping she liked the new gala plans.

"Hello, Cecilia. I wanted to let you know I received your e-mail and I'll be making some notes."

Notes. That couldn't be good. I glanced at my open laptop. A new picture had just shown up on Jasper's Instagram page, but it was just a wide shot of the crowd outside the venue.

"Okay."

There was a long pause at the other end of the line. I listened for typing, or hushed voices in the background, but there was nothing.

"Mom?"

"Yes, I'm still here," she said. "Is everything all right, Cecilia?"

The skin on my cheeks prickled. I couldn't remember the last time my mother had asked me if everything was okay. And before I knew what was happening, I was spilling the entire story. About Jasper's career and all the events and how he'd left me alone at the Young Nashville awards the other night and what had happened between us earlier today.

My mother listened to the whole thing and didn't interrupt once.

"I'm so sorry your feelings are hurt," she said when I finished.

I was touched. "Thanks."

"But if I could play devil's advocate for a moment?"

"Sure," I said, out of habit.

"This is a crucial time for him, Cecilia. All he's doing is what he needs to do to achieve his goals. He's asking you to be a part of it. If you don't want to be, that's perfectly fine. It's your choice the kind of life you want to lead—"

Ha! I thought. *Hahahahahahahahahaha!*

"But if you don't, then you need to tell him, so that you can both move on."

Oh, the irony. But I bit my tongue. Because at least she'd

tried. She'd tried to give me advice based on her own personal experience. This was progress.

"Well, I'm glad you decided not to go out, because that means you can come out to dinner with your father and me tonight," my mother continued, back in politician mode. "I've added some new, key people to my campaign and I'd like for you to meet them."

I sighed.

"I'm not really up to meeting people right now," I said, the effort of saying no to her making me tense, as always.

"Oh, Cecilia, don't be that girl who mopes around all night while her boyfriend is out having fun," she replied. "I'll send a car around to pick you up at eight."

As if having dinner with a bunch of stodgy adults was some kind of revenge. But I couldn't think of a good reason to bow out, and also, there was nothing to eat in the apartment besides cereal.

"And wear one of the outfits Matilda put together for you, would you?"

"Fine," I said. But it didn't matter. She'd already hung up.

When I looked over at the television, the *Entertainment Tomorrow* logo had just flashed off the screen and the feed cut to a reporter standing in front of the American Airlines Arena, where Jasper was performing tonight.

A glutton for punishment, I turned up the volume.

" . . . as Blake Ralston continues his record-breaking sold-out tour," the reporter was saying. "Opening for Blake is new up-and-coming star Jasper Case, who, as you know, has been dating America's Sweetheart Cecilia Montgomery ever since the misunderstanding of her kidnapping was cleared up. We caught up with Jasper outside the venue."

My throat tightened as Jasper appeared on the screen, wearing the exact same outfit he'd worn standing in my living room just a few hours ago. He looked amazing. And somehow, more tan.

"No Cecilia tonight, Jasper?" the reporter asked.

"Not tonight," Jasper said with a winning smile. "But we're gonna play some great music and have a great time."

The feed quickly cut to a crowd shot, as Jasper signed autographs for screaming fans.

"But one of Jasper's hometown friends *was* in attendance— Fiona Taylor, Cecilia Montgomery's best friend, who told our Lucy Friedman that she's considering a career in publicity."

Suddenly, Fiona appeared on the screen. It was a different angle of the crowd and I could see Jasper far in the background, posing for a picture with a twelve-year-old. What the hell was Fiona doing there?

"We've sucked you into our world, have we?" the reporter asked.

Fiona gave a practiced laugh. "It seems that way. But no, I've just had an amazing time helping Cecilia and her mom plan this gala event we're hosting in my hometown, and spending all this time on the road. . . . It's really opened my eyes to the possibilities."

"What!?" I blurted out loud. "What? You've done nothing to help! Zip, zero, zilch!"

They cut back to the Hollywood desk and I shut off the TV. The silence enveloped me and I suddenly felt embarrassed for yelling at the television, even though no one was there to witness it. I barked a laugh that was followed quickly by tears.

First Jasper, then my mom, then Fiona . . . everyone really was all about themselves.

By the time the sorbet was served I was so bored I was reciting the states and capitals in my head, in alphabetical order, backwards. The new people my mother had added to her campaign were two statisticians, and all they could talk about was numbers. The number of swing states she'd need to win in order to take the election. The number of single mothers she'd have to sway her way to secure the female vote. The number of fingernails I'd have to extract from my hands before I passed out and saved myself from this torture.

Just kidding.

My phone vibrated in my lap. It was a photo text from Britta—a picture of her and Jasper backstage.

WISH YOU WERE HERE!

My heart burned inside my chest. Clearly, Jasper hadn't told her about our fight.

"What is it, Cecilia?" my father asked.

It seemed my emotions were written all over my face.

"Nothing. I'm just tired."

"I remember that last summer before college, gearing up for a whole new life," said Felicia, the woman who sat to my mother's right. "It can be so stressful. Tell me, Cecilia, where are you doing your undergraduate work?"

My mother and I locked eyes. My father cleared his throat. I knew what I *should* say, but for some reason, I didn't.

"I'm seriously considering the Tennessee School of Design," I told her.

She blinked, then laughed. I didn't.

"Oh," she said finally. "You're serious."

"No. She can't be," her partner, Reginald, said. "Certainly you were able to get her into a reputable institution," he added, looking at my father.

"Actually, *she* got *herself* into Harvard," I said. "Not to mention Yale, Stanford, Penn, and Dartmouth. But I may *choose* to do something different."

"Cecilia—"

"In fact, Mom, I was hoping to use my design for your gala as part of my application," I said gamely. "I thought I'd include pictures from the event in my portfolio."

My mother's face froze. I could practically see her trying not to react. My father and our two guests watched us, transfixed, as if they were waiting for one of us to explode. We stared each other down, and then she looked into her lap and swiped her hands across her napkin.

"Well, if you're serious about this school, then I'm not so sure that's a good idea."

"What?" I said. "Why?"

My mother took a sip of her wine, then placed the glass down. "Because, Cecilia, the plans you sent me earlier today were pedestrian at best."

"What?" I gasped. "But I gave you what you asked for."

"Which is, of course, a very important goal for a person who intends to work with clients for a living—the customer is always right, after all—but while I asked you for a patriotic theme, I did *not* ask you to phone it in, as they say."

"You wanted traditional!" I blurted, attracting the attention of nearby diners. "You told me to throw some purple irises on the table and be done with it."

"Well, I didn't expect you to take me literally," my mother replied calmly. "And now that I know how much this matters to you, I'm a bit concerned if you think that what you sent me is in good taste, or your best work, for that matter."

My throat closed over. I'd never felt so offended in my entire life. I shoved my phone into my purse, plucked my linen napkin off my lap, and dropped it on the table next to my untouched sorbet glass. I could feel the eyes of every patron in that restaurant on me, and even though I was experiencing a rage spiral, I remembered my manners. I was not going to give them—or my mother—what they were expecting. So instead, I smiled at our guests.

"I'm so sorry, but if you'll excuse me, I think I'm going to walk home."

My father and Reginald rose slightly from their seats as I stood.

"Cecilia, I'd prefer it if you'd stay until the meal is through," my mother said. "And I'd also like you to apologize to our guests for being so rude."

"I know you would, Mother. But I really could use some air," I replied.

We faced off for a moment, and I realized that yes, I had been rude. So I glanced sideways at Reginald.

"I apologize for my outburst," I said.

And then I walked out before I screamed and shattered all the fine crystal.

"Feel better, darling!" my mother called after me, needing to both get the last word and make it look as if everything was perfectly fine and normal.

Outside, I took a deep breath of the warm evening air, but it did nothing to calm my irritation. I couldn't believe she didn't like the plans I'd sent her. I'd done exactly what she'd asked for. Exactly! I bet she actually didn't hate them. She was just trying to get back at me for announcing my design school plans in front of her staff—for acting as if I had a choice in where I went to school and what I was going to do with my life.

Why did everyone on the planet think they knew what was best for me? My mother and father knew where I should go to school, Matilda and Max knew how I should look, Jasper knew how I should react to my mother, Tash knew how I should do basically everything. They all wanted a piece of me, but they wanted it to be the piece they chose and they wanted it to look and act the way they wanted it to. Even the damn statisticians had an opinion.

Suddenly all I wanted to do was go home and tear up all the new plans for the gala. She didn't like them? Fine. Maybe she could throw her epic party without a designer. Have fun impressing your donors with undressed tables and waiters who have no food to serve. I curled my fingers into fists and started to stride across the park. I swear there was smoke billowing out my ears.

And then I heard something that slowed my steps. Sweet, harmonious voices rose up from inside the gazebo in the center of the square. It was a barbershop quartet rehearsing under the warm torchlights. Their voices blended together in such a soothing, sweet way that for a moment I paused and closed my eyes, letting the music wash over me. I took long, deep breaths and tried to calm my nerves. This was why I loved Sweetbriar. This was the reason I'd come here. It was so homey. So comforting. So welcoming.

Maybe if I stood here long enough and listened to these people sing their traditional Southern tunes, it would soothe my nerves. Maybe I would have an epiphany, think up a new idea for the gala—one so amazing that even my mother couldn't find fault with it. If I just let them inspire me . . .

A sudden shout knocked me out of my semimeditative state. The singing stopped.

"Do you guys know 'Shake Ya Tailfeather'?"

The question was followed by a round of cackles. I took a few steps closer to the gazebo and saw that half a dozen photographers were lounging around on the surrounding benches. They were drinking beer out of cans and heckling the singers.

"You've *got* to be kidding me," I said under my breath.

"Look, gentlemen," one of the singers said, "we're just trying to rehearse."

"And we're just bored," a woman with a long ponytail shouted. "Sing something upbeat!"

The four men on the platform looked at one another. They went back to the song they'd been singing, and the photographers began to boo.

Ugh. Why had did my mother have to come here? She was ruining Sweetbriar for me. For everyone.

I turned and took off at full speed across the park before any of the photographers could spot me. As I walked down the alley alongside Hadley's, I wished I had a punching bag up in the apartment. If Tank, my old bodyguard, were here, he'd spar with me. But at the moment, I didn't have anyone—or anything—to pummel. I tugged out my keys and was about to come around the corner behind the building when I heard whispered voices.

"What if this isn't her garbage?"

"Who else's could it be? There are only three cans."

"I don't know. Somehow I don't peg Cecilia Montgomery for a Bud Light girl."

I froze half a second before revealing myself. What the hell?

"Who knows what kinda girl she is at this point? You ever think you'd see her licking tequila off some dude's abs?"

The two men cracked up and I flattened myself against the wall, my adrenaline higher than ever. These guys really didn't want to mess with me in my current state. Hadn't they seen Fiona's viral video? I could kick their asses with one hand tied behind my back.

I glanced around the corner and saw the two of them— one burly and hunched over an open garbage container, the other tall and sifting through a pile of discarded trash. God, these people were *everywhere*. And they were shameless. Going through my *garbage* for inside info? My palms prickled. Maybe if they got their butts handed to them by a girl, they'd go away. Then at least there would be two fewer photographers in Sweetbriar.

Don't be an idiot, Cecilia. Call the police. The voice in my head sounded a lot like my mother's.

But if I called the police, she would find out about this. And if she found out about this, she'd definitely get me a bodyguard. Who was I kidding? If I beat the piss out of these guys, it would make front page news and she'd hire me a whole *team* of bodyguards.

"Check *this* out! An empty Cocoa Krispies box!"

"Girl has good taste at least."

They chuckled, and I deflated. I so wanted to put these guys in their place, but I couldn't. I couldn't even defend myself. My mother's reach extended everywhere. How was I ever going to figure out who I was if I couldn't make my own decisions when I was alone?

The men cracked up over a new find and I slunk off to find someplace to hide out until they were gone, cursing myself—and my mother—every step of the way.

12

"IS OKAY . . . IS OKAY . . . I KIN GET UP THE STAIRSH on my own."

Was that really my voice? And why was the striped pattern on the wallpaper moving? Everything was blurred around the edges, and no matter how many times I blinked, the blurriness wouldn't go away.

Shit. Had I lost my contacts? Or maybe I was going blind. Oh God, I didn't want to go blind.

I sat down halfway up the steps to my apartment and started to cry. Okay, so hiding out at The Roadhouse hadn't exactly been the greatest decision. Desperate for any kind of crowd on a Monday night, they had been offering two-dollar beers and not checking anyone's IDs. I had no clue how many bottles of their cheap brew I'd downed, but it was clearly too many.

If only the garbage pickers could see me now. But at least I wasn't angry anymore. Sad, yes, but not angry.

"Lia, what's wrong?" Duncan asked in an overly exaggerated way. "Did you hurt yourself?"

It was also possible that calling Duncan to join me had been a bigger mistake. He'd matched and possibly doubled every one of my orders at the bar. Now he crawled up the steps and put his hands on my shoulders, then my face, then my knees, inspecting me all over and almost knocking himself off balance. I grabbed his arm before he could tumble backward down the stairs, and after a suspended moment of panic, we looked at each other and cracked up laughing.

"Oh my God! We are *so* drunk!" Duncan announced.

He had one lock of dark brown hair plastered to his forehead and there was a weird red mark on his cheek. I had learned in the past hour or so that drunk Duncan was very dramatic. It was a good thing we lived within walking distance of all the bars.

"I know. But you're more drunk than me," I said, pushing myself up and stumbling over the next few stairs. "Drunker? Or more drunk. Is 'drunker' a word?"

Duncan laughed again. "Only you would be thinking about grammar at a time like this."

He was still laughing when we finally made it to my door. My knees went wobbly as I fished the key out of my bag, and Duncan held me up by the elbow.

"I'm definitely not drunker than you," he said.

I burped out of nowhere and the taste in my mouth was disgusting. "Okay," I said, trying to tamp down a wave of queasiness. "Maybe you're right."

We got inside and Duncan staggered directly to the

couch, knocking over one of the end tables. At least there was nothing breakable on it. He hit the cushions facedown and instantly started to snore. I clucked my tongue and tossed the keys on the coffee table, only they missed it by a mile, slid across the floor, and came to a stop under the couch. When I hit my knees to try to retrieve them, the whole world spun.

I groaned and leaned back against the couch. Duncan's hand was right next to my shoulder.

"Duncan! Wake up! I think I'm gonna puke."

Nothing. I braced one hand on the coffee table to try to shove myself up, and my fingers came down on a magazine cover. The photo was of me and Jasper, looking lovingly into each other's eyes on some red carpet. I took one look at it, turned my head, and barfed all over the floor.

Oh God. Disgusting. I was so disgusting. I had to clean it up. I got myself to my knees, and then to my feet, but the whole room tilted and then Duncan groaned. Okay. No. I needed my bed. If I could just lie down for a little while and get the world to stop moving the wrong way, then I could get it together to clean up. I turned toward my bedroom, but then my knees went wobbly again and I sank to the floor.

It was too far away. I just needed to rest. Just for a minute. I wiped across my lips with my forearm, tugged a pillow off the other couch, and promptly passed out on top of it.

* * *

"What the hell is *this*!?"

I lifted my head off the pillow and the back of my skull exploded.

"Who the hell did this?"

I pushed my face back into the nubby pillow and groaned. It was too bright. Too bright and too loud. And why was my heart throbbing inside my eyes?

"Oh God, Britta. I'm so sorry."

Duncan. What the hell was Duncan doing here?

"It was me," he said. "I'll clean it up."

I turned my face and then it hit me. The acrid, pungent scent of vomit and alcohol. Everything came back in a blink, and I sat up straight. Big mistake. My stomach heaved, my brain split open, and I grabbed the edge of the coffee table to keep from passing out.

"It wasn't him. It was me," I said.

Britta hovered near the kitchen island, looking way too put together for this early in the morning, and also way too angry.

"You don't have to clean it up, Duncan," I said, as he shuffled over to the kitchen. I assume he was going to look for some cleaning supplies, but he stopped when I spoke and sat down on one of the island stools, resting the side of his head on his hand and his elbow on the counter. "I'll do it."

"God, Cecilia! What's the matter with you?" Britta demanded. "This is our home! You can't act like this!"

"I know, I know," I said, pressing my hands to my temples.

My heartbeat had taken over my body and seemed to be pulsing heat through every one of my pores. I felt like I was having a panic attack, only everything was dull instead of sharp.

I noticed that the puke pile was dangerously close to my feet and drew my knees up. It was amazing I hadn't rolled into it overnight. There were spatters on the throw rug as well. I heaved again at the sight of it and had to swallow repeatedly to keep from spewing round two.

"Well, are you going to clean it up or what?"

"Just give me a second, okay!?" I snapped.

"Don't yell at *me*!" Britta cried. "You wanted a real life, Cecilia Montgomery? Well, here it is! I'm going down to Hadley's for breakfast and if this place isn't cleaned up and smelling a whole hell of a lot better by the time I get back, you're out!"

With that, she turned around and left, slamming the door so hard I swear the floorboards shook. Duncan whimpered.

I felt sick for a whole new reason. I had no idea Britta was even capable of getting that angry.

"What crawled up her butt?" I asked, finally shoving myself up enough to lift my ass onto the couch.

"You know that story about how Britta and Shelby's dad up and left out of nowhere one day?" Duncan asked.

"Yeah," I said, hanging my head between my knees. "What's that got to do with anything?"

"He was kind of an alcoholic," Duncan said.

I swallowed against my dry throat and looked around at the toppled table, the putrid puke, and the magazines that had somehow slipped to the floor, and I felt a heavy weight settle in my chest.

"Oh."

IN THE BOOK OF LIFE, THE ANSWERS AREN'T IN THE BACK.

I turned away from the wall and walked slowly and carefully toward Second Chances. In the last forty-eight hours, I'd fought with Fiona, Jasper, and Britta, and now I was rocking my second-ever hangover. By the time Britta returned from breakfast, Duncan and I had cleaned the apartment to a shine using every supply Britta stocked in her cabinets, but she still hadn't spoken to me. She'd simply gone into her room and closed the door. The only reason I had hope she wasn't totally mad at me anymore was that she hadn't slammed it.

I hoped she wouldn't throw me out on the street later, but I wasn't entirely sure. As I navigated the steps up to the shop, I didn't feel sure of anything. Except for the fact that I never, ever wanted to feel like this again.

I was just reaching for the door handle when the whole thing came swinging at me and almost took my face off. I grabbed the wrought iron railing to keep from falling down the stairs, and Shelby swept out of the shop in a pretty pink sundress, her hair French braided down her back. I had taken a shower and thrown on comfy jeans and a nice T-shirt, but I still felt as if I had vomit on my face.

"Wow. Did you sleep in a garbage dump?" Shelby asked, looking me up and down.

"I'm not in the mood," I grumbled.

"I wouldn't be either, if I'd pissed off Britta this morning." Shelby breezily donned a pair of cat-eye sunglasses and tilted her head. "If there's one person in this town you don't want to make an enemy of, besides me, it's her. We Tanakas hold a grudge."

"Thanks for the tip."

Shelby skipped down the steps, lifting her hand to twiddle her fingers. "I'm off to a Sweetbriar Summer Princess meeting!" she trilled. "Wish me luck."

I hope you trip and fall on your face, I thought.

But of course she didn't. This really wasn't my day.

"Okay . . . I've never been a huge eater—my mom made sure of that—so I haven't exactly chosen a menu yet."

I paused. I'd been hoping to at least get a laugh, but the eight faces around the table stared back at me as if I'd just insulted their own mothers. Fiona, who had actually showed up for this one, gave me a sympathetic almost-smile. Honestly, when she'd arrived, it had taken every ounce of my self-control not to drag her out of the room and grill her about Jasper. I hadn't heard from him all morning and she'd been with him at that concert just last night. Had he said anything about me? Had he told her we'd broken up? *Had* we broken up?

But now was clearly not the time.

I cleared my throat and looked down at my menus. Even though I'd spent half the morning trolling the Internet for ideas (Tammy had let me use her laptop during downtimes at the shop), I hadn't found any new inspiration for the décor, so my plan was to at least put the food questions to bed today. That way, from here on out, I could concentrate on event design. I'd drawn stars next to some menu items, circled others, and scrawled *X*s, numbers, and arrows all over the place. I'd made these notes at so many different times and in so many different pencil and pen colors, I could no longer make sense of any of it. By the time I looked up again, I was sweating.

"Um, so I was hoping that maybe I could get your guys' opinion," I said. "I mean, your opinions from all of you."

God. The *Titanic* had nothing on me. I was going down and I wasn't even doing it gracefully. I quickly passed around copies of the menus—at least I'd remembered to run them through the copy machine—and practically ran back to my spot at the head of the table.

"Maybe we could do a consensus thing?" I ventured, my voice reedy. "Everyone circle their favorite items and I'll tally it up at the end of the meeting."

"Tally it up? What're we voting for, eighth-grade class president?" Tash said snidely. She tossed her menus at the table, where they curled and drifted and fluttered. "I thought you were supposed to be presenting us with your final plans for the gala, Cecilia. I've already heard the design plans are a disaster. Now you're telling us you haven't even settled on a menu yet?"

My mother had told her about the design? I opened my mouth to speak, but my throat caught and I coughed instead. To my horror, a tiny drop of spittle went flying into the air and landed on the gleaming wood table. Everyone stared at the spot.

"It's called democracy in action, people," Fiona announced, rising from her chair. She wore a tasteful eggplant-colored shift dress and dangling earrings I'd just seen on the *InStyle* website that morning, trolling for design inspiration. "What better way to plan a gala for the next president of these United States than by taking the opinion of the people into account?"

Fiona gestured around at the table like a Home Shopping Network spokesperson, then gave me a big, encouraging smile.

"Exactly!" I said. "And it's not just me who wants your opinion. My mother does as well."

"Your mother wants to know what we think," Tash said skeptically.

"Yes. Yes, she does," I lied, projecting as much confidence as I possibly could. Fiona walked around the table to stand at my side, which helped considerably. It was all I could do not to squeeze her hand in thanks. But I wasn't quite there yet. I still hadn't forgiven her for talking about me on national television.

A couple of the worker bees, Victoria included, exchanged hopeful looks and acquiescent shrugs, then got down to work. Tash rolled her eyes, dragged her menus toward her, and whipped out a silver pen, the click-click sounding to me like a gun loading a bullet into its chamber.

"We really need to choose a vegetarian entrée," Victoria said, looking up at me. "There's nothing vegetarian on here."

"How many vegetarians could there possibly be? This is the heartland," Tash said with a sneer.

"You don't think there are vegetarians in Kentucky?" someone else piped up.

"We're in Tennessee, idiot."

"You don't have to be so—"

"This the twenty-first century, Tash. We have to—"

"Enough!" I blurted. They all fell silent. Wow. I'd really just sounded like my mother. Which made my head throb even worse. "I'll figure out a vegetarian option, okay? Just . . . get back to work."

"Cecilia, could I talk to you for a second while everyone else makes their selections?" Fiona asked.

She tilted her head toward the door, then slowly pivoted in that direction and walked out. I followed right on her heels. Honestly, I would have paid someone money to get me out of that room right then. The air in the hallway felt a lot less stifling.

"Hey!" Fiona said with a big smile. "So, that was intense."

"Yeah, it was." I looked down at the floor and noticed that the nail polish on her toes, which were peeking out from a pair of nude, peep-toe heels, exactly matched her dress. "Thanks for saving me."

"No problem. Are you okay? You seem a little out of it." She reached over as if to squeeze my arm, but I backed up a step.

Her smile fell. "Lia, can't we just put this behind us already?"

"Uh, no. Swooping in to rescue me at one meeting doesn't mean I'm going to forgive you for peddling my story."

"I didn't peddle your story!" she protested. "I didn't even get paid!"

"Oh, so you gabbed about me for free? Wow, Fiona, I never pegged you as a fame whore."

"What did you just call me?" she blurted, her face going nuclear.

My skin burned too. I couldn't believe I'd just said that. Especially considering how offended I'd been when my mother used a similar term about me. But now that it was out there, I couldn't take it back. I didn't want to. I was pissed. And I really wanted her to stop appearing on TV and talking about my personal life.

I wanted her to talk about my personal life *with me*. But of course, now that I'd put my foot in my mouth, that was out of the question.

"You know what? Forget it. I have to go. You really want to help me? Stick around and gather everyone's votes on the food."

"Um, you expect me to do that after you called me a fame whore? To my face?" Fiona demanded.

"You will if you want to stay on the committee," I told her. "You may have gotten my mother to give you some etiquette lessons or whatever, but she's still *my* mother, and she'll fire you if I tell her to."

I stormed out of the school, shaking, trying to wipe the sight of Fiona's indignant face out of my mind's eye. Outside on the street, a stiff, warm wind hit me so hard it almost knocked me over. Had I really just said those things to Fiona? What was wrong with me? Where was all of this coming from? I was angry at her, sure, but was I *that* angry?

Trudging over to the nearest bench, I took a breath and tried to compose myself. I knew I should go back inside and apologize, but what she'd done was wrong too, and I hadn't heard her apologizing to me. Did it even matter? Did I even want to be friends with Fiona if she'd sell me out like that? If she'd so willingly become one of my mother's minions?

I put my head between my knees and groaned. What did I really want? What would make me feel better, right now, in this moment?

Jasper. I had to apologize to him. I loved him and he loved me. It had been one argument. We needed to make up. *I* needed to make up. I wasn't going to feel like myself again until I talked to Jasper. Luckily, I happened to know his schedule and he didn't have any events on the calendar for tonight. The very idea of a chill evening in with lots of smooching got me moving again.

"Hey, pretty lady!"

I glanced over to see Frederick hanging out the passenger side of Duncan's car, which was pacing me down the street.

"Hi, guys," I said weakly.

"We're heading out to party. You want to come?" Duncan asked.

Since when was Duncan such a psychotic party animal? "Um, no thanks. I think I'm done with partying for a while," I told them. "I'm on my way to see Jasper."

The car stopped, brakes squealing, and Duncan jumped out. Good thing there was never much traffic at this time of night. He jogged around the front of the car and over to me.

"Uh, Jasper's not home."

"What do you mean?" I asked. "How do *you* know?" Jasper and Duncan didn't exactly hang out.

Duncan bit his lip and tugged his phone from his back pocket. "Don't shoot the messenger, okay?"

I held my breath as Duncan opened Jasper's Instagram feed. The first picture was of him in a lip lock with some other girl. Some tan, sweaty, big-breasted other girl. Everything inside of me clenched—from my jaw to my toes—then released just as fast. I had to grab on to Duncan to keep from buckling to the ground.

"Who the hell is this?" I demanded.

"I've never seen her before. But it looks like he's partying pretty hard with her and her friends."

He started to scroll through the feed, but I closed my eyes and turned away. "I don't want to see it."

"Sorry I just . . . I thought you should know," Duncan told me.

What is happening? I thought, bringing my hand to my forehead. Tears stung my eyes, but I refused to cry. But still. What was Jasper doing? Why was he kissing other girls? I thought . . . I thought we were going to make up. Had I really been that awful to him?

"So . . . we party?" Frederick asked.

I practically pushed Duncan aside on my way to his car. If I didn't go out with them, I was going to go home, curl into a ball, and cry all night. And I didn't want to do that. I didn't want to feel this. I didn't want to feel anything.

"Yes, Frederick," I said tersely. "We party."

13

"GERONIMO!"

There was a huge splash and then a beefy guy with more tattoos than I could comprehend popped up through the surface of the lake.

"That was awesome!" I shouted, throwing my arms in the air as the crowd on the rocky beach cheered. I lost my balance and staggered a couple of steps sideways, into Frederick's arm.

"You are drunk again, Cecilia Montgomery," he said, as I giggled.

"Not drunk," I said. "Tipsy."

"I don't know this word . . . tipsy," he replied, taking a swig of his beer.

"It means a *tiny* bit drunk," I said, holding my thumb and finger about a centimeter apart in front of his handsome face.

He smirked, and was about to say something else, when Mr. Tattoo emerged from the lake right in front of us, his boxer briefs clinging everywhere. I blushed and looked away as he sluiced water from his face with both hands.

"You going, Franco?" he asked.

"Franco?" I repeated.

"This is my new Tennessee nickname," Frederick said with a good-natured smile. "Cecilia, meet Cox. He is the captain of my football team."

"Pleasure's mine," Cox said, looking me up and down. I said nothing. How do you respond to something like that? Then he glanced over at Frederick again. "You're up."

Over on the tire swing, a girl screamed and then landed flat on her back in the water. It looked *really* painful. The crowd "ooohed" in sympathy, then cheered when she came up, gasping for air.

"I do not feel like getting wet tonight," Frederick said.

"You do, and you will." Cox locked a tattooed arm around Frederick's neck—it looked like a colorful side of beef—and dragged him toward the tire swing. I glanced around for Duncan, but he was nowhere to be found, so I hustled after them. "It's no big deal, Franco. It's just a swing. Two-year-olds can do it."

"I'm not afraid, if that is what you think," Frederick said. He put his beer down and looked at me. "I will do it if you will do it."

"This again?" I said, throwing up my palms. "Sheesh, Frederick, I'm not your crutch."

"No. But everything is more fun with you, Cecilia Montgomery."

"Awww!" A couple of girls nearby put their hands to their hearts.

Frederick stripped off his T-shirt. "We will go together."

199

Another girl swung far out over the water and dropped in gracefully, making a tiny splash. When she emerged, everyone applauded and someone shouted, "The Russian judge gives it a ten!"

Laughter all around.

It looked like fun. And, well, tire-swinging into a lake was something I'd never done. I could check it off the list. Not that I had an actual list, but if I did, this was the type of thing that would be on it.

"Okay, fine. We'll go together."

I slipped out of my sundress, glad I was wearing one of my more modest bra and panty sets, and Frederick and I strode over to the swing. I received a few catcalls, of course, but nothing too horrible, and I imagined what Jasper would think if he saw me now—giving him a mental middle finger. I climbed onto one side of the swing and Frederick stayed on his feet to swing us out. He gave a tug on the rope. The branch bowed a bit and I heard a creak.

"We have a doubler!" Cox shouted, and more cheers went up.

"Is a doubler a thing?" I asked.

"I have no idea," Frederick replied with a smile.

"On the count of three," Cox shouted. "You ready? One!" The crowd counted down with him. There were raised beer cups and half-dressed people everywhere and they sort of swam in my vision like they were doing the wave. Which I'm pretty sure they weren't.

"Two!"

I held on tight. My stomach wobbled. Maybe this wasn't the best idea. And maybe I was a tad more drunk than tipsy.

"Three!"

Frederick pulled me back, then gave a running start. My heart swooped as we flew out over the lake. I looked down and realized how high up we were just half a second before Frederick suddenly let go and splashed below me.

"Let go!" someone shouted.

The trees around me were a blur.

"Let go before you swing back!"

But I was already swinging back. The crowd was rushing at me. I had about two seconds before I slammed into Cox's face and fell in an embarrassing heap on the ground. With a cry, I finally released the tire and fell. But what was rushing up at me wasn't deep water. In fact, I could see the tiny rocks beneath the surface.

My cry became a scream. I hit the water and the ground simultaneously, and I heard my arm crack just seconds before I felt the excruciating pain.

As soon as I woke up, I knew I wasn't in my room. Maybe it was the smell—antiseptic mixed with floral air freshener. Or maybe it was the scratchy weave of the blanket beneath my fingers. Or it could have been the fact that my mother was sitting in a chair five feet away, scowling at me.

I turned my head and the back of my skull radiated pain. For a half second the parking lot light beyond the window danced and swayed. I heard the sound of gathering voices and realized it was coming from outside.

The vultures were circling again. I wondered how long it had taken them to hear about my broken arm. Someone at the party had probably live-tweeted the whole event.

"Cecilia," my mother said.

Tears stung my eyes. I went to roll onto my side, but I couldn't. My left arm was in a cast. An involuntary cry escaped my lips.

"What is it? Does something hurt?" my mother asked, coming around the bed.

The concern on her face was so unfamiliar, I felt like I was having a fever dream. Maybe I was. Maybe they'd pumped so many painkillers into me that I was hallucinating.

"M'fine," I mumbled. My mouth tasted foul. "Is there water?"

My mother picked up a pink plastic pitcher, poured water into a plastic cup, and held it out to me. I shimmied up in my bed until I was semi-upright, and took the drink. Nothing had ever tasted so perfect.

"Do you remember what happened?" she asked. She was wearing the same light gray suit she'd worn to dinner, only the skirt was wrinkled. I'd never seen her wrinkled before.

"Yes," I said, wincing at the memory of the ground rushing up toward me. "Why? Do I have amnesia?"

My mother snorted. "No. You do not have amnesia. I just wanted to make sure you were aware of how stupid you've been this evening."

I tried to sit up a little farther and winced as my skull cracked again. "Yes, I'm aware. Can I go home now?"

"No, you may not go home." She straightened her suit jacket and huffed. "You have a concussion and your arm is broken in two places. They want to keep you overnight for observation. If I had my way, they'd keep you indefinitely."

"Of course they would. New state, new prison."

My mother's green eyes flashed. "You see, this is why I kept you cloistered away all that time!" she snapped. "To save you from becoming this."

"This?" I asked, my face flushed. "I thought you were protecting me from the outside world."

"Yes, and as an added bonus, I never had to worry about you making ridiculous and idiotic decisions!" she shot back. "I never had to worry about *you*. Now, as you keep helpfully pointing out, you're an adult, and I'm worrying about you all the time!"

She paused, and her chest heaved with each breath. Her twisted logic hung in the air between us.

"You're not worried about me," I muttered finally. "You're worried about how this is all going to reflect on you."

My mother drew up to her full height. Her lips pressed into a thin line. "If that's what you think, Cecilia, then we have nothing more to talk about."

She grabbed her Louis Vuitton purse and stalked out. A few minutes later, the murmur outside grew to a roar and cameras flashed. I heard a car peel out and knew my mother was gone.

Silent tears leaked out the corners of my eyes as I leaned back against the pillow. My head throbbed. My arm felt like dead weight and the skin was incredibly tight, like it was bracing for the pain that would return once whatever was in my system wore off.

I couldn't believe I'd broken my arm. I'd never broken a bone before in my life. Definitely *not* something I wanted to cross off the list.

Was my mom serious? Had she really kept me locked away and out of the public eye for this long so that I wouldn't rebel? So that I *couldn't*? If so, she was even more messed up than I'd originally thought.

"Hey."

I looked up, startled, and flinched in pain again. And then my heart all but stopped. Jasper was standing in my doorway.

He looked gorgeous, as always. Blond hair tousled, light stubble on his cheeks, white shirt tucked into perfectly distressed jeans. I didn't even want to know what I looked like. I turned toward the window, where the ruckus caused by my mother's departure was just dying down. The pain in my skull moved to my temples. Maybe I hadn't been given any painkillers after all.

"Cecilia, are you okay?" Jasper asked.

He walked around the bed and into my view, tugging a chair away from the wall to sit at my bedside. He reached for my hand—my good hand—but I tucked it under the blankets. I felt like an idiot. And I was also pissed. All I could see when I looked at him was his lips plastered on some other girl's face. I just wanted him to go away.

"Wow. It must be bad if you won't even hold my hand."

I swallowed, which was damn near impossible. There was a jagged rock inside my throat causing tears to prickle behind my eyes.

"Jasper, I really can't right now."

"Really can't what?" Jasper asked. "I know we haven't spoken today and after last night . . . but, Lia, you're hurt."

"Yeah, I broke my arm, but that doesn't change anything," I said, glaring at him.

My heart throbbed, trying to make me smile or frown or cry—anything that would take the sting out of what I just said, but I refused.

"Look, I'm sorry if I made you feel used or whatever—"

"Or whatever?" I shot back, and scoffed.

He went wide-eyed—incredulous. "But you have to know that was never what I meant."

I did know that. Or maybe I didn't. I wasn't sure what I knew anymore. Except for the fact that Evan Meyer saw me as a publicity boon. And he was with Jasper way more than I was these days. Who knew what sort of crap he was whispering in Jasper's ear. Maybe he'd put Jasper up to kissing that girl. Maybe all of it was for publicity. Maybe it was all fake.

But it didn't look fake, and it definitely didn't feel fake.

Jasper took a deep breath. This time when he took my

fingers, I let him. Only because I was tired and it seemed silly to try to play keep-away in my current state.

"I'm going to be down in Austin for a few days. Maybe you should come with me?" he said hopefully. "You wouldn't even have to go to any of the shows or have your picture taken at all. We could just hang out in the hotel . . . order room service . . ."

Oh, so now I was his kept woman. The words were on the top of my tongue, but I bit them back. He was trying. And part of me wanted to say yes to him. Those two days we'd spent in Nashville together on the record label's dime—holed up in a nice hotel with no one to bother us—were two of the best days of my life.

But things were different now. He was famous. I was famous. There was no way we could go anywhere without anyone bothering us. I was sure if we were together, Evan Meyer would find a way to exploit it. And then, there were the girls. Girls I didn't want to bring up because I wasn't sure my ego could take another hit.

"I can't," I said. "I have work. And there's so much to do with the gala."

And I was starting over from scratch, without a single good idea or even a clue how to begin.

"C'mon." Jasper gave me his most charming smile. "Just a coupla days? I'm sure Tammy will understand. And who cares about your mom?"

Something inside me snapped.

"I care," I said. "I care about my life and my family and yeah, even my work. You do remember that I'm doing all this so I can get into design school—so that I can stay in Sweetbriar. This stuff actually matters to me—to my future. I don't have time to run off and be your groupie girlfriend."

Jasper's face went hard. He dropped my hand and stood up.

"Fine. You're clearly exhausted," he said. "So I'm just going to chalk that one up to you being tired and on painkillers."

"Whatever," I said.

"God, Lia. I'm trying, okay? But if you keep acting like this, then I—"

"What?" I asked. "Then you what?"

He took a step back and started for the door. "Never mind. Let's just talk about this when I get back."

"No. You know what? I think you should enjoy your little tour without any strings attached," I said.

What? What was I saying?

"Excuse me?" Jasper asked.

"You heard me," I said. "Go. Go have fun with all your fans. Post whatever the hell Evan wants you to post on Instagram."

"Is that what this is about? My Instagram feed? I don't even control that thing anymore. Evan has some intern taking care of it."

"So you're saying that *wasn't* you kissing some random girl last night?"

Jasper's face was the color of ripe eggplant. But he wasn't denying it. How could he? The photo had thousands of likes.

"That girl basically threw herself at me, Lia," he said finally. "And I didn't know that picture had gone up. I—"

"Do you have any idea how humiliating that was? All those people know I'm your girlfriend and then they see that and I—"

"I'm sorry, Lia, okay? I'll have them take it down."

Great. So they'll take that picture down. But how long before another girl "threw herself" at him? How long before an even worse picture showed up? I knew firsthand how one stupid moment could be memorialized forever—how it could hurt people. And I didn't want to keep getting hurt.

"Just forget it, Jasper. I'm done."

Done. I'd said the word "done." Maybe Jasper was right. Maybe I was too hopped up on painkillers.

"You've got to be kidding me. Lia, you do realize that I wouldn't even have to be doing half this stuff if it wasn't for *your* mother."

"My mother didn't make you kiss that girl!"

"I just *told* you I didn't kiss her. She kissed me!"

"But what about the next girl and the next? I don't want to spend my life wondering what you're doing and with whom and when I'm gonna be blindsided by another photo. I can't do it. Not anymore."

"I'm sorry, just to be clear, you're breaking up with me?" Jasper asked, grasping the plastic bar at the end of my bed and squeezing.

"Yeah," I said, my voice breaking. "I am."

"Well, I don't accept." He stood up straight and crossed his arms over his chest.

"You . . . what?"

"I don't accept," he repeated. "You and me. This. Isn't over. I'll talk to you when I get back."

With that, he turned and walked out of the room.

"We're broken up!" I shouted after him.

"No, we're not!" came the muffled reply.

And then, I was totally alone.

14

"I MADE GRILLED CHEESE."

Britta stood in the doorway of my darkened bedroom with a plate and a glass of what looked like iced tea. I hadn't seen her since the puke fight, so even though I was in prime moping mode, I pushed myself up enough to really look at her.

"I'm so sorry I barfed on our floor," I said.

She walked in and put the food on my bedside table.

"It wasn't so much that you barfed on the floor as the fact that you didn't clean it up."

"I couldn't," I said. "I was kind of a mess."

"And still are."

I grimaced, but didn't argue. After all, I was lying in bed in the middle of the afternoon in sweatpants and a cropped T-shirt with a pudding stain on the front of it. Plus, there was the cast.

My phone vibrated next to the grilled cheese plate.

"You gonna get that?" Britta asked.

"No. In fact, would you mind turning it off?" I rolled over and pulled the blankets over my head.

I heard it stop vibrating.

"You have twenty-one missed calls and, like, a zillion texts," Britta said. "From Jasper, your mom, Fiona, Duncan, my mom, Frederick, and . . . ugh . . . Tash."

"Delete them," I muttered.

"Uh, no. I'm not your personal assistant."

The sheets in front of my face lifted up and Britta placed the phone in my hand.

"Deal with your drama," she said. And then I was enveloped in darkness again.

The phone felt warm in my hand. I didn't want to talk to anyone. I didn't even want to know what their texts said. I just wanted to be left alone. Didn't anyone get that? I was recuperating over here.

Okay. I was wallowing over here.

I pushed myself up against my pillows and, ignoring the many notifications, opened my web browser. It wasn't easy, typing into the phone with one hand, with the phone propped up on my leg—it kept sliding off and hitting the pillow until I figured out how to hold it down with my cast while I typed. Finally I managed to type in two short words—"Jasper Case."

I held my breath, my heart pounding a frantic beat against my breastbone while I waited. Then the first headline came up.

"Jasper Case to Play the Juke This Friday Night!"

I scrolled down.

"Jasper Case Leads Wave of Young New Talent"

"Jasper Case Plays to Sold-Out Blake Ralston Crowd"

The more I scrolled, the more the air went out of me. There was no mention of us breaking up. No mention of us being on the skids—one of the tabloids' favorite phrases. So Jasper was for real. He wasn't accepting my breakup. Or at least, he hadn't told Evan about it yet. I wasn't sure whether to feel even more pissed off—or relieved.

I mean, it was one thing to think that my life was lame, but to totally ignore my wishes and not even allow me to break up with him? Who did he think he was?

But then again . . . did I really want to break up with him?

I couldn't believe I'd yelled at him. He'd come to visit me in the hospital after a long night working, when I was only there because I'd done something stupid, and I'd yelled at him. I felt like such an asshole. Which only made me feel angrier somehow.

But he had kissed that girl. And done God knew what else. Plus he kept trashing my mom. And yes, she'd done some awful things, but he didn't have to keep harping on her. Especially not when he knew I was working with her and that I was only doing it to get into TSoD and stay in Tennessee—with him. And also, he kind of kept belittling my life. Was I supposed to just not care about that?

I briefly considered getting up and trying to do some work

for the gala—trying to find some way to meld my mom's request for the traditional with high style and turn it all into something I could use for my portfolio—something I could be proud of. But the idea exhausted me.

My phone vibrated and fell off my leg again, landing face-down in the sheets. When I picked it up, Duncan smiled out at me. My heart thunked. I couldn't even remember seeing Duncan after I face-planted onto the rocks. Was he the one who'd called the ambulance? Why hadn't *he* come to see me in the hospital?

Feeling icky and sour inside, I hit ignore. Then I turned the phone off, rolled over, covered my head with my pillow, and screamed as loud as I could.

"Cecilia Elizabeth Montgomery, this has to stop."

I pulled the pillow off my head and blinked in the ridiculous sunshine. Someone had thrown open my curtains. My mother, it seemed, since she was the one staring down at me wearing a sharp pink suit and a light gray silk shell top. Or perhaps it was Max, who was busy unpacking his bag of tricks on the desk, humming as always. He'd shoved aside my computer and restacked my papers on the dresser. Now he was busy lining up pots of lip gloss.

"Mom," I groaned, "go away!"

I tried to pull the pillow over my head again, but she snatched it out of my grip and flung it across the room.

"Not today, young lady. Today you are getting up and coming to a community fundraiser with me, where you will remember who you are and what it means to be a Montgomery. Today is the first day of the rest of your life."

"Mmm-hmmm," Max agreed, momentarily interrupting his theme song.

"Not you too," I chided him.

"Matilda is here as well," he said, nodding toward the living room. "She's got two rolling racks outside."

I groaned and rolled over on my stomach, yanking the blankets over my head.

"I told you I wasn't going to be doing any photo ops with you," I said, my words muffled.

"This isn't a photo op. It's a community gathering."

I sat up and glared at her. "Come on, Mom. If we're going to have this new relationship . . . whatever it is . . . let's at least be honest with each other. It's a photo op."

Huh. Apparently my misery was making me stronger.

My mother narrowed her eyes slightly and huffed a sigh. "Fine. It's a photo op." Max snorted and her gaze flicked at him. He quickly turned away. "But I also think it will be good for you to get out of this room. To get some fresh air. To be among people." She gave me one last look and left the room.

"She's not gonna give up," Max said wisely.

"I'm aware," I replied.

And somehow, I forced myself out of bed and into the shower, ignoring Matilda's greeting on my trudge across the living room. She was busy laying out colorful outfits across the couches, which she'd lined with sheets lest there be a stray stain that could transfer to the clothes. I thought of my recent vomit and shuddered. Smart girl.

Of course, the doctors hadn't given me a waterproof cast, so I had to wrap a garbage bag around my arm and then hold it outside the shower as best I could while washing myself with one hand. Awesome. At least I didn't have to deal with my hair. All it ever needed these days was a quick finger styling. I was down to one wash a week.

Back in the living room, I glanced at the three outfits Matilda had laid out on the plaid couch and did a double take. One of them was straight out of the window at Second Chances. It was an outfit I'd styled, actually—a forties-style shift dress in deep purple with a little marigold-colored crocheted caplet and brown leather peep-toe booties.

"Don't you love that? Your mother picked it out."

"Really?"

I glanced over at my mom, who was busy barking into her cell phone near the front door.

"I'm the one who put that in the window at work."

"You have a great eye," Matilda said. "Want to try it on?"

"What's this event we're going to anyway?" I asked.

"Your mother said it was a garden party," she said. "I think it's perfect."

I felt this tiny flutter in my heart area. My mother had appreciated something I did. She might not have known I did it, but still. It was nice to feel something other than the sadness, anger, and confusion I'd been floundering in for the past two days. If she liked this outfit, she liked my taste—even if she didn't know it. Maybe I could still come up with an overall look for the gala that she would approve of. Perhaps all was not lost.

"Sure," I said, trying not to sound too enthusiastic. "I'll try it on."

An hour later I was standing on a plot of untilled soil behind a church, in the blazing hot sun, holding a shovel. All around me, people in T-shirts and shorts and gardening gloves chatted and laughed as they assembled supplies and curiously eyed the cameramen my mother had brought along.

"This is not a garden party," I said to my mother.

"I never said it was. It's an event for a community garden," she replied through her smile, giving a wave at some random person on the other side of the yard.

"It's *working* a community garden," I said, looking at my freshly painted toenails peeping out from my heeled booties. "We are *not* dressed for this."

"Tash must have gotten her signals crossed," my mother said. "Just pose for some pictures and then we'll politely excuse ourselves."

A few women walked over and gamely introduced themselves to my mom. I took the opportunity to slip away.

"Lia! What're you doing here?"

I turned around to find Duncan and Fiona walking toward me, decked out in work clothes. Of course. They probably went to this church. They probably had a reason to be there. A real reason. They belonged here and actually wanted to help their friends and neighbors build a garden. They were part of something. While I was a complete poseur. And not even of my own free will.

"My mom," I said, wishing I'd gotten out of here just five seconds sooner. I wasn't sure where I stood with Fiona, and the last time I'd seen Duncan I'd been swinging through the air toward my doom. Just being near him made me feel idiotic. "She wanted a photo op."

"Are you okay?" Fiona asked, eyeing my cast.

"Fine," I said, lifting my heavy club of an arm. "It doesn't really hurt anymore."

But it was hot. And it itched like crazy. There was a huge patch of sweat in the center of my back and it was all I could do to keep from squirming. I had to get out of there. Any flicker of hope or positivity I'd felt earlier was long gone.

"I'm really sorry," Duncan told me. "I should have stopped you guys from getting on that tube together."

"It wasn't your fault," I told him. "And honestly? You probably couldn't have stopped me anyway." I turned and tossed my shovel back onto the pile of shovels with a clang. From the corner of my eye, I saw my mother look around for me, and I knew I had only seconds to escape.

"Well, it's been real," I said finally. "You kids have fun."

"You're leaving?" Fiona asked.

"It's not like I could really help in these clothes anyway," I told her, walking backward toward the gate. I caught my mother's eye, and she looked murderous, but I just kept moving. "Really, Fiona," I said, shoving through the garden gate, "what's the point?"

I let it clang behind me, thinking it would make me feel better. It didn't.

Lia Washington probably would have gone home, gotten changed into shorts and a T-shirt, and come back to help out. Or she would have said *screw it* and gotten down on her hands and knees in that dress. Or maybe she would have had something cool to do today and wouldn't have been lying around when her mother stopped by to drag her out of bed, and then none of this would have happened. Honestly, I had no idea what Lia Washington would have done in this situation. Not anymore. And that depressed me more than anything.

On the way home, I caught a glimpse of the Book Nook's wall. It read:

I DO NOT REGRET THE THINGS I'VE DONE, ONLY THOSE I DID NOT DO.

15

I HATED FEELING LIKE THIS. LIKE MY BODY WAS SO heavy I couldn't move. Like someone was pressing an iron down on my chest. My brain was full of fog, and I was so bored but I couldn't think of a thing to do. And even when I did think of something to do—like clean my room or make my bed or figure out *some* kind of design plan for the gala, which was just over week away—I couldn't put together enough enthusiasm to lift my head.

What I really needed to do was call Tash and surrender—tell her to do it herself or hire a professional—but I couldn't do that. I couldn't admit defeat. Even though I felt so very defeated.

You're depressed, Cecilia.

Gigi's voice came out of nowhere, and I realized I hadn't thought about her in a few days. Which was weird, because I'd thought about her every day of my life, even before she died. Gigi had been my go-to ear when anything went wrong, and there had been days when I'd considered calling her eighteen times, but somehow managed to save it all up for one long blubber-fest.

But now, she was gone. And I had no one to blubber to.

Stop feeling sorry for yourself, Cecilia.

But I couldn't do that. I didn't know how.

I wasn't sure how long I'd been lying on the couch, staring at the wall—I hadn't had the energy to find the remote—when there was a pounding on the door. I sat up straight. It sounded like there was a mob coming up the stairs. I heard voices and laughter, and shushing, then giggles.

"Who is it?" I called.

More giggles.

I shoved myself off the couch and immediately all the blood rushed from my head, so I had to steady myself against the kitchen island. My arm throbbed inside its cast and I realized, suddenly, that I was starving. When was the last time I'd eaten? As I was reaching for the door, whoever was on the other side pounded so hard, the whole thing shuddered.

"Who is it?" I asked again, my voice cracking this time.

"Party Patrol! Open up! You're under arrest!"

I let out a breath and rolled my eyes. "Duncan!"

When I yanked the door open, Duncan was standing there with Fiona, Frederick, Ryan, and a few other kids I recognized from town. Everyone had a brown bag and everyone was smiling.

"We figured we wouldn't be able to get you to come out and party, so we brought the party to you!" Duncan announced.

He breezed past me and dropped his bag on the island, sending some of Britta's magazines sliding to the floor.

"Duncan, no," I protested as Fiona, Frederick, and the others filed in. "You heard what Britta said the other day. We can't have a party here. She'll kill me."

And she'll throw me out, I thought to myself.

"We will not let this happen, Cecilia Montgomery," Frederick said, slinging one arm around me. He reeked of cologne and looked like he hadn't shaved in two days. "It is a small party. Nothing crazy."

I glanced around as people settled themselves on the couches and Ryan turned on the television, scrolling quickly through the stations. Frederick was right. There were only nine people there. I could keep control of nine people. But the question was, did I want to? Answer: Hell no.

Fiona placed a couple of plastic bags on the counter and started to pull out takeout containers from the diner. I smelled fries and my stomach sat up at attention.

"You brought food?" I asked weakly.

"Oh, the Taylors always bring food," Fiona said over her shoulder. She shot me this cautious/hopeful look and I realized we should really talk. The stalemate between us couldn't go on forever. Also, she was holding fries.

"Okay, fine," I said, inspiring a high-five between Frederick and Duncan. "But no belly shots. And no daredevil crap. I don't want anyone trying to jump out our front windows into a bouncy house or something."

Duncan glanced over at the front of the apartment and the street beyond. "Actually . . ."

I whacked his arm with my cast.

"Ow!" we both said.

"I was just kidding," Duncan added.

"You'd better be," I said as Frederick popped open a beer. I glanced at Fiona. "Tell me you have some fried green tomatoes."

And Fiona smiled.

There were a lot of people in my apartment. Definitely more than nine. When had they multiplied? And why was it so hot? And sticky. My fingers were very sticky. I pressed them against the wall to see if I could climb it like Spider-Man, but instead I ended up on my ass.

That caused a lot of laughter.

"Oh my God, Lia, you are *so* drunk!" Fiona cried, clinging to a longneck beer bottle with one hand as she pulled me up with another.

"I am not! I'm sticky!" I told her, flexing my fingers in front of her face. I couldn't be drunk. Not again. I had promised myself I wouldn't.

"Ew! Disgusting! Stay away!"

She screeched and ran and I tore after her, knowing I looked like a dork and not caring. I stepped on something soft, then something hard, then almost went sprawling. Frederick caught me before I could hit the deck and break my other arm.

"You okay, Cecilia Montgomery?" he asked.

His eyes looked a little swimmy. Or were those mine?

"Yes, thank you," I said primly, standing up straight and holding up my arm. "One cast is enough for this girl."

Oh crap. My cast. Someone had drawn a huge penis on my cast.

"Who did *this*!?" I shouted.

I heard a snort and a laugh, but no one claimed responsibility. Duncan seemed to be laughing the hardest though.

"You!" I shouted, and somehow couldn't help laughing. "Both of you Taylors are dead to me."

Everyone "ooohed." Fiona threw a marshmallow at me. I have no idea where she got a marshmallow.

"This means war!" I cried.

"I will defend my sister to the death!" Duncan announced, climbing up on top of the coffee table and raising his beer high.

This, of course, got a rousing cheer from everyone. I chucked a pillow at his head and he tumbled off onto the floor, then sprang up, grabbed Fiona's hand, and ran for the door shouting, "Retreat!"

"Attack!" I yelled.

And suddenly, the entire party was barreling out the door and down the stairs. I felt sweat drip down the back of my neck as I made the turn, clinging to the railing. The stairwell tilted and I tried to pause, but a dozen pairs of feet pounded the stairs behind me and I was shoved out of the way into the brick wall. My stomach heaved, and I clung to the coarse grain of the bricks until everyone else had passed me. Their hoots and hollers echoed out into the night.

I took a few deep breaths. I could just go back upstairs. Go back upstairs and lock the door and none of them would be able to get back in. I'd be back where I'd wanted to be when the night began. Alone.

But I didn't want to be alone anymore. There was nothing to do but follow the crowd.

I slowly made it down the last few steps and along the alley onto the street. Most of the partiers had run across Main to the park in the square and were chasing one another around, screaming and laughing. The cool evening air hit me and I felt instantly more awake and less nauseous. I felt free. I jogged across and spotted Duncan and Frederick near the head of the pack. Duncan's back was exposed. I sprinted across the park and jumped on him.

He staggered sideways but stayed on his feet. I clung to his neck and wrapped my legs around his waist.

"What're you doing?" He laughed.

"You were supposed to go down! I was trying to tackle you!" I cried.

"Nice try," he said, his hands cupping my thighs to steady me.

"Cecilia, come," Frederick said. "Let us get you down from there."

He wrapped one arm around me from behind, between

my stomach and Duncan's back, and tugged. I didn't immediately let go, and Duncan tripped backward.

"Frederick, don't!"

Before I knew what was happening, their feet got tangled up together and we all landed in a knot on the ground. My arm throbbed. I groaned and looked left and there was Frederick, his face just centimeters from mine.

"You are very beautiful, Cecilia Montgomery," he said.

And then he kissed me.

He tasted like beer and Cool Ranch Doritos. I almost threw up in his mouth. And then a bright light blinded me.

"Hey! What the hell!"

Frederick broke off the kiss and sat up. Duncan was already on his feet. A swarm of photographers had surrounded us. Someone's heavy boot came down on my good hand and I cried out in pain.

"Cecilia, are you all right?" Frederick asked.

There were people running everywhere. Feet and legs and bright lights. Hands grabbed at me and someone screamed.

"Cecilia! Cecilia! What's the new guy's name!"

"Cecilia, turn this way!"

"Where's Jasper? Are you guys planning a threesome?"

Oh my God, now I really was going to throw up.

One of the photographers reached down and nudged my shoulder. I looked over and he took a close-up of my face.

"Get your hands off her," Duncan shouted.

Frederick cursed in French and advanced on the man.

"Give to me your camera," he demanded.

The man kept the lens glued to his face, firing off shots of Frederick even as he backed away. I scrambled to my feet.

"Are you crazy?" the photog said.

"I am not crazy. You did not ask to take her picture. You are a heathen," Frederick said. "Give to me your camera or I will take it from you."

The man lowered his camera slightly. "Who the hell do you think you—"

Frederick reached out, grabbed the long zoom lens, and flung the camera to the pavement. Something cracked, but that wasn't enough for Frederick. He lifted his foot and brought it down—hard.

Everyone started shouting at once. The photographers, the partiers. Shirts were grabbed. Shoulders shoved. A fist flew. Someone hit the ground next to me and I jumped out of the way.

"You guys, stop!" I screamed. "Someone's gonna get hurt!"

But they were still taking pictures. Some of the photogs were circling the fight, snapping away. One of them got right up in my face, so close I could smell her perfume and see a tiny scar on her wrist. She noticed the penis on my arm, laughed, and snapped a close-up of it.

"So much for America's sweetheart, huh, Cecilia?"

There was a whoop of a police siren. I saw red, but not because of the lights.

"Screw you, you psycho!" I shouted.

And before I knew what I was doing, her camera was in my hand, and then I was hurling it as hard as I could. It hit the back of a police car.

Five seconds later, I was in handcuffs.

16

MY EYES PULSED. THE BACK OF MY HEAD FELT ICE cold. I had never known my back could ache so much. This was misery. This was the worst I'd ever felt.

And then my mom showed up.

"Get. Up. Cecilia."

I lifted my head off the cold metal bench inside my teeny, tiny jail cell. There were only four barred cubicles inside the police station, and I had been given my very own, while everyone else had been crowded into the other three. The police had been worried about my personal safety. Now was when they really needed to be worried. My mother looked murderous.

Slowly, I lifted myself off the bench and made my way over to the metal bars.

"Congratulations," my mother said. "You have sunk to a new low."

"Thanks. I appreciate you noticing," I muttered.

"Don't be smart," my mother shot back.

The two officers working the desk on the far side of the room looked up.

"I've posted your bail," my mother said. "And you are coming home with me."

"Home to Boston?" I asked, my voice breaking.

"No. Thanks to you, home is here now. You're coming back to the house your father and I have rented, and you will stay there until we can figure out what to do with you."

She yanked down on her jacket. I waited for her to tell me that I was ruining her career. That if I kept this up and lost the election for her, she was going to make my life a living hell.

"Guard! We're ready."

Okay. So maybe that lecture was going to wait until we got "home."

"What to do with me? I'm an adult, remember?"

"I'll believe that when I see it," my mother said with a sniff.

An older officer shuffled over and unlocked the cell door. When he shoved it aside, it made a clang that was somehow worse than the one it had made when he locked me in here a few hours earlier.

"You, my dear daughter, had better start thinking about what sort of person you want to be," my mother said through her teeth. "And what sort of life you intend to have. Because from where I'm standing, you are going nowhere fast."

She flicked her fingers at me, and when I didn't move, she grabbed my arm and steered me out of the police station ahead of her.

* * *

My father gave me a look I'd never seen before. It wasn't just disappointed—it was pitying. My father pitied me. As I trudged through the gleaming modern kitchen of the huge colonial they'd rented, trailing behind Tash, whose heels click-clacked primly, I kept my head down so I wouldn't have to see his face.

Tash led me up the freshly waxed stairs, lined with detailed paintings of the Tennessee plains, and paused outside the first bedroom door.

"This is your room."

Her lips pursed and she seemed to be holding her breath. I was sure I smelled, but not badly enough that she was caught up in some kind of toxic cloud. I wanted to tell her off, but I just didn't have the energy.

The room was large and airy, with a huge bed covered in puffy white pillows and a down comforter. There was a dresser and a vanity table, but no TV, no computer, not even a desk.

"What does she expect me to do in here?" I asked.

"Sleep it off, I imagine," Tash said.

Then she closed the door. I wouldn't exactly call it a slam, but she did it with conviction.

"Welcome to your new ivory tower, Cecilia," I whispered.

Then I careened facedown into the bed. It smelled like lemon and lilac, and after spending all those hours on a cold metal bench, it was heaven. I groaned and rolled over, pulling the comforter around me like I was a veggie wrap. I wasn't going to let my mother lock me away again. I wasn't going to let her control my life. But that didn't mean I couldn't sleep. Just for a little while.

My phone vibrated in the pocket of my jeans and I quickly fumbled it out. Jasper's face smiled at me.

"Hello?" I said, my heart already hammering in my chest.

"'Sweetheart Threesome'? Are you for real?"

I sat up straight. "What?"

"Have you even been on Perez today? Buzzfeed? Twitter?"

"Ummm . . . I haven't exactly been near a computer."

"Oh, right. Because you spent the night in jail."

Wow. I'd never heard him sound so bitter.

"You want to run around kissing French guys and tangling with Duncan Taylor? What is this, payback? Real mature."

"I . . . I . . ."

"Fine then," he spat. "Message officially received, Cecilia. We're done."

The line went dead. It was the first time he'd called me Cecilia. Tears burned behind my eyes, but I blinked them away. I was the one who'd thrown him out of the hospital room. I was the one who'd told him to go have fun on his tour. What did I expect? For one of the most sought-after new stars in America to pine away for me forever?

Okay, yeah. Maybe I kind of did.

I brought a pillow to my face and cried. What the hell was I doing? How had I ended up here? Why did I keep doing and saying all these things when I knew they weren't the right things? And why did I feel so angry all the time?

There was a knock on my door. Had to be my mom. I lifted my face.

"Go away," I said, my voice thick.

"Cecilia, it's your father."

Shit.

"I can't talk right now, Dad."

There was a pause, and I waited to hear his heavy footsteps retreat down the hallway. They didn't. Instead, the door creaked open.

"Cecilia, are you all right?"

What do you think?

"No."

My father blew out a sigh. His white shirt was tucked neatly into gray slacks that were fastened with a shiny black belt. Even in the midst of crises, my dad was dressed for a business lunch. He stepped inside and sat down on the edge of the bed, with me behind him. I didn't want to move. He reached back and patted my thigh, which was wrapped up in the blanket.

"Sweetie, you know I'll always love you no matter what, and if there's anything you want to talk about, I'm here."

I bit down on my tongue to keep from crying again. "Not right now, Dad."

"Okay then. That's fine. You don't have to talk. But you do have to listen." He took a deep breath and talked to the wall ahead of him while I curled farther into myself at his back. "It's . . . well . . . I always thought that you had a good head on your shoulders—that once you were given the independence that comes with adulthood, you'd make good choices. But that's not what I'm seeing here."

I squeezed my eyes closed and two tears slipped out.

"Maybe we coddled you for too long, I don't know."

Coddled me? Try controlled *me.*

"But if there's any advice I could give you, it would be . . . from here on out, try to look before you leap. It's an adage for a reason." Another pause. "And it's something I wish I'd done more of when I was young."

I held my breath. What had he ever done wrong when he was young? The man was an angel—a saint. He won a scholarship to Harvard. He was a Rhodes Scholar. He'd graduated number one in his class from Georgetown Law.

Was he . . . was he talking about marrying my mother? It was pretty much the only impetuous thing he'd done in his life—popping the question at the age of nineteen, when they'd been together for only eight months.

God, my family was so screwed up. If he regretted marrying her, then why was he still with her? Why did he always let her have everything she wanted when it came to her career, their life? When it came to me? What about what *he* wanted? Why didn't he matter?

So many times when I was younger, I sat alone in my room and imagined what my life would be like if my dad took me and left my mom. I imagined us in a little apartment, making dinner together and eating on the couch in front of the TV, going to the beach or to ballgames every weekend. The two of us—we'd have had actual fun. We would have had a life.

But that would never have happened. Nobody left a Montgomery. Except maybe Jasper. But even as I thought that, I knew it wasn't fair. I'd broken up with him. And then, when he wouldn't accept it, I'd done to him exactly what he'd done to me—shown up on social media kissing someone else.

I wished my dad would look at me. I wanted to ask him about a zillion questions. But then the weight on the bed shifted and he walked out, closing the door silently behind him.

The next morning, I texted Tash as soon as I woke up, in answer to about four thousand texts and e-mails from her demanding to know where we stood with the hiring of a country act for the gala. Now that Jasper was done with me, there was no more putting it off.

Jasper unable to find band for gala. Need new plan.

Her response came five seconds later.

I already hired a classical quartet and a cover band JIC. ☺

Nothing like a mocking smiley-face emoji to start your day.

I knew that if I spent more than one night at my parents' house, I'd end up staying there forever, so I got up, stole a mug of French-press coffee made by the staff, and snuck out. It was a long walk back to town, and I spent the entirety of it composing a speech to Britta containing all the reasons she shouldn't throw me out. Or trying to.

Unfortunately, I couldn't come up with many.

How badly had we trashed our apartment? Had anyone gone back to clean it up? How horrible was I for hoping that Fiona or Duncan or anyone had done it? It was my responsibility. My home. And once again, I'd disrespected it.

By the time I found myself trudging up the stairs to the apartment's front door, the speech-brainstorming was over. Instead, I was imagining how I'd manage to carry all my stuff back to my parents' place with a broken arm.

The door opened the second I pushed my key into the slot. Britta was standing there with a rolling suitcase. It took me five seconds to process the fact that it was hers and not mine. That she wasn't about to shove it in my face and tell me to get lost.

"You're back," she said flatly.

Silence. I had no idea what to say. Finally, she angled herself to one side.

"Come in."

Relieved, but still very much on edge, I stepped inside the apartment. It was mercifully clean, aside from the pile of tabloids and newspapers that always covered the kitchen island. Maybe Fiona had come back to clean up.

"I heard about your party." Britta closed the door and placed her suitcase next to it. "Everyone on the planet heard about your party."

"I'm so sorry, Britta," I said, hanging my head. "I tried to make them leave, but I . . ."

I trailed off, realizing I hadn't tried very hard. And I didn't feel like defending myself. It made me feel like a jerk.

"I'm just sorry."

"It's okay," Britta said. "Nothing was broken or anything. I talked to Duncan and he said he's pretty sure the action moved to the park before anyone got really out of control."

She gave me this look. *Anyone but you,* it said.

"Oh."

"So." She paused and gestured at her bag. "I'm going to Austin to cover the Firebrand Three's three-night stand at the Whiskey, and I need you to do something for me."

"No parties, I promise."

"Not that," she said, crossing her arms over her chest. "Well, yes, that. But also, I need you to take care of the wall."

My heart thudded. "The wall?"

She couldn't mean—

"Yes. The wall. I am the anonymous wall painter."

I blinked. Britta looked me dead in the eye. She wasn't kidding. I couldn't believe it. All this time I'd been living with the person whose message on the wall of the bookstore seemed to speak directly to me? How was this possible? How had I not known? How the hell did she manage to do it when she was constantly attending concerts and going on the road? Did the girl never sleep?

I opened my mouth to ask all these questions, and she held up a silencing hand.

"Don't ask. All you need to know is I started doing it at a time in my life when I needed inspiration. Direction," she said pointedly. "And now, I think it's your turn."

"No. No way. I have no idea what I'd say," I told her, flopping down on the couch. "And besides, I suck at painting. *And I have a broken arm.*"

And also . . . it means too much to me. I didn't want to touch the wall because . . . because I wasn't worthy.

"I could never come up with something that would inspire people."

"Excuses, excuses."

Britta moved to the door and pulled out the long handle of her rolling bag.

"Let's put it this way, Lia." She yanked open the door, her bangle bracelets clattering. "You don't do it, and tomorrow there's no message up there and thousands of people will be disappointed."

She couldn't be serious. "But you can't . . ." I looked around the apartment as if it could somehow save me. "Where do I get the paint? And the ladder? How do I get it all over there without getting caught? What should it say?"

"That's for you to figure out," Britta reminded me.

"Oh, come on. You have to have a book around here somewhere. Something with lists of quotes and platitudes. For when you get stuck?"

"I am offended that you would even suggest such a thing," Britta said.

And then she walked out.

I was exhausted, I was hungry, the only thing in my system was caffeine, and now, I was panicking. People freaked out when the message didn't get painted. Fiona had told me that on my very first morning in town. What would happen if there was no message tomorrow and people somehow found out it was my fault? They'd slaughter me. I was already a joke. Now I'd be the joke who ruined a town tradition.

I walked into my room and opened my laptop to Google "inspirational quotes," but as it came out of its sleep mode, it hit me: This wasn't my problem. Britta had created this responsibility for herself. It wasn't my fault she'd addicted an entire town to her wise words. Why should I be the one to stress about it?

By the time the screen came to life, I was already crawling into bed. But my heart was still pounding and my breath seemed superloud. Between the adrenaline and the caffeine, my body was on high alert. In the corner were piles of poster board and cloth samples, printouts of floral arrangements, and brochures from local vendors. The gala was one week from today, and nothing was getting done.

You need to start thinking about what sort of person you want to be, my mother's voice said in my ear.

I didn't know what sort of person I wanted to be, but I knew who I wasn't. I wasn't the person plastered all over those tabloids. I wasn't some drunk slut looking for attention. I wasn't a loser who shirked my responsibilities, who didn't go to college, who had no future.

I'd hoped you'd make better choices than what I'm seeing: my father this time.

But how was I supposed to make good choices when everyone around me seemed to want me to do something other than what I wanted to do?

You don't seem to be scared of anything! It's one of the things I like best about you, Jasper told me.

And then it hit me. I knew exactly what the wall should say. I sat up straight and held my breath. Maybe if I did this, it would make me feel better. Maybe if I could complete this one task, I'd be able to face all the other crap I had to do.

Now I just needed to figure out how to get it done.

17

"WHAT THE HELL, CECILIA?"

I launched myself inside the Taylors' house, nearly taking Duncan down in the process. The six or seven paparazzi that had followed me over stayed rooted on the other side of the white picket fence. Rumor had gotten around that the woman who lived here was a badass lawyer. They knew better than to trespass on her private property.

"Sorry if I scared you." I'd knocked kinda frantically. "They won't stop taking pictures."

I peeked around one of the eyelet curtains and saw the crowd freeze, readying their next move.

"It's all right," Duncan said. He was wearing a T-shirt and cotton shorts, dressed for a day of lazing around the house, it seemed. "Are you okay? I can't believe you got arrested. I swear, no more mobile parties at your place."

"I'm fine," I said. "That's not why I'm here. I just . . . " I glanced around him into the darkened kitchen and cocked an ear toward the ceiling. "Is anyone else here?"

"Nope. Dad and Fiona are at the diner, and Mom's down at the county courthouse." He narrowed his eyes at me with interest. "What's up?"

I took him by the wrist and led him over to the living room, where I basically shoved him down onto the couch before perching on the coffee table across from him.

"I need your help with something, but you have to swear on your life that you'll never tell anyone what I am about to tell you."

Duncan's entire face lit up. "Intrigued," he said, leaning forward.

"First, do you have any paint?" I asked.

"Paint."

"Yeah, like spray . . . paint?" I assumed that was what one would need to paint over a brick wall, but how the hell would I know?

"Maybe out in the shed," Duncan told me, speaking slowly—cautiously. "Why? Are you planning some kind of political protest?" He gasped and covered his mouth with one hand, pointing at me with the other. "Are you gonna spray paint moustaches on your mom's campaign posters?"

"It pains me that this is what people think about me now," I said. Then I stood up. "Show me."

Duncan led me through his house and out the back door to a pretty blue shed in the far corner of his family's yard. The door creaked as it opened, and inside, along the right wall, were dozens of cans of paint. A few tarps were balled up in the corner, and three different sizes of ladders hung on the back wall.

"Wow. You have everything I need."

"Britta got to you, didn't she?"

I turned to him, shocked. "What do you mean?"

"You can drop the act. I know all about Britta and the wall."

"You do?" I couldn't help feeling disappointed that I hadn't gotten to tell him. "How?"

"Because I'm her backup." Duncan grinned. "I'm the one who paints the wall when she's out of town."

I stepped back, clunking my head against a bucket hanging on a hook behind me. Apparently during those two normal weeks of my otherwise abnormal life, I'd been completely oblivious to the world.

The wig on my head itched like a nightmare and sweat poured down the back of my neck. It was pitch dark on Peach Street now that Duncan had doused the lights—one of Britta's secret methods for nondetection—and I cursed as I tripped over a curb, dropping several cans of paint with a never-ending clang.

"Shhhhh!" Duncan admonished, and turned on his head-lamp.

"Like I didn't already know that was loud," I whisper-hissed back. "Why do we have to be quiet, anyway? Everyone in this town turns a blind eye to this street at night, right? If they want the messages to keep appearing, they have to avoid it."

"Yes, but there's still the tourists. And your best friends, the paparazzi."

"Don't remind me," I said, scratching the back of my neck under the synthetic blond hair—the wig from an old Halloween costume of his mom's. As disguises went, it was pretty shoddy, so we'd snuck out the back gate of his house after midnight and taken only back roads to get here. So far, so good. We hadn't seen a photog or a news van yet. But we had to get this done as quickly as possible.

"Find the black paint," Duncan said.

"How am I supposed to do that? I can't see anything!"

Suddenly a bright light flicked on and I blinked at Duncan. He'd strapped the headlamp to his forehead.

"It's this one," he whispered, and tossed me the can, which I fumbled thanks to my cast, before finally grabbing it. "Man, your reflexes suck."

"Gee, thanks."

"Shake it up and test it on the bottom of the wall to make sure it works."

The aerosol can clicked loudly as I shook it, then sprayed a small dot near the sidewalk.

"Well. That's a very specific smell."

Duncan smirked and handed me a white painter's mask. "Welcome to the world of the street artist, my friend."

We strapped matching masks over our noses and mouths and he found, and tested, another can of black paint. "We have to cover up the old saying before we paint the new one," he said. "I'll go up the ladder. You and your cast stay on the ground."

"Thanks."

We got down to work. Between the mask and the wig I was sweating pretty profusely, and breathing wasn't exactly easy. In fifteen minutes that felt more like an hour, we managed to paint over Britta's old message. Duncan jumped to the ground next to me from the second rung of the ladder, and placed his can on the ground.

"Okay, Lia Washington, what's this wall gonna say?"

I took a breath. "It's going to say, 'You can't be brave if it doesn't scare you.'"

Duncan took a couple of steps back and looked up at the still-glistening paint.

"I like it."

I grinned. "So let's do this. What's the plan? What's the procedure?"

Duncan grabbed two cans of white paint. "The most important thing is to get the message on the wall. As long as the words are up, if you get caught, the job is done. Only get fancy if you have more time."

I nodded. "Got it." I hadn't felt this excited—this exhilarated—in days. Maybe since my foot hit the gas on that car I'd stolen back in Florida. Was it possible I was an outlaw at heart? Or maybe it was just that I'd been so good for so long that stepping any teeny toe out of line felt like an accomplishment.

Actually, it felt kind of awesome.

"I suggest you start at the top," Duncan said, lifting his chin.

"Me?" I said dubiously.

He stood up. "This is your deal. I'll shine the light up at you from down here."

"What happened to, 'You and your cast stay on the ground'?"

"Hey, this is your deal. I can't do *everything*." Duncan gave me a shrug. "If you fall, I'll catch you. Promise."

I snorted, rolled my eyes, and took the paint can. It was slow going, climbing the wooden ladder with one hand in a sling and the other holding the paint can, my face covered by a paper mask, and by the time I got to the top, I was dripping with sweat.

"Screw this," I said, and knocked the wig—and the baseball cap that had been holding it on—off my head with my cast. The night air rushing over my scalp felt like heaven.

"Um, Lia? I think you owe my mom a new Marilyn Monroe costume," Duncan called up to me.

I looked down and saw that the wig had caught some of the black paint on the way down.

"Oh God! Sorry!"

Duncan chuckled. "It's okay. She—"

He stopped abruptly and glanced over his shoulder. My heart stopped. "What?"

Silence. He held up a finger and I held my breath. Finally he relaxed. "It was nothing. But let's get this show on the road."

My hand was shaking as I started to paint, but somehow I managed to eke out the *Y* and *O* in "You." Then I had to climb down so Duncan could move the ladder, then climb back up to finish the word. When I leaned back to check my work, I saw that the *U* was a lot bigger than the *O* and the *Y* was crooked.

"It looks like crap," I grumbled.

"It's fine," Duncan replied. "The lettering takes some practice, but no one expects it to be perfect."

I took a deep breath and shook off my type A side, which was screaming at me to go back and fix it. I wondered if that was really me, or if I'd gotten that perfectionist thing from my mom. I wondered if I'd ever know.

I climbed back up to paint the words "can't be brave," which seemed to take three hours. My arm hurt from holding it in the same position, and the nozzle of the can had permanently embedded itself in my fingertip. By the time I finished up the *E* at the end, I felt as if I'd run a marathon.

"I'll do the rest,'" Duncan offered, taking pity on me as I climbed back down the ladder.

"Bless you," I replied.

I was just handing him the paint can when the first camera flashed.

"Oh crap," Duncan said.

"It's her! It's Cecilia Montgomery!"

There was no telling how many there were, but they rushed at us from the direction of Main Street, sounding like a herd of buffalo. I dropped the paint can and Duncan grabbed my hand and ran, the light from his headlamp bouncing in front of us, disorienting me to the point of nausea. We ducked around a corner and Duncan turned off the light, pulling me into a tiny garden outside a little brick home and shoving me to the ground. The mulch was fresh.

Duncan and I held on to each other, panting for breath as quietly as possible, as the stampede went by. Two photogs stopped not inches from the bushes we hid under, one of them wheezing.

"Where the hell did they go?" someone asked.

"I don't know." The wheezer paused to wheeze some more. "But did you get the shot?"

"I did. I *so* did," the first voice answered.

There was a click and some laughter, and then the two of them walked back toward town. I looked at Duncan.

"That can't be good," he said.

I groaned and hid my face behind my hands.

18

"PRINCESS VANDAL"

That's what the headline read the next morning. At least, the headline I was staring at as I sat in one of the window booths at the Little Tree Diner, my face throbbing from a sleepless night. Duncan sat across from me, wearing the most hangdog look I'd ever seen outside the Cartoon Network.

"Cecilia! Cecilia! We know you're in there! Come on! Just one smile. Just look out and give us one smile!"

The blinds over the window next to us were drawn, but that didn't stop the paparazzi from banging on the glass, trying to get a shot of me angry or tired or hungover. Hal had spent half the morning chasing them out of the diner and had finally posted a sign that read NO PHOTOGRAPHERS ALLOWED! That was when they'd moved to the street, and after chasing them off with a baseball bat five times, he'd called the cops. Now there were two police officers out there, and a yellow tape perimeter keeping the crowd a few feet back from the window. But they were still there. They were always going to be there.

Hal brought a couple over to the table next to ours. They were chatting happily until they saw me sitting there. Then the woman's face soured and she whispered something under her breath. Next thing I knew they were seated on the far side of the restaurant.

"It's official. I'm a leper," I said, hanging my head in my hands.

"Ignore them," Duncan said.

"How can I? They're everywhere. The entire town hates me."

Duncan didn't argue. He couldn't. The few townspeople who didn't mind putting up with the paparazzi stamping through the park and patrolling the streets and hanging around outside my apartment waiting for me all night, and who weren't annoyed by my mother and her posse barreling them over on the sidewalks wherever they went, had finally turned on me now that I'd messed with the wall. The scowls and stares I'd endured on my way to the diner this morning had damn near broken my heart. It was as if they thought I'd murdered the real wall painter in a coup so that I could take over the job and scrawl a half-assed message.

Honestly, that was what bothered me more than anything. I'd been given a chance to say something, and I hadn't even been able to finish.

"Cecilia! 'You can't be brave'?" one of the photogs shouted. "What kind of message is that to send to the young people of America?"

The whole diner turned to look at me. I folded my arms

on the table and my forehead slammed into them. Duncan reached over and squeezed my shoulder.

"Ugh, I can't believe this. I hate this town all over again."

Fiona huffed as she dropped into the seat next to Duncan and shoved him aside with her hip. For the first time in weeks, she was dressed like herself—jeans, a black T-shirt, and a colorful fringed scarf slung loosely around her neck. Her hair was now too short for the ponytail I'd gotten so used to, but it was shoved haphazardly behind her ears and she wore no makeup.

"What happened?" Duncan asked.

"I just came from a Summer Fest meeting and Marissa Millstone told me I should ask Cecilia to leave town."

My head popped up.

"What?" Duncan blurted.

"Who's Marissa Millstone?" I asked.

"The town bitch," Fiona replied, grabbing Duncan's soda and taking a sip. "She runs the Sweetbriar Summer Princess program. So I told her if that was the kind of town we were living in, I didn't want to be its princess. And I quit."

"Oh God, Fiona, I'm sorry," I said.

"Don't be." She grabbed a fry off my plate. "It's not your fault. Actually, it felt kind of good. I don't know why I joined up in the first place. It's so not me. And wasn't that the whole point? To be the real me? I think I got confused between doing something brave and doing something I actually wanted to do. And also? I've always kind of liked me. And kind of hated Sweetbriar."

Duncan leaned over and wrapped his arms around his

sister, pressing his cheek into her shoulder. "My sister is back!"

"But you hate that I hate this town," Fiona protested, laughing.

"Yeah, but I like *you*," he replied, letting her go.

"Well, you're not going to like my other news," Fiona said, eyeing me warily.

I gulped. "What could be worse than the town bitch leading the charge against me?"

"There are more newspeople camped out in the park," Fiona said. "Real newspeople. With big trucks and satellite dishes and everything."

Duncan jumped up and over the back of the bench to run to the front windows. I would have gone with him, but I couldn't show my face. Also, I suddenly felt too heavy to move.

"Dude. They're literally camping there. Some of them are putting up tents," Duncan said, wide-eyed upon his return.

"Can't the cops get rid of them?" I asked.

Fiona shook her head. "They tried. Apparently there's no law against it. They can stay there as long as they want."

"I'm so going to have to move," I said with a groan. "I wonder what Reno is like this time of year. Isn't that where people go to disappear?"

"I think that's TJ," Duncan replied. "Do you speak Spanish?"

"Fluently. Also French, Mandarin, Italian . . ."

"Oh my God, then go to Italy. Is this even a discussion? You could—"

"You guys, stop. This isn't funny," Fiona said. "Lia, you can't move. You can't let them drive you out of town."

"But it's the only way to get these people out of Sweetbriar. Forget Reno. I'll go back to Boston and take my parents with me. Then they'll have to follow us there and you guys can go back to living in peace. Plus the town can stop hating me. They'll probably forget I ever existed."

"No one hates you," Duncan said.

Someone nearby—I couldn't tell who—snorted derisively. I glanced at Duncan and, oddly, we both smiled.

But no matter what I did, I couldn't seem to gather the energy to even sit up straight. I couldn't keep going on this way. Britta was right. Working on the wall had made me feel better— it had made me feel energized and like I had a purpose—until it had all fallen apart. But now that I'd felt *that* way, even for a few hours, I didn't want to feel *this* way anymore.

So what was I supposed to do? Travel the country painting walls? I needed some advice, but I had no idea who to talk to. The very idea of facing my parents made me want to crawl under the table, assume a fetal position, and never come out again.

The door opened and everyone in the diner seemed to tense. Would it be another reporter for Hal to kick out? A Secret Service agent scouting the place for my mom? But instead, Jasper walked in. Most of the clientele relaxed, but my face felt as if it was on fire.

Jasper sidled over to the counter, looking gorgeous in dark

brown jeans, cowboy boots, and a light blue T-shirt. He was about to order when his gaze flicked around and met mine. I felt a shock of hope, but then he frowned, waved the waitress off, and walked out.

My eyes brimmed with tears. I couldn't believe he'd just looked at me that way. I felt like a piece of dirt.

But I also knew, suddenly and with absolute certainty, who I had to talk to.

"I have to go," I said, standing.

"Are you all right?" Fiona asked.

"I don't know," I said, heading for the kitchen and the back door. "Check back with me in a couple of hours."

Dee Case's entire house smelled like hummingbird cake. The sweetness of the vanilla cream mixed with the tangy, nose-prickling scent of the pineapple was like nirvana. It was my grandmother's favorite dessert—something she baked for me every time I visited. And as I sat at the kitchen table, I could hardly breathe for the tightness of my throat. What was it about scents that brought memories back with more vivid detail, more heartbreaking poignancy, than anything else?

"I can't believe I didn't see it," Dee said as she sat down across from me. She had made her hummingbird into cupcakes, which were cooling on a wire rack near the window, the bowl of frosting sitting ready to be glommed on. "You have her smile."

"Do I?" I asked, and cleared my throat.

"You do." Dee's gold bracelets jangled as she lifted her hand to rest her chin on her palm. "And right about now you have the same sad glint in your eye."

"Was she sad?" I asked.

Dee shifted in her seat. "Not always, baby, but for a while after your daddy left." She gave me a wan, apologetic smile. "But then you came along. You, Cecilia, were the light of my best friend's life."

An ugly sob escaped me and tears poured down my cheeks. "I'm sorry," I blurted. "I don't know what's wrong with me."

"Oh, honey, don't apologize." Dee slipped a napkin out of a wicker napkin holder on the table and handed it across to me. "She was your best friend too."

Those words hit me like a nuclear bomb, because although they were true, no one had ever said them aloud. I unfolded the napkin, covered my face, and just wept, letting out all the sorrow over Gigi, all the anger at my mother, all the confusion of the past few weeks. When I felt like I could possibly breathe again, I looked up.

"I wish she was here." I sniffed, toying with the edge of the napkin. "I really need to talk to her."

Dee reached her arm across the table, palm up. I hesitated for a second before taking her hand, and when I did, she squeezed it, her fleshy fingers warm.

"I'm here though, Cecilia. I know it's not the same, but why don't you tell me what's troubling you?" she asked. "Maybe I can help."

I took a deep, broken, breath and spilled out the whole story. How I kept doing the wrong things even when I knew they were wrong. How, even though I knew they were bad decisions, it annoyed me when my mother and father scolded me for them. How I'd never wanted to be famous but now, whether I was with my parents or Jasper or on my own, there were always cameras there. How things with Jasper had gone south and I didn't know how to fix them.

And then I talked about the gala, and the Tennessee School of Design. And how the two were intertwined. I told her that I hadn't worked on the event design in a week because every time I tried, I started second-guessing myself.

"It's just exhausting," I told her. "And I need to do a good job. It's the only thing I'll have for my portfolio, and the application for the spring semester is due at the end of July. But my mother . . . it's like no matter what I do, it's not good enough."

Dee watched me as I caught my breath. I'd barely taken a break the whole time I'd been talking.

"It sounds to me like you want to do a good job, not just to get into school, but to impress your mom as well," she said finally.

I scoffed. "Please. There's no impressing her."

"But that doesn't mean you won't try."

My throat felt tight.

"She's your mother, Cecilia. That's what we're wired to do. To some extent, every child on this planet wants to make their parents proud."

I rested my cheek on my hand. "Well, clearly that's not about to happen anytime soon. I tried to do something creative, and she trashed it. Then I tried to do what she wanted, and she trashed that, too. So what am I supposed to do?"

"You're putting a lot of pressure on yourself," Dee said. "Why not give your mom what she wants, but in a creative way?"

I rolled my eyes. "Yeah, that's not pressure."

"I have a feeling that if you just take a breath and stop overthinking it, the answers will come to you," she said with a smile. She got up, iced a cupcake, and placed it in front of me.

"What you need, my friend, is time," she said, then licked a bit of frosting off her finger. "Time and cake."

I managed a short laugh and tugged at the wrapper. "What if I don't have time?"

"Are you kidding me?" She went into the fridge and poured me a glass of milk. "Look at you. You've got all the time in the world."

"Okay, maybe, like . . . in your eyes," I said, and she shot me a wry look. "But the gala is next weekend, and the application deadline is right around the corner."

"That gala is going to happen whether or not you design it," Dee told me. "And that school isn't going anywhere."

"Okay, well . . . what if Jasper moves on before I can figure out how to make things right?"

"If that's what he does, then that's what's meant to be," Dee said as she closed the fridge. My stomach hardened, but then she put her hand on my back, right between my shoulder blades. "But, honey, I'd be right surprised if that's what he does. That boy loves you."

"Really?" I asked, as she came around to sit across from me again.

"Absolutely." She leaned forward over the table and looked me squarely in the eye. "Here's my advice. That's why you came to me, right? For my advice?"

I nodded, spinning the cupcake between my fingers.

"Take two days. Two days to completely focus on yourself. Don't answer the phone, don't talk to your momma or to Jasper or to anyone else who might confuse things. All you're to do during those two days is sleep, eat, and think about what you want. Where do you want to be next week, next year, in five years? And once you've figured that out, you'll know how to get there."

"You think?"

"I do," Dee said, then narrowed her eyes. "Now eat that cake before I do it for you."

Britta wasn't home when I got there, so I left the Tupperware box full of cupcakes on top of the magazine mountain and went to my room. The place was a mess. For someone who had always kept my living space as neat as a pin, I'd certainly gone over to the dark side. There was no way I was going to be able to think in this mess. I immediately went about straightening it up—flicking the sheets over the mattress and then tucking them in tight, throwing used tissues into the garbage can, and shoving clothes into a pile to be washed later.

Once everything was clean and organized, I grabbed the sketchpad I'd bought when I first started envisioning ideas for the gala and tore out everything I'd come up with so far. Those pages got balled up and tossed in the trash can. Then I sat down in the middle of my perfectly made bed, the pad open on my lap, a pencil in my hand, and I closed my eyes. For a few minutes I meditated, clearing my mind and controlling my breathing.

Dee was right. I knew what I wanted. Now I just needed to figure out how to get there.

Finally, I opened my eyes and got to work.

19

I HOVERED IN THE WINGS AT BAR VERDANT IN AUSTIN, Texas, two days later, clutching the neck of my violin so tightly the strings were cutting into my fingers. All I'd done for the past two days was work on my new vision for the gala and think about what I was going to say to Jasper, who now stood center stage, crooning into his microphone, while at least fifty girls swooned in front of him. He was coming to the end of one of his more upbeat songs, and when the last drumroll faded, the crowd went crazy, screaming, cheering, and clapping. Some girl in a black tank top threw a bright pink bra at his feet.

What, exactly, did she expect him to *do* with it?

I was supposed to walk on stage now. That had been my plan. To walk out between songs. But now, Jasper bent to pick up the bra and twirled it around his finger.

"Thank you, darlin'," he drawled.

"It has my phone number on it!" she shouted, and the people around her hooted and whistled.

Oh. So that explained it.

Jasper raised his eyebrows, then made a show of shoving the bra into the back pocket of his jeans.

Okay. So maybe instead of going out there, I was just going to barf on my shoes.

The next song began, and I realized with a stomach-lurch that (A) I had missed my window of opportunity; and (B) he'd just launched into "Meant to Be," the song he always dedicated to me.

And as he began to sing, he just didn't seem that into it.

My already shallow spirits sank even lower. What was I doing here? Clearly, Jasper had meant it when he'd said we were over.

"Are you going out there or what?" Evan Meyer whispered in my ear. "I mean, I went to all the trouble of getting you past security."

I turned to look him in the eye. He'd spent more time with Jasper the last few weeks than anyone else. "Right. And why did you do that, exactly?"

"Are you kidding? The two of you are a publicist's dream!" he exclaimed, as Jasper neared the chorus. "If you get back together, my job will be *so* much easier."

It was all I could do not to strangle him with his own scarf. Instead, I rolled my eyes and turned away.

"Wait wait wait." Evan touched my arm lightly with warm fingertips. "I'm just kidding. Well, no, I'm not. That's all true. But honestly, Cecilia, Jasper has been miserable without you. And I kinda like the kid. I'd rather see him happy than mopey."

"Really?" I asked, feeling only a little bit guilty that Jasper's misery was making me happy.

"Really. Now get the hell out there!"

Evan gave me a little shove and I tripped onto the stage. Wow. He was pretty strong for a little guy. The bass guitarist noticed my stumbling entrance, as did some of the audience members, who gasped, but Jasper was too into his performance, his gaze trained on the swaying crowd.

He finished the chorus and began the second verse. I held my breath, lifted my violin, and began to play along. The crowd cheered and Jasper glanced over his shoulder.

To his credit, he didn't miss a lyric, but I could see the total shock in his eyes. I walked slowly toward him, my whole body shaking as I tried my hardest to keep up with the melody. Our eyes were locked as he sang his beautiful words, and I played the notes from my heart.

Jasper lifted the microphone off the stand and approached me. The spotlight followed him. The girls in the audience were going crazy, which was a surprise, since it was pretty clear every last one of them had been daydreaming of going home with my boyfriend. Ex-boyfriend. Whatever.

Whoever he was, he was mere inches away now, singing his lungs out, gazing into my eyes. And then the song was over. I held my bow to the strings until they stopped vibrating. My hands never stilled, though. In fact, my whole body was vibrating.

"Hey," I said to him, against the din of the crowd.

"You're here," he said.

And then he pulled me against him and kissed me. His lips tasted salty and his hands were warm and strong against my back, and the only coherent thought my brain could form was, *Thank God. Thank God. Thank God.*

When I finally pulled back, I wasn't sure what was louder, the screams of the girls in the front row or the pounding of my pulse in my ears.

"I know you can't come home right now, and I know we have a lot to figure out," I told him, breathless. I had to shout in his ear to be heard. "But I know that we can do it. I know that we belong together," I said, and my voice cracked. "So when you do come home, you're coming home to me."

Jasper's lips touched my earlobe. "You bet I am," he said.

And then he picked me up and twirled me around for all the world to see.

We stood on the balcony of Jasper's Austin hotel room the next morning, watching the sun come up over the Colorado River. Jasper held me from behind, his arms around my waist, and I leaned back into him. We'd been up half the night talking. And smooching. And crying a little here and there. But for the most part, it had been good. One of those nights I'd only ever read about in books where everything comes out—hopes, fears, stupid daydreams, stories, and memories you thought you'd forgotten—and you emerge on the other side feeling like you've never known anyone better in your life.

"I'm really glad I came to Austin," I said.

"I second that." Jasper kissed the top of my ear.

I turned around to face him and placed my hands on his chest, up close to his shoulders.

"From now on, when things get crazy, we take a deep breath and think of each other first," I said.

"That's the deal, Red Sox. Whether there's a camera in your face or your mom is on your butt or some French dude wants to take you for a ride on his . . . what do French people drive, anyway?"

"Tricycles?" I suggested.

Jasper laughed. "I like it. Yeah. His tricycle."

"And whether a fan is accosting you or Evan is whispering in your ear or we have a date you know you should keep."

He bit his lip. "We think of each other first."

"Deal?" I said, and leaned back to offer my hand.

He grasped my fingers and pulled me into him, and just before his lips touched gently down on mine, he whispered against them, "You've got a deal."

"Honestly, ma'am, I'm not sure how we can spin this one. The girl was caught on camera with a paint can in her hand."

I paused outside my mother's office, my heart in my throat, as I clutched my laptop to my chest. It wasn't every day I walked in on high-level government employees talking about me.

"He's right. We managed to sell the broken arm as a

run-of-the-mill accident, but between the threesome thing and this—"

"I was not having a threesome!" I blurted, stepping into the room.

"Cecilia!" my mother snapped, standing up from behind her desk. "I'm in a meeting!"

"Yeah, a meeting about me," I replied, glancing at the two men sitting in chairs before her. "And as for the paint, that wall is a tradition. Every night someone writes a new message up there. Ask around town. They'll all tell you. It's not a vandalism thing, but a community thing. Everyone checks the wall each morning for inspiration!"

"And you thought 'You can't be brave' was inspiring?" Tash asked sarcastically. She was standing behind my mother's desk with her iPad ready, as always.

"I didn't get to finish!" I replied. I looked my mom in the eye. "Mom, let me have a press conference or something. I'll explain everything."

The man on the left snorted. "If you try to explain, it will just sound like excuses."

"He's right, Cecilia. The only way around this is spin," my mother informed me. "We could say it was an art project. That the photos were taken out of context."

"They *were* taken out of context! That's what I'm trying to tell you!" I shouted.

Everyone stared at me. I took a deep breath. "I'm sorry. I just . . . I can't live like this anymore, with photographers watching my every move." I put my bag and laptop down, sat on the arm of the nearest couch, and looked up at my mom pleadingly. "Mother, you have to move your campaign head-quarters back to Boston."

"Excuse me?"

"I apologize for interrupting your meeting," I said. "But you're ruining this town, and everyone hates me for it because they know you wouldn't be here if it weren't for me. Please, Mom. Just go home and take the press with you. I promise I won't get caught doing anything else stupid. At least I'll try really hard not to. And I'll make some campaign stops with you . . . as long as they don't interfere with school."

My mother lifted one eyebrow ever so slightly. "You've decided to go to Harvard?"

My throat closed over. "I've decided to go to school."

There was a beat of silence. The two men seemed afraid to move or even blink. Tash was on high alert.

"May we have the room please?" my mother said.

They were out of there in ten seconds flat, taking their briefcases and computers and tablets with them. My mother rose slowly from her desk. She walked around it and then leaned back against it to talk to me, crossing her arms over the front of her red silk blouse.

"Tell me you're not talking about that design school."

I pressed my lips together. "Before you say anything else, I have something to show you."

My mother waited as I took a few cloth samples out of my

bag—my hands trembling—and opened my laptop. I had an entire PowerPoint presentation ready, full of photographs of centerpieces, wall swags, floral arrangements, lighting concepts, and table settings.

"I'm calling it 'patriotic chic,'" I told her, turning the screen so that she could see. "Understated elegance with a nod to the colors of the flag. Everything will be muted, elegant, but still completely American."

I'd found photos from a wedding held in Washington, D.C., a few years ago—one in which a congressman's daughter married a justice's son. They'd used burgundy, cream, and navy instead of red, white and blue, and the effect was sophisticated and luxe.

"We'll use this color scheme, but take it a step further, draping the walls with silks and satins, and cream-colored hydrangeas will be the base flower for all the arrangements. Lit by candlelight, this is going to be seriously gorgeous, don't you think?"

My mother scrutinized the photos as I clicked through, still as a stone gargoyle. I filled the silence with detailed descriptions of every sample flower arrangement, vase, and candlestick I'd found online, and weighed the pros and cons of each china pattern and flatwear set. At the end I'd added pictures of historical events in Nashville and Memphis—sepia-toned shots of rallies and speeches—that depicted the mood I was going for.

"Mom?"

She leaned back and sighed, rolling her shoulders. I braced myself.

"I like it," she said.

I blinked "What?"

"It's patriotic, yet elegant. Understated and refined. Well done, Cecilia."

I almost dropped my computer. "Really?"

She stood up straight and strode to the far side of her desk again. "Never sound surprised when someone tells you you've done a good job," she said pertly. "The response you're looking for is, 'I'm so glad you're pleased.'"

I cleared my throat and clicked the laptop closed. "Then I'm so glad you're pleased."

Actually, I was freaking ecstatic. My insides were having a trampoline party.

My mother faced me across the wide expanse of her desk. "But I still think you should go to Harvard."

"Mom, the Tennessee School of Design is a well-respected school," I argued. "And if I go there, I can live here and commute. I don't want to go to Harvard and become a lawyer. I want to spend my time with artists. I want to learn how to become a stylist, or an interior decorator, or a clothing designer. Maybe even an event planner."

I expected my mother to snort, but she didn't. "Cecilia, you're one of the smartest high school graduates in the entire country. Do you really think those careers will be challenging or fulfilling for you?"

It was my turn to lift an eyebrow. "I don't know. Maybe I'll be like Matilda and style politicians. Or their daughters."

My mother smirked. "So you want to be Matilda," my mother said flatly.

"Why not? Matilda is talented," I said. "And honestly? I don't know. I want to go to school so I can find out what's out there."

"And don't you think that Harvard will give you a broader pool of subjects to explore than the Tennessee School of Design?" she asked.

"I think that if I go to Harvard, we'll go right back to where we were—you controlling every single thing I do, and me . . . well . . . hating you," I said, standing. I was sort of amazed that my knees didn't buckle beneath me. My mother lifted her chin, but there was a horrible, deep sadness in her eyes. "And I don't want to do that anymore, Mom. I don't want to hate you. I don't . . . I don't want to feel like that anymore."

Tears brimmed in my eyes. My mother was so still it was eerie. There was a long silence. Then she pushed herself up straight and said, "Well, I don't want you to feel like that anymore either."

"Fine," I said automatically. Then blinked. "Wait. What?"

"Go ahead. Go to this random university." She walked slowly around her desk. "Defer your acceptance to Harvard. I guarantee that at the end of one year, you'll be begging them to give you a dorm room assignment." My mother smoothed her skirt over her backside and sat, opening up her laptop. "But if you're staying here, you'd better get used to the townspeople hating you. Because those paparazzi aren't going anywhere."

"Mother, please. You won't even consider moving back to Boston?" I asked. "I know you'd rather be there. It's your home. And you can't be happy about what this heat is doing to your hair."

Her hand automatically fluttered up to touch her blond 'do. Which was, of course, perfect. I smiled—gotcha!—and she rolled her eyes.

"What you fail to understand, Cecilia, is that those reporters and photographers are not here for me. They are here for you."

A snort of disbelief escaped me, but it was cut short when my mother opened a drawer and dropped a copy of *OK! Magazine* in front of me. The cover was a picture of my face, eyes half-mast, mouth hanging open, and the headline read "Sloppy Princess." She dropped another on top of it with a thwap. Me and Jasper. And another. Me and Frederick and Duncan on the ground. And a fourth. Me on the red carpet at some random event of Jasper's. And a fifth. Me, wide-eyed, caught with a can of spray paint in my hands.

"Make no mistake about it, my dear. These people are not here for my campaign. They're not even here to cover the lauded Montgomery family." She slammed the drawer shut and folded her hands on her desk. "They're here to see what *you* do next."

20

"THAT'S IT. I'M JUST GOING TO MOVE. START OVER somewhere else."

"NO!"

So many voices spoke up at once, I actually jumped, spilling some of my soda over the rim of the plastic cup. Sitting around me in the Taylors' living room were all my friends in Sweetbriar—Fiona, Duncan, Britta, Frederick, Ryan, Hal, Tammy, and even Shelby. Jasper was there too, but via Skype on Britta's open laptop, his face hovering against the backdrop of his Austin hotel room. Duncan and Fiona's mom was in the kitchen, waiting for the microwave to finish popping the last batch of popcorn.

"Okay, I appreciate your enthusiasm," I said as I reached for a napkin, "but how else are we going to get these vultures to leave? I mean, if I go, they'll follow me and leave the town in peace."

Fiona shook her head. "I honestly can't believe how bad it is. I mean, I'm not surprised you bashed that guy's camera.

Do you know one of them tried to follow her into the bathroom today? It was insane!"

"I had some dude *waiting* for me in the bathroom the other day," Jasper said. "I had to call the police."

"What'd they do to the guy?" Shelby asked, nibbling on popcorn.

"Nothing! He claimed he was just in there taking a pee and he didn't do anything wrong," Jasper replied. "Like he didn't have a two-thousand-dollar camera in his hand."

"Unbelievable," Britta muttered.

"That's what they always say," I told them. "Either that or it's their constitutional right."

"Unfortunately, it's true," Mrs. Taylor said, walking into the room with another full bowl of popcorn. "They have a right to make a living, so as long as they don't physically harm you, they're within their rights."

"Just like it's their right to camp in the park," Fiona said.

"Did you hear they're thinking about canceling Summer Fest?" Ryan said.

"What?" Hal demanded. "They can't do that."

"They can if there's nowhere to have it. Those people have taken over the square and we can't make them move," Ryan replied.

Shelby shot daggers at me from her eyes and I dropped my head into my hands. "This town is going to burn me at the stake."

"It's so stupid!" Duncan said. "They can take over our

park and take pictures of Cecilia wherever she goes, and we just have to accept it? There should be a law. We know the mayor. Can't we make a law?"

We all laughed, but out of the corner of my eye, I saw Shelby's face go slack. She jumped up out of her seat. "I've got it!"

"Got what?" Duncan asked.

"Remember in seventh-grade civics when we had to do that project on local government?" Shelby asked, swinging around to look at Duncan and Fiona, her plaid skirt fluttering.

The twins exchanged a look. "Sorta . . . ," Duncan said.

"Um, no," Fiona added.

Shelby rolled her eyes impatiently. "Why am I the only person who cares about this town?" she asked, throwing up her hands. Then she turned and looked at me. "Well, *I* did my project on the Sweetbriar judicial system."

Her expression was so triumphant that I wanted to shake her.

"And?" I asked.

Shelby cocked one eyebrow. "And you, Cecilia Montgomery, are about to owe me," she said. "Big time."

"Britta! Wake up! It's happening!"

One second Britta was asleep on her stomach with her face half-pressed into the wall, the next she had shot out of bed and was grabbing the extra mug of steaming coffee from my hand. Together we ran on our toes to the front windows of the living room as if it were Christmas morning. Outside, the sky was lightening from gray to lavender to pink, and the flashing lights of the Sweetbriar Police Department cars seemed all wrong set against the dawn—in pretty much the same way that the shouts and protests of all the photographers who were getting arrested—and some of those who weren't—sounded wrong against the peaceful trilling of the birds in the trees.

"Get your hands off me! You can't—"

"Dude, let a guy wake up before you throw him in the—"

"This is police brutality! There's no law against camping in this park."

"No, but you have been found to be in violation of Sweetbriar ordinance number twenty-four D." The police officer who said this barely kept a straight face as he led the cuffed photographer over to a waiting patrol car. I had a feeling he was speaking extra-loud on purpose, as if he knew he had an audience.

"What the heck is Sweetbriar ordinance number twenty-four D?" the photographer asked sarcastically.

The cop shoved the man inside the backseat and then leaned toward him. "I think I'm gonna let the chief explain that one."

Then he slammed the door, turned around, and winked up at our window. Britta and I raised our mugs and high-fived.

The five police cars holding offending photographers took

off, and all the rest of the paps in the park packed up quickly and jumped into their cars and vans to give chase. They knew a good story when they smelled one. Within minutes, every one of the tents was gone and all of the random people had cleared out.

"Ah. So quiet," Britta said with a sigh, and took a sip of her coffee.

I smiled—a real smile that seemed to melt away every bit of negativity in my body. For the first time in ages I felt light inside. I felt . . . happy.

Britta, Fiona, and I entered the slam-packed Sweetbriar court-house through a side door, and the din inspired by our arrival was deafening. It was all I could do not to duck my head and cover my ears, but I wanted to look as mature and in control as possible. I wanted to look like the exact opposite of the way I did on those magazine covers. As of today, the world was going to meet a whole new Cecilia Montgomery.

Seated along the front row of the gallery was an assort-ment of familiar photographers, all of them with hands cuffed behind their backs. They stood up when they saw me.

"This is all your fault!" one of them shouted.

"Who the hell do you think you are?"

"You're the one who should be thrown in jail."

I already was, thanks to you losers, I thought. Though yes, I knew I had played a role in that mess. I swear I am never drinking again.

The bailiff ushered us over to what would normally be the jury box—the only free seats left in the room—and on our way past the judge's desk, I noticed that my mother was standing there in a pressed gray suit, having a chat with the judge. I also noticed that this side of the room was much more welcoming. People began to clap as we approached, and by the time we'd sat down, the cheers overpowered the jeers.

I bit my bottom lip to keep from smiling too wide. But it was nice to feel not-hated for the first time in days.

Duncan, Frederick, and Ryan were already seated in the jury box. I slid in next to Duncan and nudged his shoulder. "I don't understand. Shouldn't we be at the police station?"

"That's where they took everybody, but it got way too crowded way too fast. And if there's one thing Chief Marshall is serious about, it's the fire code. As soon as they counted over a hundred people, he made the call to move everyone here."

Britta whipped out her laptop and started to type into it.

"What're you doing?" I asked.

"This is a historic moment," Britta replied. "Someone should be taking notes."

"And the *reporters* are a tad tied up at the moment," Fiona joked, saying the word "reporters" as sarcastically as possible.

"Speaking of, did you guys notice there's a podium set up outside on the front steps?" Ryan asked. "What's that about?"

"We came in the side entrance," I said, narrowing my eyes. "But that's weird. Is someone giving a press conference?"

Before anyone could answer, the judge banged her gavel.

"Order in the court! This court will come to attention!" She was a large woman with tight, dyed-red curls and coffee-colored skin. After a few more slams of her gavel, everyone shut up, but she gave the room a narrow-eyed look that said we hadn't shut up fast enough.

"Thank you. For those of you who don't know me, I'm Judge Rosalie Williams, servant of the municipal court of Sweetbriar, Tennessee," she said. "Now, this is a very unusual situation. Normally anyone arrested in Sweetbriar is made aware of the charges being levied against them and then brought to the police station for processing. But the citizens of Sweetbriar clearly have an abundant interest in these particular arrests, so here we are."

While the judge was speaking, my mother walked slowly over to the corner of the room, where Shelby stood, holding a big leather-bound book to her chest. She watched my mother's approach, wide-eyed, as if Beyoncé herself was coming to talk with her. Or maybe Godzilla.

"Chief Thomas Marshall, would you care to read the charges?"

The chief stood up from the front row, across the aisle from the perpetrators, and cleared his throat. "Your honor, these people have been found to be in violation of Sweetbriar ordinance number twenty-four D."

The far side of the room erupted in protests all over again, until the judge banged the gavel a few more times. I rubbed my palms together between my legs, giddy with anticipation.

"Order! Order in the court!"

The room went quiet again and Judge Williams took a long, deep breath. "Chief, would you mind explaining to these fine people what Sweetbriar ordinance twenty-four D is?"

The chief opened his mouth to speak, but a voice from the corner interrupted him. My mother's voice.

"Actually, if it pleases the court, I'd like to read the law aloud."

I glanced at Britta. Her fingers froze over her keyboard.

"Why not? It's already a circus in here." The judge leaned back in her chair until it creaked. "Senator Montgomery has the floor."

Shelby handed the book over and my mother walked to the center of the room. Her heels clicked on the hardwood floor, the sound echoing against the silence. There were at least a hundred cell phones raised, recording her journey for posterity. At the center of the room—the optimal vantage point for all—my mother paused, cleared her throat, and opened the book. With one toss of her hair helmet, she began to read.

"Township of Sweetbriar ordinance number twenty-four D, signed into law December 12, 1840."

There was a murmur among the crowd, but the judge sat forward and everyone clammed up.

"Within the city limits of Sweetbriar, Tennessee, no person shall be allowed to photograph a female citizen of

Sweetbriar under the age of twenty-five without express per-
mission of her father or husband. Penalty for infraction is
arrest and twenty days' jail time."

My mother closed the book. The room erupted. She smiled
over at me, handed the book to Mrs. Taylor, and strode out
of the room, her Secret Service agents jumping up to follow.

21

AFTER THAT, THE FINE MEN AND WOMEN OF THE Sweetbriar Police Department took over, calming down the crowd and ushering out the prisoners. A slew of people came over to congratulate me, and to thank me for dealing with the scourge of the paparazzi. Apparently I was no longer the town's number one enemy.

"You should really be thanking Shelby Tanaka," I told them, shouting to be heard. "She knows Sweetbriar law better than anyone. Vote Shelby for Sweetbriar Summer Princess!"

Britta rolled her eyes at me and I shrugged. Shelby had told me what I owed her for helping, and now that Fiona was out of the race, I had no problem joining her campaign.

"Um, guys? We need to get outside. Now," Fiona said. She held up her phone and I saw a live feed of the front of the courthouse. Across the bottom of the screen, a red headline flashed: "Breaking News: Senator Rebecca Montgomery Press Conference About to Begin."

"What is she giving a press conference for?" Duncan asked.

My heart sank to my toes. Oh God, no. She wouldn't. She couldn't. I shoved my way through the crowd toward the big double doors leading to the lobby and then the marble steps beyond. By the time I sidestepped all the well-wishers and made it through security, my mother had already begun speaking. My father stood behind her and, from the corner of his eye, saw me hesitate.

She wasn't really going to bow out of the race, was she? Just because I was a train wreck? Because she couldn't figure out how to spin my front-page headlines?

"I'm here today to talk to you all about someone who's been in the news quite a bit recently—my daughter, Cecilia Montgomery," my mother was saying.

My insides quivered as dozens of faces and microphones and cameras trained on me, hovering ten steps above and behind the podium. My father lifted a hand, beckoning me to come join him. Somehow I made it to his side on wobbly knees and he put his strong arm around my waist.

"Cecilia is a unique young woman," my mother continued. "She has led a very cloistered life. After the attempted kidnapping when she was only ten, my husband and I made the decision to do everything we could to keep her safe, which meant keeping her out of the limelight, keeping her close to home."

She paused and took a deep breath. A light breeze cooled the back of my neck and made goose bumps pop up all over my skin.

"But that also meant she was denied something that, as American citizens, is our birthright. She was denied freedom," my mother said, and the crowd murmured. "Denied the freedom to make her own decisions, the freedom to try new things and meet new people. The freedom"—she paused—"to make mistakes. And to learn from those mistakes the way each one of us must do if we are to grow up to become responsible people."

My breath caught in my throat. I couldn't believe my mother was doing this—was saying these things to the entire country—the entire world.

"I'm here today to say that while I did what I thought was best at the time, I now regret the decision we made. Because of our overly protective instincts, our daughter never got to be a real teenager. She never got to rebel or explore or find her independence. So yes, in the past couple of weeks, she may have made a few ill-advised decisions, but my husband and I take part of the blame in those decisions. If we'd let her have any sort of fun in the past few years, maybe she wouldn't be having *so much of it* now."

She said this with a wry smile and the crowd chuckled.

"I realize that this country has a special fascination with fame, and I know that the road ahead won't be an easy or overly private one for Cecilia. But I ask that—if you can find it in your hearts—you give her a chance to find her footing and not prejudge her by every photo or every headline you see. Cecilia is a straight-A student who was accepted into every top university to which she applied. She's a hard worker, a good friend, and a stellar person. And she hasn't even lived up to her full potential yet."

There was a pause and I had to swallow over and over again to keep from crying.

"Thank you all for indulging me here today. And God bless America."

My mother turned around, putting her back to the hundreds of shouted questions, and without even thinking, I threw my arms around her. It took a moment for her to hug me back, but when she did, it wasn't stiff or perfunctory or calculated. It was a real, warm embrace.

"Shelby Tanaka for Sweetbriar Summer Princess!" I shouted, handing out hot pink flyers at the entrance to Summer Fest. "Vote for Shelby Tanaka!"

Most people smiled at me as they took the flyers, but I wasn't sure if I was on their good side again, or if it was because I was wearing a big, full-color photo of Shelby on my chest. Either way, I didn't care. Things were back to normal in Sweetbriar. The air smelled of fresh-baked pies and cotton candy, country music blared from overhead speakers, and everyone was in a dang good mood. It felt like home again.

"How long do you have to do this chore, Cecilia Montgomery?" Frederick asked, sipping from a huge plastic cup of lemonade as he sidled over to me. "I was hoping you would teach me how to do the line dancing."

"Oh, I have no idea how to line dance," I said, glancing over at the wooden floorboards where dozens of people stomped and twirled. "But it does look like fun."

"So let us go." He reached for my hand.

I bit my lip and slipped a few flyers to passersby. "Frederick . . . about the other night . . ."

His brow knit and he tilted his head, as if he had no idea what I was going to say.

"You kissed me," I said. "But I have a boyfriend."

"Oh, that was nothing," he told me. "I have a girlfriend as well."

A girl on the tilt-a-whirl screamed so loud it made the people waiting on line laugh.

"Then why did you kiss me?" I asked.

"I have a girlfriend, but that doesn't mean I do not enjoy the kissing." Frederick grinned and reached for my free hand again. This time, I let him take it. "I also enjoy the dancing. Come. We will dance as friends."

I glanced at my stack of pink flyers. There were maybe twenty left.

"But I promised Shelby I'd distribute all of these," I said.

Frederick took the stack from my hand and tossed them high into the air, where their hot pinkness fluttered and flipped against the setting sun. Everyone around us whooped and started to grab for the papers like it was a game or the papers were dollar bills.

"Now they are distributed," Frederick said, taking my hand.

"You are a bad influence, Monsieur Valois," I said with a laugh.

He narrowed his eyes. "Why is everyone always telling me that?"

We joined the dancers just as they were finishing up a song, and fell into line for the next one. Ryan, Duncan, and Fiona were already there and did their best to help us as we kicked up our heels, spun the wrong way, and tried to figure out what a pivot step was. Mostly, we were doubled over laughing. At the end of the song, my phone vibrated. An incoming Skype call from Jasper. I dove off the stage to take it.

"Hey!" I said, out of breath and probably flushed.

Jasper was in the back of a limo. His hair was mussed and he had day-old stubble, and somehow he looked more gorgeous than ever.

"You look like you're having fun," Jasper said with a smile.

"I am!"

"I can't believe I'm missing Summer Fest. First time in my entire life."

I wished he was there too, but I didn't want to make him feel worse. "Hey, you've got a job to do," I said. "And Summer Fest will still be here next year."

"True," he said. "But I miss you."

"I miss you too. Where's this gig tonight?" I asked.

He rolled his eyes. "Some new venue. I lost track of my own schedule a good three days ago. But listen, have fun tonight and tell everyone I said 'hey,' all right? I'll be back before you know it."

"Okay. I will," I said, a touch of melancholy in my voice. "I love you, home-wrecker."

Jasper's smile widened. "I love you too, Red Sox."

We hung up and I was about to rejoin my friends, when Tash came flying up to me wearing an extremely fancy black ball gown. She grabbed my arm, gasping for air. I'd never seen her so out of sorts.

"What's wrong? I told my mother I'd be at the gala by eight," I said.

"It's the caterers!" she cried, gripping my wrist so tightly I thought her fingers might break. "They say you never ordered a vegetarian option."

My stomach zipped up tight. "Oh God."

"You really never ordered a vegetarian option?" Tash squealed.

"But you said we wouldn't need one!" I replied, though I had realized this was in no way true.

"Do *not* put this on me, Cecilia," she snapped, releasing my arm. "Do you have any idea how many Hollywood people we have coming to this thing? They're *all* vegetarian! What are we going to do?"

I took a deep breath, but it did no good. My heartbeat was pulsing against the inside of my skull. All I'd done for the last few days was work with the set-up crew and the seamstresses and the florists and the lighting engineers, trying to get the look for the gala exactly right. I couldn't let one menu snafu ruin the entire thing. I glanced around as my friends tumbled off the line dancing stage, Duncan and Fiona hanging on to each other as they laughed.

"Taylors!" I shouted, and they both looked up at the desperation in my voice. "We have to find your dad."

I had a lot of begging to do.

"So you just happened to have over-ordered hundreds of green tomatoes?" I asked, as Hal, Duncan, Fiona, Britta, Ryan, Frederick, Caitlin, and I unloaded huge trays of fried green tomatoes from the back of Hal's delivery van.

"I like to be prepared for any culinary emergencies that might arise," Hal replied, giving me a wink.

I handed a tray over to one of the waiters near the back door and stopped myself before wiping my hands on the front of my deep red gown.

"Seriously, Hal. Thank you for doing this. I can't believe how fast you and the guys whipped these up," I said. "And I'm sorry I blew you off the other day. I was going through some stuff."

Hal put his warm hand on my bare shoulder. "We've all been through some stuff," he said, looking into my eyes. "That doesn't mean we stop being family."

My heart skipped. "You think of me as family?"

"Of course," he said, and reached into the van for a couple of juice jugs.

"What's that?" I asked, still smiling happy.

"I also brought some of my famous sweet tea," he said with a wink. "Just in case."

I laughed as I followed him inside, more wait staff streaming out past us to finish unloading the van. I slipped along the least-busy wall of the kitchen and out into the gymnasium, where dozens of tables were draped with dark burgundy tablecloths and navy and cream accents, decorated with gorgeous modern glass centerpieces that invoked the three stars on the Tennessee flag. The guests milled about in their gowns and tuxedos, as classical music played out on the patio. I found my mother chatting with my dad and one of the senators from Florida, and walked over to join them.

"Cecilia, you did a wonderful job," my mother said, leaning in to kiss my cheek. "You remember Senator Rashad?"

"Yes, hello, Senator," I said, extending my hand. "Lovely to see you again."

"You planned this event?" the senator asked, shaking my hand and bringing her other to her heart. "The décor is absolutely stunning. I might have to hire you for my next fundraiser."

I laughed as my father beamed. "I'm not responsible for all of it," I said. "In fact, my mother's assistant, Tash, picked up a lot of my slack and did some serious troubleshooting."

Tash, who was at my mother's side as always, shot me a stunned look and I smiled gracefully in return.

Gigi had always told me it was in our nature to rise above, and from now on that was going to be one of my mottos. *Rise above. Learn to say no. Alcohol=evil.* I'd learned a lot in the last few weeks.

The music on the patio stopped abruptly and there was a shout of surprise, followed by a quick screech of feedback. Tash and I locked eyes. What now?

We were both three steps across the room when a voice stopped me cold.

"How y'all doing tonight? I'm Jasper Case. And I'm here to give y'all a little taste of authentic Tennessee."

Suddenly, I was running in my ridiculously high heels. The guitar-heavy opening of Jasper's "Midnight Run to You" blared through the speakers as I emerged through the French doors. Everyone on the patio was rapt with attention as Jasper began to sing. He had shaved since I'd last seen him—how?—and wore a perfectly cut tux with his signature black cowboy hat and a pair of black and teal boots. The first time he looked up from his guitar he caught my eye, and his smile almost made me swoon.

"I thought you said he couldn't find us a country act," Tash said.

"I guess he decided to take it upon himself," I replied.

"Your boyfriend is very talented, Cecilia," my father said, coming up behind me.

I sighed happily and touched the strand of pearls around my neck. "He is, isn't he?"

I wove my way through the crowd, which grew by the second with people spilling out of the gym and onto the patio. When the song was over, the volume of the response surprised me, and Jasper looked down, clearly impressed with himself.

"I thought you had a gig tonight," I shouted.

"I told you it was a new venue," he said with a satisfied grin. "I brought you a little somethin'."

He turned and the guitarist handed him my violin, which he held out to me.

"Care to join me for this next one?" he asked.

I hesitated half a second. What would my mother think if I took the stage at her gala to play backup to my country-star boyfriend? But then I realized, it didn't matter. It was time for me to start making my own decisions, and I wanted to play. I wanted people to see me play. I wanted people to know I was about more than the tabloids made me out to be.

"You're on."

I stepped up onto the stage and readied my instrument. Jasper leaned into the microphone.

"Accompanying me on this next song is the one, the only, Cecilia Montgomery."

The polite applause was punctuated by loud cheers from my friends in the back corner. I shot them a grateful smile and Jasper and I began to play. As we moved through the first verse of "Meant to Be," I scanned the room, my eyes landing on my mother, my father, Tash, and my friends. And then I started to focus on the strangers in the crowd—the Hollywood moguls, the veteran actors, the politicians and the business people and the few esteemed reporters. They were a rapt audience. Every one of them was enjoying the music. And yeah, maybe they were judging me or judging Jasper or wondering how we came to be or how long we would last, but who cared? I knew what we were, and I knew that together, we could do anything.

The song ended, and the crowd cheered. My mother raised her clapping hands above everyone else's, and for the first time in a long time, I saw pride in her eyes.

Jasper leaned in for a quick kiss and then spoke into my ear. "What're we doing after this, Red Sox?" he asked.

I looked into his eyes. "Anything we want."

Acknowledgments

Huge thanks to everyone who helped bring Cecilia's story together, including Alyson Heller, Sara Sargent, and Liesa Abrams, as well as the production and design team behind the awesome covers and interiors of *Escaping Perfect* and *Finding What's Real*. Thanks to my agent, Sarah Burnes, for all your support, and to my family, as always, with love.

Turn the page for a look
at where it all began
for Cecilia Montgomery
in *Escaping Perfect*.

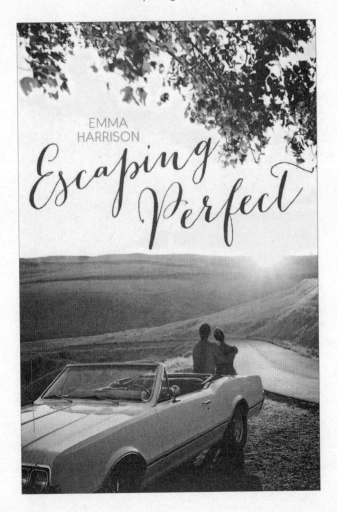

"Senator Montgomery! Senator Montgomery! Roll down the window! Just for a second! Senator Montgomery!"

There was a bang and a shout—some photog getting so close to the limo that he tripped and slammed his camera into the side of the car—and so the most hellish part of my day from hell truly began.

The rest of the paparazzi crowded around the limousine's tinted windows as it eased through the wrought-iron gates of the South Palm Memorial Cemetery. They couldn't see me or my mom and dad, would only go home with pictures of their own cameras' reflections. But that didn't stop them. Nothing ever stopped them. Some people made a living just by selling whatever pictures they could get of our family. And now the one unfamous person in my world had died, and of course the photographers were still here, clamoring for shots of the living.

Sometimes I really wished their cameras would sponta-
neously combust in their faces. But only when I was feeling
truly pissed at the world. Like now.

"Five minutes, Cecilia," my mother said tersely, glancing
up from her tablet to check her Cartier watch. "We have to get
this show on the road. I have a briefing at three."

I felt my father's body go rigid, even with him sitting clear
on the other side of the limo.

It's Gigi's funeral, I thought bitterly. *You couldn't take one day off?*
What I said was, "Yes, ma'am."

Outside the windows, rows of white and gray headstones
stretched into the distance for what seemed like miles. It was
all so anonymous. My grandmother didn't belong here, camou-
flaged by the dreary sameness. She belonged someplace special.

My mom's eyes narrowed. "Don't take that tone with your
mother."

The great Rebecca Montgomery, aka dear old Mom, loved
to refer to herself in the third person. Ever since I was a toddler,
it was:

Look, Cecilia, Mommy's on TV!

*Mommy will only be gone for three weeks, but don't worry. Miss
Jessica will take care of you!*

No, no! Mommy can't hug you right now. This suit is couture.

Yeah. The word "maternal" was not in her vocabulary.

"It's not as if I can take the time off right now," she added,
reading my mind. "Not when there's so much work to do."

Of course there was. It was an election year. Nothing was more all-consuming for my mother than an election year.

She huffed out a breath and placed the tablet aside, opening a compact to check her perfectly bobbed chestnut-brown hair.

"I still don't understand why we had to fly all the way down here to this godforsaken swamp for her funeral when we have a perfectly beautiful burial plot back in Beacon Hill."

"Because my mother lived *here*," my father said, still staring out the window. "She wanted to be buried *here*. You never gave her anything she wanted in life, Rebecca; you'd think you could at least give her this."

"Oh. So I see everyone's ganging up on me today." My mother clicked the compact closed and shoved it back into her black Birkin bag. She had a right to be surprised. My father, a high-powered defense attorney for Boston's wealthiest residents, usually saved all argumentative tones for the courtroom. I hardly ever heard him raise his voice or even snipe at my mom, unless it was from behind very firmly closed doors. "It wasn't entirely my fault that Maura and I didn't get along. She did play a hand in it, you know."

"But she's still Dad's mom," I said quietly. "And my grandmother. And we're never going to see her again."

You could at least pretend to be sad.

My mother sighed her impatient sigh. "Cecilia . . ."

"Mom, please," I said, my voice shaky. "Could you maybe not be a bitch right now? Just for today?"

My left cheek exploded in pain. I didn't even see my mother move until she was settling back into her seat across from mine, tucking the hand that had just slapped me into her purse.

My left eye prickled over with purple and gray spots. I brought my quaking fingers to my cheek.

"Was that really necessary?" my father asked.

I blinked, surprised he'd even bothered. He'd never said anything to her the many other times she'd smacked me.

"Stay out of it," she growled at him.

My father clenched his jaw and looked out the window. Mother tugged down on her suit jacket and glared at me. "How dare you?"

It had been a long time since she'd hit me. Possibly because I had hardly seen her for more than an hour or two here and there over the past two years. Maybe I hadn't had time to piss her off enough. But now? On the day we were burying my grandmother?

"Gigi was my best friend," I muttered to the door, turning the stinging side of my face away from her. "Just leave me alone."

"What was that? If you're going to speak, at least enunciate," my mother said.

I sat up straight, trying very hard not to tremble. "I said, Gigi was my best friend. And she was more like a mother to me than you've *ever* been."

My mom made an indignant noise at the back of her throat.

"I should throw you right out of this car, young lady."

"Like you'd ever do that," I shot back. "You'd rather die than let me see the light of day."

I hadn't even been allowed to go out for my eighteenth birthday last month. Instead my mother—or rather, her assistant, Tash—had sent me a gift at boarding school, but she hadn't otherwise acknowledged it. No call, no text, no e-mail. Just a hand-delivered box from Tiffany containing an ugly ladybug pendant I immediately donated to my graduating class's silent charity auction.

I crossed my arms and sat back, but the huge bun her stylist had fashioned out of my mane of curls held my skull away from the headrest at an uncomfortable angle. My irritation spiked. Even though I was sitting here declaring my ability to be my own person, I'd spent the entire day letting her order me around as always.

I said the Kenneth Cole, Cecilia, not the Calvin Klein.

Take off that god-awful lip color. Did you pick that yourself? When was the last time we had your eyes checked?

And then, when she'd seen my hair hanging loose around my shoulders: *I'll have Felicia come take care of you next. How you deal with all that hair, I have no idea.*

And what had I said all morning long? "Yes, ma'am."

Sometimes I really loathed myself. I should have asked her how she dealt with having a stick up her butt all the time.

Of course, my hair wasn't the only thing about me that my

mother couldn't wrap her brain around, but it wasn't surprising, considering her hair had always been tame and shiny and cut above the chin. I had inherited her skinny bones and angular face, and my dad's extreme height and dark curly hair—though he kept his almost entirely shaved. My skin color was all my own, somewhere between his dark chocolate and her milky white. I pushed my butt all the way back so I could straighten my posture, barely containing the urge to rip out the three hundred bobby pins stabbing me in the skull.

"Please, Cecilia," my mother said with a derisive chuckle. "If you want us to treat you like an adult, you should stop moping like a child."

My face burned.

"We're here," my father said gruffly. "Five minutes, Cecilia."

Of course he was agreeing with her timeline. He always agreed with everything she said. Which is how I'd ended up with her last name instead of his. But I felt suddenly too exhausted to argue anymore.

The mound of dirt and the casket on its metal lift were situated about three rows in from the car. My grandmother's grave site sat beneath the shade of a huge weeping willow. She would have loved it, and the thought brought fresh tears to my eyes.

I stepped shakily out of the car. It was stiflingly hot and humid.

My mother's security team sat on alert in the Town Car behind ours along with Tim "the Tank" Thompson, the former pro wrestler who had followed me around for the past ten years. I sensed their eyes on me as I slipped my sunglasses on and walked over to the grave site, alone, feeling oddly exposed without Tim there as my shadow. But he'd been told, I was sure, that I was to have these five minutes.

Because my mother refused to let anyone ever get a glimpse of me, I would not be allowed out of the limo during the actual service and burial later. Ever since I was eight years old and a man named Scott Smith had attempted to kidnap me for ransom, my mother had kept me on a short leash. Well, more like locked up in a cage and transported from place to place only by heavily armed professionals.

It was why I had spent the past ten years cloistered behind the brick walls of the Worthington School, where no camera phones were allowed and every student signed a confidentiality clause. Why I'd never seen the inside of a movie theater or a Starbucks or a commercial airport. Why I'd spent every summer trapped in our house on Martha's Vineyard with a team of tennis coaches, academic tutors, and etiquette experts grooming me for the day I'd emerge from the suffocating cocoon in which I'd spent most of my life.

Suffocating like the starched jacket of the black suit I'd been forced to wear, which now itched at the back of my neck under the glare of the sun as I approached the grave. The length of the pencil skirt—just above the knee—clamped my legs together and made my steps small and awkward in my black kitten heels. I finally came up alongside the white coffin and lost my breath, imagining Gigi inside. Instead I trained my eyes on the sky as blue as cornflower and dotted with white clouds. I wanted to say the right thing. Tell her how much she'd meant to me. But she knew all that. And the first words that came spilling out of my mouth weren't so much a grateful homage as a selfish plea.

"How am I supposed to do this?" I asked, my voice cracking. Sudden, hot tears streamed from the corners of my eyes. "How am I supposed to do this without you?"

It was all I could think to say. Then I bowed my head forward, covered my face with my hands, and wept.

An hour later, it was all over. At least a hundred friends and family members stood alongside her grave while the pastor spoke and my father and his sister cried and my mother's lip wobbled dramatically.

Our driver stood under the shade of a palm tree alongside the car, which was parked at the front of a winding line of limos and Town Cars awaiting their passengers. He watched the proceedings while I stared through the window, open half a centimeter so that I might catch a stray word. My face and eyes were dry, my skin itching from the tears I'd shed earlier. And the longer I watched, the angrier I felt.

The whole thing was a sham. My parents hadn't even told my grandmother's real friends where she was being buried. This was not about her. It was about my mother. The senator. The glamorous Senator Montgomery, fourth child of Jack and Marianne Montgomery and niece of former vice president Frederick Montgomery. Currently, my mother was the highest-profile Montgomery in the country with her ascension to the US Senate, and she had no intention of stopping there. She had turned my grandmother's funeral into a networking party.

Finally the flowers were strewn, the dirt was tossed, and those in attendance were saying their good-byes. I sat up straighter as my parents approached the waiting cars, my father supporting my mother as if she were the one suffering.

I steeled myself for round two, but my parents and their entourage of bodyguards slipped between parked cars and walked up a slight incline on the other side of the roadway. I had to turn around and crane my neck to see where they were going. The driver moved away from the car to join the rest of the security team. They stopped at a spot atop a grassy knoll near the brick fence that surrounded the cemetery grounds. I saw Tim find a position midway up the hill. My father stood just behind my mother's right shoulder. Always, always, he stood behind her.

"We'd like to thank you all for coming and showing your respect for my husband's late mother, *our* late mother, really," my mom began, her hair shimmering in the sun. "One of the great matriarchs of our family."

Bile. I tasted actual bile. Matriarch? *Our* mother? My

mother had treated Gigi like crap. Any overtures from my father's mother were swept under the rug. Any offers of advice or assistance were scoffed at. How dare she get up there and act like Gigi had meant something to her?

"Maura also meant a good deal to our daughter, Cecilia," my mother continued, gazing down at the car. "The two of them had a special relationship, and for that we will always be grateful."

My fingernails dug into the flesh of my palms. I was sweating under my arms and along my upper lip. She was such a liar. Such a fraud. And I hated her. I hated what she'd done to my life. I'd never had a boyfriend or even a real friend. Never been allowed to invite anyone to my house, go to a regular party or out to a concert. I was hardly even a functioning human being.

Heat crept up my neck as my heart pounded out of control. I unbuttoned the suit jacket and yanked the tight sleeves from my arms, straining my shoulder muscles in the process. It didn't help. I couldn't breathe. I needed air. I had to get out of there. I had to.

My hand fumbled for the door handle, but then I froze. If just one member of the paparazzi happened to turn their head, they would be on me like starving crows on roadkill. I wouldn't get two feet from the car before the security detail easily caught up with me and tossed me back inside.

My eyes darted around the confines of the limo as my pulse raced and raced and raced. Suddenly I felt a cool breeze on my ankles and realized that the air-conditioning was blowing. The car was running. I turned and glanced at the ignition. There dangled the keys.

Without thinking, I got on my knees and shoved myself through the open window that divided the driver's seat from the rest of the car. Within seconds I was behind the wheel— thank God the Tank convinced my mom that my learning to drive was necessary for my safety. The crowd was at least six or seven cars behind me to the left, eyes and lenses riveted on the senator. There was nothing in front of me but open road.

I clicked the car into drive, put my hands on the wheel, and pressed my foot down on the gas pedal.

I had been on the road for fifteen minutes when my phone began to ring, but I refused to look at the screen. I gripped the steering wheel with slick fingers, hardly able to take a full breath. But even in all my panic and elation and terror and sadness, my logical side was still functioning, and it was telling me that the cops were going to be on me in about thirteen seconds. A scrawny black girl behind the wheel of a stretch limo with livery plates? *That* was something people were going to notice.

I had to get off this highway. But where the hell was I supposed to go?

I had barely asked myself the question when a sign appeared before me. An actual sign for Everglades National Park. Gigi used to take me there every December 26 for a picnic at a secluded spot near the water. No one would ever look for me there, and there were enough trees to hide the limo, even if my mother somehow got NASA to train a satellite on the area. Which she could totally do.

I just had to find the right turnoff once I got inside the park area. Then maybe I could stop for a while, give myself some time to think, figure out what I was going to do next. I eased the limo off the road.

A few drivers peered curiously out at me as they blew by in the other direction. I noticed that the driver had left his black hat on the passenger seat, and I jammed it down on top of my hair. Not the greatest disguise in the world, but better than nothing.

More signs pointed off to various sections of the park. Fishing piers, wildlife preserves, designated water sports areas. Finally, I found what I was looking for: an old, chipped sign that read PICNIC GROUNDS with a red sticker slapped across it— CLOSED. I ignored that, just like my grandmother always had. I almost laughed, remembering how her irreverence had stressed me out, how I'd spend the first half hour of any picnic worried that we were going to get caught. Never the rule breaker, and now I was breaking every rule in the book.

As soon as I turned onto the packed dirt road, the trees and undergrowth bent in around me. High above, the canopy of leaves blocked out the sun, and long green grasses swished against the sides of the car. I eased my foot off the gas and realized that my ankle hurt from being in the same tense position for so long. Finally I found myself able to breathe. Able to think.

What the hell was I doing?

Did I really think that this stunt would prove anything? That I could escape my mother? No, in fact, I didn't. When I'd crawled through that window, I hadn't been thinking at all. I'd been working on instinct, hopped up on emotion. I had wanted to get away, plain and simple. I'd seen my chance and I'd taken it.

The question was, what to do now? I took a deep breath and considered my situation. I had a ton of cash in my backpack—the bag I never left home without—from the tutoring services I offered at school. Okay, the flat-out writing-papers-for-other-kids business I'd been lucratively running behind Tim's back for the past five years. Most of the money was hidden under a floorboard in my room back home in Boston, where I made deposits every break, but I'd brought my latest haul—about two thousand dollars—with me, in case the school did one of its random sweeps while I was away at the funeral. If I could just get somewhere, somewhere off the grid, maybe I could really and truly be free.

I came to the end of the road and hit the brakes. The car stopped soundlessly. Fingers trembling, I shoved the gearshift into park. Before me was the bog where Gigi and I had picnicked just this past December. Where we'd tossed out a couple of lines and sat munching on cold fried chicken, not catching anything and not caring. I'd leaned my head against her shoulder and we'd daydreamed about going to Europe together. We'd talked about how once I turned eighteen, I could do anything I wanted, I could escape, and she'd be here to do it with me.

Except that she wasn't. Thanks to one tiny blood clot, she was gone.

I leaned back in the seat and cried. I cried in total earnest and abandon in a way I hadn't since Tash had called me to tell me Gigi had passed. For the first time in forever, I was truly and completely alone, no bodyguard hovering, no driver or personal assistant or tutor listening in. I cried with everything I had in me.

And by the time I stopped, I had a plan. By the time I stopped, I knew I wasn't ever going back.

EMMA HARRISON

has written several YA romances, including *Escaping Perfect*, *The Best Girl*, *Tourist Trap*, and *Busted*, as well as many TV and movie adaptations. When she's not writing, she loves to bake, work out, read, and watch way too much TV. She lives in New Jersey with her incredibly awesome husband and two perfectly adorable sons.